CARNIVÀLE DE LA LLUM
PART ONE

MEGAN CROWE

Dedicated to Daisy and Violet Hilton,

Simon Metz (Schlitzie),

and Stefan Bibrowski (Lionel the Lion-Faced Man)

★ ★ ★ ACKNOWLEDGMENTS ★ ★ ★

The Ritter family: Darla, Scott, and Sierra. You helped when no one else would.

Mom, Terry, Darla, and Sierra, thank you for reading this novel in the early drafts, and the final draft.

To my best bud Sierra, all the thanks for being my wall to bounce ideas off of, for listening to my venting and empty threats about deleting my entire document, for writing neato songs just for my novel, and for begrudgingly acting as a guinea pig in solving the mystery of the killer. *You are the only one who knows his true identity.*

The Written in Red Podcast: Aron Beauregard, Daniel J. Volpe, Carver Pike, and Rowland Bercy Jr.
Your show convinced me to move forward with self-publishing, and supplied great advice as I began the process. You are an awesome group of guys, and I love your books!

Ville Valo, your music has, and continues to get me through the darkest days.

Mom, special thanks to you for putting up with your weirdo of a daughter.

☆ INTRODUCTION ☆

THE HIERARCHY

OF

FRK-32

IN
⚬ HIS ⚬
WORDS

There is no better—*more horrible*—place to view so many in a single go, than a cesspit like this.

Carnivals, circuses, sideshows, Freak shows. All presenting Sickos for profit. Fear for pay. The privilege of vomiting for only two bits a pop.

Freaks, the worst of the Sick. More than Sick! Damned, cursed, revolting monsters!

Things one cannot fathom. *Things* that should not be. *Things* against nature. *Things* unmeant for this world. For sustainable life. For quality life.

What good is a man without the use of his arms? Legs? Body? How can birth go so horribly wrong?!

Useless, squirming trunks of flesh attached to heads. Faces formed of curdled cottage cheese tumors, and growths beneath the skin. Three legs, four! Arms aplenty or none at all! *Biological amputees.* Furred and scaled animals walking about on two legs with the ability to speak. One-eyed babies, conjoined twins, bigheads, pinheads, bearded women!

These, *these* things, are the result of a *cure. The* Cure.

FRK-32. A preemptive strike against sickness, a vaccination for all current and future strains of virus, disease, or defect. Able to adapt and strike out against any mutation found within its human host. The Cure that would save humanity from sickness and early graves.

What a load of shit.

First it healed the masses, then it killed their babies.

It's what they deserve.

All of them. They *all* deserve to die.

A blurring of lines. The Sick in disguise.

Playing dress-up until the costumes are dropped, make-up smeared away, and wigs snatched from heads.

Superior only for the ability to hide the sickness lying in wait.

Once illness sets in.

Always will.

Paling, turned skin and bones, losing hair.

For a time, *until that time*, a life of peace. No judgment. No restrictions. Free. Unlike the Freaks.

Their death sentence is not branded at birth by clawed hands or crocodile-plated flesh.

Disease *will* find each and every one.

In the early years: *before a child knows what life is, before understanding their purpose.*

Middle-age: *settled with a family, married, the peak of happiness.*

Or in the last stages of life: *when old age has become a burden, and one prays for the end.*

Death will be at their side.

He takes many forms. Cancer, failing organs, heart, brain, kidneys, liver. Throw a rock at any part of the human body and the stricken target will turn against its host. Nature will always find a way to destroy her children.

She writhes in the blood of her babies, screaming in ecstasy as they perish.

They caused it all. Thought they could beat the order of the world.

Believing, trusting, a single injection would cause all disease and sickness to disappear. To become extinct, as if it were some animal. A sentient being capable of compromising. *They forget, a rattlesnake recoils before striking.*

Untouchable, our ancestors thought.

Never considering the consequences. And thusly paid with everything. In debt even after one thousand years and counting. The future, innovative discoveries, technological advancements, gone, erased, rewound.

Fucking fools!

Look what you did to us!

You are all damned.

The unworthy. Cheats, filthy cheats at birth with a card up their chromosomal sleeves.

Why are *they* rewarded? What did *they* do to deserve it?

Fucking cheating bastards! Why them!?

Looking down their noses at the shit stains that are the Sick, the Freaks, the Normal! Deeming themselves better. *It's a painful, envious truth.*

Superior, not only in Health, but pedigree. Entitled to life, unlike the rest. Descending from those few who did not greedily inject a yellow serum into their bloodstream.

It means nothing!

Nothing… except for Health. *Immunity.*

The expectation of FRK-32.

No sickness, ever. Death arriving with old age, winding down as a slowing clock… or accident.

They hide. Hide because of fear. Pathetic as a baby deer lost in the woods, left by mother with a gimpy leg. At the mercy of predators and the elements.

Scared, terrified it will be taken away. Title. Birthright. Disease exemption. The Sick will come looking, hunting, stalking. Consume the Immune, hoping to take the Health for themselves.

Eat your enemy's heart to gain strength. Bathe in the blood and live forever.

Death. He is at a distance, waiting. Watching for his first opportunity to strike.

Even an immortal can die.

Arkansas — Oklahoma Border

Year 3094

CARNY CURSES

❦ TOD ❧

"Do you believe in curses?

"You will. Give it time my love, and you will *believe.*

"I promise this is no joke. Ask any man, woman, or child on the circuit and you will be assured, carny curses are not to be trifled with. They are not mere wives' tales or children's fables. But warnings of what is to come. Truths of the inevitable.

"Seven total, as were the archaic sins of the pre-Cure faiths.

"Fire, Weather, Accidents, Mobs, Rape, Murder, and the Law.

"Some may appear throughout a season, minor nuisances. Winds and rain cancelling a show. A lawman requiring a larger cut of the take. A man slipping from a ladder and spraining an ankle. Other instances will devastate. Townies setting the Ten-In-One alight with performers trapped inside. In the dead of night, men ransacking trailers and tents, dragging those who sleep from their beds with nefarious intent whether fueled by lust or hatred or both.

"I will not lie to you. You will *encounter the seven. Each one. Whether recounted by a trouper, rumored on the road, or lived. Witnessed. Suffered.*

"I will ask you once more, will you accept this fate?

"For once you are one of us, you too are cursed."

Wish, Arkansas

Year 3134

Present Day

CARNIVÀLE DE LA LLUM

~o DAWN e~

"How did he die?"

"Otis found 'im outside the cook tent this mornin'. Seems he stumbled over a guy line with'a belly full'a hooch an' fell noggin first on a stake. Still holdin' the bottle I'm told. Not a drop spillt."

"Poor fella," she sighed, the frown on her face affected her voice.

"Yeah. Season's still fresh an' we're two men down. Can't hardly believe it. Curses're workin' strong this year."

"Did you get in contact with his family?"

Dawn's veil click-clattered, "Nah, no address in his wallet. Thought about listin' his name in the Banner-Line, but no one reckons his last name. Can't send in *Jeb*. Jeb died. *Jeb who?* It's a shame. Don't know if he got himself a family waitin' on 'im back home. Never know."

"Aww, that's awful… What about Dell's widow?"

"Sent off the belongin's at the post an' wired his last month's pay. *Plus,* what he woulda' made rest'a the year, had his ticker held up."

"A year's pay? Can you afford that?"

"No. But a grand gesture fer a troubled soul, such as poor ol' Dell's wife, durin' a time'a need is somethin' the Baron woulda' done, even if it were to his *de-tri-ment.*"

"He sure would've."

For a few moments Dawn de Barcsy and her companion Sherilyn—*'Venus,'* to the marks—strolled along the outskirts of Carnivàle de la Llum in carnival silence. *Which is none too quiet at all.*

Children's laughter. Awe for the sights and sounds. Shrieking as the tykes rise with the orbit of *The Shadow's Eye*, de la Llum's Eli wheel. With black framework and monochrome seats, the ride is promoted across the country as: *The World's Only Dark Wheel!*

From bally stages drifted the shouts of barkers—*talkers, lecturers, to other outfits, but not here at de la Llum.*

Catcalls whistled and yipped for the Kootch girls out back.

The second *rousing* performance of the evening would begin soon enough.

"Daddy says we ain't going to Florida this year?" Sheri asked, moving away from the last subject. *Death. Accidents.*

"Nah," Dawn answered, flapping away with a wooden fan. Hairs gone rogue from auburn ringlets tickled her throat, she itched with a red fingernail. "Hear they ain't allowin' nobody on the circuit." Not even the *Railey Brothers*. A traveling troupe made up of *not one* Freak. *Boring.* Dawn didn't much care for their show. "Tryin' ta run out *anyone* ain't Normal," she shook her head, "*Didn't use ta be that way.*"

Carny community goes full bloom in Florida during the off-season.

Gibsonton, carny mecca since pre-Cure days. Whether calling the town home during the winter or settling down permanent in the twilight years.

If Gibtown ain't sacred, what is?

"*I know,*" Sheri said quietly. Hemmed blouse sleeves rippled across narrow shoulders in a sudden gust of wind. Blonde hair stayed pinned tight at the back of her head, except for two loose curls on either side of her face. "Are we drivin' through?"

She seemed worried. The girl's face didn't allow for hidden emotions. Squinting, pursing lips, gaze straying.

Can't blame her. Sheri remembered Texas.

Eleven, but plenty old enough to vividly recall the wrongs committed. The havoc, confusion, and death. Knowing it could go that way again anytime, anywhere.

"Nah, honey. We ain't passin' through," Dawn answered. "Got us a month or so booked in Louisie then on ta the Missus. Ain't expectin' straw house sales till Jackson, but at least they won't run us off till then."

She hoped.

"That'd be nice."

"*Mmm-hmm,*" Dawn nodded.

"Where will they go?"

The others. The circuses, the carnivals, the Freak shows, during the off-season, where would they set up camp if not Gibtown? Where will they live? *Hide?*

"Can't say I know." Cali, *de la Llum's winter haven,* or Nevada maybe. The two states aren't *so* hostile to their kind. "Sure they'll make out fine."

She glanced at the young woman.

Head hung low, searching the ground for nothing at all.

Sheri don't believe a damn word.

That meant she worried where *they* would go this year. If *Florida* was out, surely *the Black State* could be next. Where the fuck would de la Llum bed down then?

Truth was, Dawn didn't know. *This world seems to get smaller and smaller every passing day.*

Dawn changed the subject this time, asking, "So how ya been honey? You sure been busy… And yer daddy, how's that old geezer dealin' with it? If *I'm* noticin' *he* must be down in the sawdust lookin' fer marbles."

Dawn knew the first answer. Saw the girl every damn day, hard not to know just what she did, when, and where. It was her father, Sunny, and his wife Vie, that piqued her nose's interest.

Sheri smirked at the reference of her father being a geezer, *a man sixteen years Dawn's junior.*

"I'm doin' alright, just finished another jacket for Evro. He only had the one after all." *A fresh greenie, but a trustworthy greenie. Runs Carrie while the gate's open, and his mouth for the rest of the time. Dawn likes him.* "And Daddy's fine," vibrantly, "He and Vie've been real happy lately. Won't say why, the cuckoos," she laughed.

Not uncommon for the couple. Noticeably *abundant* as of recent. All smiles and giggles after hours. *The Hel are the pair up to?*

"Hi, Vincent!" Sheri called. *Dawn's heart fluttered at the name.* "I thought you had a show?"

Wait? Vinnie? What the Hel's he doin' out here?

She held the half-collapsed fan above her eyes to block glare as he grew nearer. Neck ticking back the closer he got.

He should be in the Ten till closing.

Dawn's son stopped behind the broadside of a red and white top. Years of baking in the heat and soaking up rain left the colors in a sad ashen state.

He did not lower the hood of his cloak.

Good boy, just as he was taught growing up. *Keep hidden.*

If they ain't payin' for the privilege don't let 'em gander fer free.

A quick smile for Sherilyn before relaying, "Serene's tank has begun to leak again…"

"Oh *Hel!* Not again!" Dawn gripped the sides of her face, beaded veil clenched in fists. *Why always openin' night!?* "An' the show's goin' I reckon? All packed full an' now it decides ta bust?"

He nodded. Shiny blonde beard brushing up and down the front of a blue vest fastened with silver buttons.

"*Damn it!* Ev'ry time, *ev'ry time* we set up! It's somethin' else! First Dell, then Jeb, now this! *Them fuckin' rousties!* I tell 'em, load up Serene's tank last!" Dawn stomped toward the Ten-In-One, Vincent at her side. "Glass ya dummies, it'll break when shit's been piled on it."

Sherilyn remained behind. Five minutes till her next showing in the Single-O's: threading a needle, sipping from a cup, and signing autographs using only her toes.

THREE'S A CROWD

～ SHILZIE ～

Shilzie, Elvi, and Nylee peered between the curtains separating stage three from the crowd. *The eventual reveal would be all the grander if kept hidden.*

"Please... Muckers, can I get out of here!?" the mermaid's delicate voice did not dare rise too high.

Elvi and Nylee hugged one another, listening to Serene's plea as the glass tank crackled audibly within the canvas walls of the Ten-In-One.

Shilzie watched, helpless, but *wanting* to help.

She couldn't. Neither big enough nor strong enough.

"Hep err, hep err preez!" Shilzie begged of a man below.

He recoiled from the garbled speech. Jerking as one might from an aimed gun between the eyes.

Oh, what is that thing!?!

This unintelligible language could be a curse from the little girl. The strange little creature. *An Aztec Daughter of Xipe-Totec,* if the banner outside were to be believed.

Muckers held his arms wide, cane in one hand, assuring the crowd all would be well in a few moments. Please remain calm. Stay where you are. All is under control. *Anything* to keep the patties quiet. Patties, patrons. Rubes, marks, townies.

Do not speak to strangers, unless Mother or I are with you, she forgot her brother's rule in the panic when asking the man, *the patty,* for help.

However, men or women working for the show are safe.

Never did she speak to *that* man on stage one.

The extent of Muckers' responsibilities began and ended with the pats. Corralling the herds before each stage, giving a short lecture, arousing curiosity with the mysteries of the Annex. Something never seen before! A mystery of nature! Shocking!

Amazing! Alive! See it with your very own eyes! *For an additional fee.*

Anything more, he considered free labor.

Why do that? This ain't charity!

Why should he have to help? Get himself all wet? What if the damn tank busts open? He ain't gonna get himself cut for a Freak. Fuck her! For now, he'd stand clear of shattering distance. The Boss's monster should be back soon enough.

"Oh! *Oh!* It's going to break!! Please get me out! Muckers!"

Lightning cracks struck from the pressure of the mermaid's hands on the edges of the tank. Water dribbled off the planked stage to the floor. Droplets turned to a drizzle, forming puddles, wetting the feet of those at the forefront of the crowd. Customers squelched in sawdust turned to an unpalatable woody oatmeal.

Serene's fin tensed: to stand, to jump? Surely she would slip and take the tank with her without aid. She remained seated, eying the glass, jerking at creaks.

"*Okaaaay, okaaaay*, calm down, help is on the way."

The girls reached and pled for Shilzie when she stepped outside the curtain.

Come back, come back! Their combined voices echoed in her mind.

No one noticed the small child move between partitioned stages. Not even Serene saw the tiny performer cross stage two, disappear in the blocked corner of the L-shaped stage, and slip onto stage one across from the tank.

Too busy were the mermaid's dark eyes. Wet with tears, cheeks flecked with splashes of water, willing the spreading lines to freeze, halt, stop until *real* help comes. Until someone came to get her out of the water.

Vincent had been unaware of the continuously splintering glass. *White, pulsing veins on the translucent surface.* He only noted water, steady drips at its base. Mother should know about it right away. She would tell the boys to fix it, *Johnny*, most likely.

On the way back Shilzie's mother and brother would call Rocky from the Midway. Serene can't perform in a leaking tank. It isn't safe. Mama cares too much for her people to allow one to be hurt.

Best be paranoid than sorry, she once said. *Worrying today will prevent a tragedy tomorrow.*

Precaution cannot always protect or prevent. Look at Dell and Jeb, one bumped his head—*and couldn't get up in the morning,* like the ancient rhyme. The other fell over while raising canvas at the last stop. He couldn't get back up again either. Not without heartbeats.

A gulp for courage. Serene wouldn't be accident number three.

"Preez, hep err!" Shilzie tugged on the barker's greasy tweed coat.

It stunk of smoke and sour body odor. Stitching stood out around one shoulder, and the adjacent armpit in white. Flannel fabric patched the left elbow and replaced the entire breast pocket.

Sherilyn, or Lavi, could repair the jacket for him.

Muckers doesn't like the thought of Freaks touching his things. Or the thought of paying for it—*though the ladies mend show outfits free of charge.*

Muckers wouldn't know that. Would never ask. Not a Freak.

"Hey!" his curtness quieted, realizing the identity of the grabber. The cane, tight in a fist, prepared to whack an unruly mark.

In Barnum's fuckin' name did a pat think they were gettin' on his *stage! What're they gonna do? Help her?*

Not a pat. One of the Pins from stage three.

Ugly things, he thought. *Heads no bigger than a coconut, and bright as a broken bulb shoved half way up a loon's ass.*

With one narrowed brow he said, *"Get back where you were."* His breath reeked of hooch and browned teeth gone without brushing for weeks. *Maybe years.* A lack of proper wash habits wafted from each raise of arm or shift of leg. Food, dirt, and feces turned the underside of his fingernails black. Dry skin peeled in tiny chips between furry brows working to become one.

Shilzie glanced at Serene. *She needs help.* The water, the glass.

"I said... *get back where you were."* Even more silent, and close he came until hot, rancid breath made the girl's eyes water, *"We don't want the nice patties seein' what happens when a cane cracks a tiny head like yours all over the stage.* Hmm?"

Shilzie bit her lip, hands lacing over an aching belly, and backed away.

Shilzie come back!

Come back, come back.

The fragile young girl peeked at her sisters through the spread curtains of stage three. Elvi motioned with big waves, up and over her shoulder. Nylee hugged tighter at her sister.

They could be twins with those matching petite noses, tiny smirks, teeny triangular jaws, and beady sparkling eyes. All three shared the same chocolaty brown hair and green irises.

Coloring is where similarities ceased between Shilzie and her sisters.

A triplet? A sister? In what resemblance? With such an opposing jut of brow, severely over bitten jaw, hooked nose, and wide toothy mouth.

Shilzie backpedaled, waving a hand for the curtain. She slunk behind it, and closed the red cotton, covering Muckers' snarl.

She let out a long breath, gripping the material in small fists. *He won't do it. Not really. Not in front of the crowd. Not ever!* Her mama wouldn't allow it! He would be punished if he hurt them. She knew he would.

He can't. It is the rules. Carnies *never* hurt their own. *Especially Freaks.*

Avoiding a podium and the gaff whose beak squawked toward the ceiling, she returned to stage three.

Wrapped in the arms of her sisters they barraged Shilzie with questions.

What did Muckers say?

Is Serene okay?

What's happening?

Where did Vincent go?

Is he getting us candy?

He is with Mama. Shilzie knew this. Could hear them on the midway, see them, even from inside the Ten, on stage, behind the curtain.

It leakin' real bad? Mama asks.

Not terribly. Vincent tucks down his chin in the crowd.

Think we oughta get Rocky?

Ahead, the man in question is leaving Midway Stage West, giving one last gaze to the smiling banner advertising a beautiful Armless Wonder.

I feel it would be wise to remove her, if only for precaution. She was quite frightened.

Alright. Hey Rock!

The three met and crossed to the Ten-In-One.

A leather hand slipped through the tent flap, pushing it aside for the incoming group. First, the muscled form of Rocky. His body blocked the entirety of the tent opening. Then came Dawn. Vincent lowered the canvas and followed, pinching the cloak closed, keeping his head low, away from the crowd.

"*Vinza-*," Shilzie began to call, excited, forgetting Muckers. *Remembered Serene.* Shilzie could wait for her brother. *Help Serene first.*

The waterlogged beauty moaned, gaze paralyzed and steady on the glass threatening to shatter and cut vulnerable arms and belly.

"I got you, don't you worry, I got you."

Strips of animal fur swung from the belt of Rocky's costume. Leather straps bound from upper forearm to wrist, and wrapped sandals to his feet, crisscrossing ankles and calves.

Carefully, the strongman dipped thick, dark arms into the water, curling under the mermaid's knees and across her back. Vincent stood on the ground floor. Gloved hands hovered, watching for a sign the water might push through and send shards into the audience.

"Oh, careful, careful…" Serene worried.

"He's got ya darlin', Rocky'll get ya outta there," Dawn reassured, fan frantically flapping.

The veil's teardrop beads clicked and clattered, swaying with each gust. Shilzie could make out the form of a beard beneath the semi-sheer black fabric, only because she knew it to be there. *A pat would not think to look for such a thing.*

Its conical shape flowed off the point of her mother's chin. The curling tip briefly became visible where it touched at the center of her collarbone.

Serene removed a hand from the frame and grasped Rocky's arm, raising her fused feet up and away from the water.

The crowd inspected the anomaly closely now without water to mug up the view.

A woman cringed, backing into the man behind her. He covered his mouth. Many sneered. All seemed to gasp. Shilzie could only spot one or two looking on the woman with intrigue, not disdain.

Curious, fascinated, in awe of the beautiful mermaid. She is that indeed. With straight black hair hugging the length of a sun-kissed back, and wide narrow eyes a deep dark brown, black as the undiscovered depths of the sea. Serene could have swum right out of the fairy tales Vincent reads to his sisters.

Shilzie tilted her head to listen to the conversation off stage one.

"You okay, dear?" No cuts as far as Mama could tell.

"I'm fine…" the mermaid quieted, Shilzie watched her lips, *"I'm not getting back in that tank tonight. Next time it's going to break, I just know it!"*

"No no, gonna git a man in here ta drain it pronto, an' I'll send Johnny inta town fer *new* glass an' he'll repair it *hisself* this time. Ain't leavin' it up ta no gazoonie." She patted Serene's hand once, twice, between her own. Stepping towards the crowd Dawn called, "Ya'll will have ta excuse Serene fer tonight Ladies an' Gentlemen!"

Boos.

"We need ta get our mermaid ta water before she dries up!"

They grumbled, some chuckled, few scoffed.

"Don't ya'll worry, the show'll go on, and *after*, you'll *all* be granted a ticket fer the ride'a yer choosin' fer the trouble."

There were claps, noises of disappointment, and muted conversation. The people turned to the stage when Muckers tapped his cane. *Show time!*

He started in on a story about a monster the show came across in New Mexico.

A strange dog-like creature, a monster known as the *Chupacabra. The Goat Sucker.*

Not true. Only a gaff made up of a chicken beak, feet, and sharpened bones for spines. Feathers from any bird the boys could find, and snakeskin. All stuck, wrapped, and glued to the body of a dirtied-up children's stuffed dog. A prize from the Duck Pond outside. Any patty could have one right now, stripped of its disguise.

"Did you behave while I was gone?" Vincent teased from the steps at the back of the stage. The black cloak hung over his arm. Bright red tickets curled over the top of the inside pocket.

Carnies may be considered liars, but Dawn de Barcsy certainly isn't one. Most of the time. She tries to keep her lies a whitish hue.

Nylee and Elvi stood by the partition, holding hands, agape smiles overtook earlier concern at the sound of their brother's voice. A whisper sweet as a swirl of caramel on the tip of the tongue.

They hurried to him, hand in hand.

"What trouble did my sisters get into, *hmm?"* he kissed the tops of their heads. "Was Muckers kind while I was away?"

No! But Shilzie didn't tell him that.

She grinned at the *Gentleman Beast of York.* The back of her tiny head nearly touched her shoulders as she looked up at the handsome velvety face framed by golden waves and an equally gilded beard. The second tallest man at the carnival, only two inches shorter than Rocky who stood six foot eight inches.

Both men, no matter how big, would seem average in height beside the giantess, Sabina Samson. An elegant lady of seven feet two inches. *Promoted as eight foot two inches for the crowd.*

Is she okay?

Did Serene get hurt?

Where are Mama and Rocky taking her?

What about the show?

Will she really dry up?

Still smiling big at the Beast, Shilzie asked, "Sreen ay?"

"No worries my beautiful girl," he bent to one knee and wrapped an arm around Shilzie, pulling her close. "Serene will be just fine. Johnny is on his way to fix her tank, and tomorrow she will be ready to sing for the crowd."

She leaned into the embrace, laying her head against his shoulder. Small hands disappeared in the long golden locks cascading down his chest.

Is Vincent going to finish the story tonight?

Ask him Shilzie!

We want to know what happens.

Vincent stood, meaning to return to stage four. The triplets lecture would begin as soon as the pats finished inspecting the *Chupacabra.*

"Vinza," she took his large and hairy hand, no longer hidden by leather. "Tory niht?"

"Of course," soft fingers brushed her cheek. "We will finish the story tonight. We must see how it ends," with a smile he gently squeezed her hand, and turned to the curtain. Lifting it, he passed by, and let it fall.

"Ladies and gentlemen for our next exhibit of human curiosities we have the last remaining members of an ancient Aztec tribe..." Muckers droned with neither the enthusiasm nor innovation required of a proficient carnival barker.

Shilzie sighed. *Time to dance for the people.*

TWO KINDS OF JOHNS
∽ HILLY ∾

Hot and hard muscles shifted beneath her hands. White thighs hugged the waist delving deep and fast between her legs. Eager breaths rustled damp hair.

She bit her bottom lip to stifle a cry.

Men gathered outside for the next show.

"Oh, honey!"

"Hey, pretty lady!"

Whistling, howling.

"Gentleman, this fine woman, she will DAZE you! Drive you CRAZE-y!" The spiel and calls waned in and out.

He wrapped both arms around her and buried his face into her neck, gritty breaths and guttural moans vibrating flesh. Next, he would pull her close, mashing her breasts, lifting her against his chest. With trembling legs, hips striving forth toward the end.

She took a handful of hair and gripped his shoulder, holding on when they climaxed. Their bodies quivered, clenching and shaking in unison until the pleasure ebbed and his body went lax.

Hilly welcomed the weight of him, his warmth, even his smell.

Dirt, and the faint scent of oil and metal. Not typically a woman's most favorite aroma. She inhaled it deeply, enjoying each distinct note.

Dust and grit. Iron, handling tools. Sweat from work and passion. His hair hinted at shampoo, it melted away beneath the rest. Mostly she inhaled the warmth of his own masculine scent. She couldn't describe it, other than heat, and earth, burning leaves in October damp.

After a few much-needed breaths the man lifted his head. Brown eyes traced the arch of her brows, the fullness of her lips, the sleepy slant of sated eyes. One hand lifted to pinch a strand of pale blonde hair between his fingers and hooked the curl behind her ear.

Her gaze kept with his, lips parting when she turned it to his mouth.

They never kissed. She never kissed *any* man. Passionately, or otherwise.

Never on the mouth. *Rule number three.*

A cheek occasionally, *the closest she ever got.* Swift, and precisely placed.

Hilly believed a *real* kiss, one involving lips and tongue, is reserved for love. Far from what she did with the Johns.

The Johns require no warming up, *in the romantic sense.* Tender kisses or gentle petting. Paying customers want her on back, and knees. The floor, the bed, gripping the baseboard, headboard, her ankles. Any way to quench their needs. To bring lewd and exotic fantasies to life. A quick tug of hand or a flick of tongue finished most off instantaneously. Easy money.

Majority arrive hard before entering the tent. Too ready for the thrill of a stranger. *The blasphemy of sex without the goal of procreation.*

They pay for sheer pleasure without consequence of children, and nothing more.

Labor-roughened fingers touched her chin, pulling her back into the man's studious regard.

Those familiar brown eyes held firm. Cocoa outlined the irises at the rim, honey and maple syrup drizzled toward the pupil. The sticky sweet gaze fell to her lips once more.

Pink, flushed red from release, and softened with lip balm.

Would his lips be dry from the sun? Chapped? Rough like his palms? Smooth like the skin of his back?

She *wanted* to kiss a man. The wait had gone on so long she did not want to throw away the first carelessly. It would happen at the right time, with the right man. A man of her choosing. A man she loved. She would *have* to love him. Fully, unconditionally. The kind of love she ached for at night.

Outside a shadow approached. Gangly and carrying a cane. A warped top hat off-kilter to the right.

The thin form, *Sunny*, called softly, "Hey, *uh*, Johnny... *buddy*, don't mean ta rush ya, but... the lady is requested on stage."

Shouldn't have done this, should have turned him away... or should *he* have turned *her* away?

His stop by the Kootch had been for professional reasons, to fix the stairs after Vie's fall. To prevent another accident from cursing the show's season. So no one else would be hurt. So *she* would not be hurt.

Hilly thanked him for the repairs. He smiled. She returned it.

Pondered aloud that the next show would start after her break ended. Casually informed she would head back to her room to change. *She didn't have long until the next dance.*

Her lip may have slid from nibbling teeth, she may have taken a deeper breath than necessary to drag his eyes under the swell of her breasts like a drowning man helpless against the ocean's rising current.

Today's costume lay on opposite sides of the tent. On the edge of a costume trunk the brassiere clung by a single hook. A bead fringed skirt landed on the bookcase. Panties tented atop one kicked shoe.

Johnny sighed, the warmth of his breath fanned her face, fluttering strands of platinum hair. "Yeah... Hilly'll... she'll be right out." Without another look, he rolled to his side and sat on the edge of the small creaking bed.

She gathered up the sheet at her breasts, covering a bare, and glistening body. A circlet of tangled rawhide Johnny used to tie his hair fell from the linen folds. She picked it up, undoing the knot as she watched him.

He covered his face and scrubbed at a stubbly jaw. Wide tan shoulders tensed, covered in red marks and fingernail indentations.

"I ain't got no cash on me," he didn't want to say it. Guilt forbade he look at her.

She dismissed the comment with a head shake. "I'm sorry you can't stay longer…"

What is she doing? Never during a show! Before, after, but *between* shows now?

"Ain't yer fault…" he sighed, eyes on his lap, a hand moved there.

"Maybe you could come back tonight?"

"You ain't busy?"

Right. The Johns after curtain drop itching for a *private dance.*

Daze couldn't take care of them alone.

Her mouth opened-

"Thought so." He stood, pilfered three tissues from a box on the end table, and made his way to the tin trash can by the vanity. Red paint chips littered the floor like autumn leaves around its rusting bottom.

A rubber—*slick with feminine arousal, no coital gel required*—dropped from his hand, next, a tacky wad of tissues.

More rubbers stood at the ready in a repurposed candy tin under the bed. Beside it: the lid, a jar of unnecessary coital gel, and a hastily torn pink and white box reading: *'Avoid Sickness! Trust Hughes Brand Condoms.'*

"Are you heading back to Shadow?"

"Nah," Johnny kicked up the rumpled heap of brown material beside the vanity with the top of his foot. Caught it by the belt still looped. The muscles of his thighs and backside flexed. Hilly admired them shamelessly. "Gonna head over to Carrie. Heard talk she's bein' stubborn today."

Smiling, lifting perusing eyes, "She's an old woman. Of course she is."

"Ain't that the truth," he pulled up his pants and buttoned the fly. Sat to tug on an old pair of socks, stood. Slipping into scuffed black boots he squinted, scouring the rug, beneath the nightstand, "Where the...?"

A sleeveless white undershirt tangled within the sheet.

She leaned for it. "Here."

When he grabbed, she retracted.

"Gonna hand it over?" his expectant hand hovered midair, halfway between them. His eyes struggled to avoid the now exposed breasts he'd moments ago worked with his hands, mouth, and tongue. Hiding the quick looks, *unsuccessfully*, with squinting.

Hilly didn't mind.

That's what they're there for, Aunt Babs use to say.

"Come by later? After we've closed."

The Kootch show started at dusk and ended early after a handful of dances and blow-offs. Time enough before closing for Johns to finish their business and head back to wandering wives calling out names.

Johnny smirked, the left side of his mouth tugging tightly, "You tryin' ta bleed me dry woman?"

"Doesn't have to be for that," she said, grinning. "I like *talking* with you, you know."

He huffed, doubting, "Yeah 'cause I'm just *swell* at conversatin'."

Soft shoulders shrugged. Johnny watched them lift, eyes going up the side of her neck, before following down once more to her breasts. Quickly his eyes found the nearest side pole. He gave it a pat with his fist for good measure, mock testing its security.

"It's good enough for me."

He laughed once, more of a grunt, "Yer easy ta please."

Smirking she assured the contrary. "*No*... not really. But *you* get the job done."

Johnny coughed, eyes gone again to the tent. Knocking the wood for a second time.

This man's modesty is a rarity. Something she found utterly provocative in a man. *This man.*

"Come on, we could *just* talk. Drink some of that hooch Sunny picked up before leaving Cali."

The good kind. Not the Tub Rust rousties pass around campfires.

Rust *is* cheap and abundant. Homemade most often in tubs as the name suggests. Questionable when it comes to ingredients and the cleanliness of the vat whence it had been brewed. Nevertheless, the stuff is inexpensive enough the workers' wages can take a hit. *Quality* hooch is hard to come by on the road.

Doesn't make it taste any better. Stuff is like sucking on a filthy nail found lying in a gutter.

He hummed indecisively, able to look at her once more. He did enjoy a good nip now and again. "Tell ya what. If yer free after closin', meet me at the Eye," taking the shirt, he put it on. She held up her index finger, rawhide curled around the tip. Taking that as well, he headed for the exit finishing, "Bring the drink," he winked. "Bye Girly."

"See you there..." she smirked, *"Mr. Rollercoaster Man."*

"Ah Hel, not you too."

Laughter shook the bed. *"Can't you see I am your biggest fan?"*

Mr. Rollercoaster Man. Oh, what a man. Mr. Rollercoaster

Man.

"Stop!" he groaned. "Why're ya'll tryin' ta ruin that tune for me? Swear I used to like it a good deal. *Not no more…*"

Not since the Sherry Vena hit inspired a feature film and returned to its previous hype. Including a cover by an up-and-coming gal by the name of Kitten Belle.

Nice, but sung too fast in comparison to the original's slow vocal roll.

The song's resurgence on the radio sparked the carnival crewmen to tease their boss relentlessly. *Hilly included.*

"And ya know I run a *big wheel,* right?"

A gasp, "You do?"

His smile yanked hard to one side, widening his lips. The expression took years off of his face. Rendering him boyish and adorable.

Johnny didn't mind the little nickname. *Not from her.*

The boys, yes. Sunny, definitely. Blake, you bet ya. The young man can't seem to stop boasting that his name is featured right there in the lyrics:

> *Oh I know,*
> *Back when that Blake was mine,*
> *he ran all over town!*
> *night and day,*
> *he'd run away,*
> *I couldn't make him stay!*
> *But, he's just a, Good ol boy,*
> *And you're oooooo, What a Man!*
> *Mmmm Mr. Rollercoaster Man*

"Alright," still smirking, "bye-bye."

"Bye Johnny."

Hilly leaned against the pillows, grinning at his shadow.

It brushed together hair the color of brass. Dark, tarnished, in need of shining at the root. Lightest at the top where the sun hits most directly. Scooping, gathering, smoothing down the sides from the temple. He tied a double knot and bent for his toolkit before disappearing.

Once gone her gaze went to the vaulting dingy white ceiling.

That man, she thought, and nothing else. Her hands touched where he touched, running up each arm and across the collarbone, knees squeezing. A familiar pulse beat with her heart between them. If it weren't for the show. For the inevitability of Sunny's return—*a five-minute warning, four, three, two, one*—she may have considered rubbing her fingers against the thrumming that thoughts of Johnny reawakened.

Who am I becoming? Daze? She laughed, scoffed, and shuddered, in succession. *This isn't like me at all.*

Dangerous thoughts, her mother's voice.

You only like him 'cause he gets you off, Daze's.

Do not! He's only a friend.

Men and women can't be only *friends. Our parts are opposite. And opposites attract. Magnets drawn together. Prongs into sockets.* A mother's wisdom. *Besides, men aren't* friends *with* whores.

"Five minutes Hon!"

The smile disappeared. Thoughts dimmed from bright to dark. Friends and whores. Johnny to faceless Johns slathering wet, perhaps even drunken lips on her body. Hot hands giving chills. Phantom illness in her belly. Shame. Dirtiness.

Hilly stood from the bed smelling of the man, *her friend*, who made her smile, and prepared herself for the next performance.

DEVIL IN DISGUISE
◟ MORGAN ◞

"Ladies and Gentlemen what you are about to see will *shock*, and *amaze* you… This man you see before you, *believe me* when I say, he has the luck of a Devil. This young man right here, is the *Man* with the *Devil's* Lucky Streak!

"The day I met this man I was sittin' on my front porch and the sky turns black as pitch. It began rainin' so fiercely the drops left dents the size of silver dollars on the hood of my car! Now this man, while I cowered under my roof, prayin' to all there is, that my home and my very life would be spared by such a heinous storm… well he just kept walkin'… without a care. I tell you I could hear him whistle! Well, he weren't whistlin' for long. No! From above I hear a terrible sound! Like drums poundin' in my ears. Then there was a flash of light and a CRACK!… The old elm in front of my house set aflame, and the branch, right from the very top, I saw it fall. Fall right down to this man here. Why he looked up, couldn't let out a yell before that branch went right down his throat! I turned away, knowin' no mere man could survive such a thing… then I saw him… *Alive*… He grabbed that branch and pulled it out his mouth like a finished-off chicken bone! I could not believe my eyes, but this man was unharmed! Untouched! All but for one thing… his hair had gone *white* from the fright of it all… 'cept for one streak, *straight down the back*. His lucky streak…

"Now won't you all give Lucky a hand!"

Lucky, as known to the crowd; to the residents within the canvas walls of Carnivàle de la Llum, he was Morgan. Few used this name, some did not know it, most forgot it.

What's the archaic saying? *Use it, or lose it?*

None spoke to Morgan in any regular conversational sense, how could they utilize this supposed name of his? So, it was lost. Rather, they stuck to Lucky. It is written across his banner, much less of a hassle to remember if requiring his attention. One look toward the Midway and there it is. *The Man With the Devil's Lucky Streak.*

Hey you, pal, punk, little mouse, shitheel, fucking waste, were also acceptable when his name escaped the tongues of coworkers.

The majority did not bother with him. Did not have the chance. Morgan didn't give them one.

Wells, *the barker at the helm of Midway Stage East,* Morgan interacted with more than any other individual in the carnival.

You ready?

A nod.

Alright kid, let's give 'em those thrills they paid for.

That initial step on stage is the hardest.

The eyes. Marks, patties, rubes, parents, children, strangers. *People.*

Breathe. Don't look at them. Breathe.

The thud of his heart skipped beats. Hurried, slowed, lagging. Pumping, faster, faster, failing, urging, heavy, crashing wildly. The contractions seemed to cease, the muscle lifting as an enemy's head flaunted in the fist of the victor, before slamming against his sternum. Bashing itself awake, into regularity.

Breathe, breathe, breathe.

He gulped the air. In deeply and out to further steady the rhythm. To calm himself, to ease the familiar dizziness. The coolness of panic rubbing its hands across his belly, stroking his cheeks and neck. Combing fingers through his hair, caressing his scalp with claws.

Morgan took that first hesitant step from the banner line. Held his gaze above the edge of the crowd, down a lane of game joints, where Star's fence herded a waiting line into order.

Breathe.

His lips thinned, chin dipping toward the applause, the closest he could muster to a smile and a bow.

Randall watched with lackluster interest from the Bottle Ring joint, stoop-shouldered on a stool, arms crossed as pats tried their best to throw rings. Betting coins from their own pocket one might land around the necks of bottles varying in size.

The bigger the bottle, the more difficult to fit the ring, but the better the prize if successful.

The grand prize, a cheap radio, was not one Morgan's boss, Dawn de Barcsy, worried over keeping in stock. In Morgan's eight years with de la Llum, he could count on his hands the instances he witnessed a young man, or father, *always a man,* walk away with a shiny new radio under his arm. Though by that time, he paid the cost*, if not double*, of buying a radio of better quality from the nearest *Hughes Brand Electronics & Appliances.*

The thrill of winning kept customers paying for those red wooden rings. Of having conquered. Beating the impossible.

The thrill is what maintains the attention of every crowd.

Whether the thrill be excitement, fear, disgust, or lust.

These people will fear Morgan's performance. Fear *for* him. His safety. Scream and fidget, even gag or faint. But they would clap and cheer, exhale in relief once the show came to a close, and he survived.

At center stage, he held three items. One he would set to the side for now: a torch. The other lifted, slowly twisting in the air as if intimidating a sparring partner. Real steel, shiny and smooth. With the third item, a cooking oil-dampened rag, he clamped the blade and stroked once, end to end, hilt to tip. Some licked the metal for lubrication, others used nothing at all.

Morgan tossed the rag. Displayed the blade once more. *Real, all real folks. Solid steel.* The weapon glimmered above his open mouth. Light bounced off metal edges, winking, assuring the audience before easing down the performer's vulnerable throat. Passed the esophagus it dived deep. Between the lungs, beside a live, beating heart, and into an empty stomach.

The cross-guard rested in the corners of his mouth. He raised his arms. Nothing would keep the blade from shifting inside his body.

A resounding awe rose from the ground below.

Morgan put both hands on the hilt, making as if he were going to save himself from further danger and remove the sword from his body. With a quick turn, he rotated the sword from front to back. A woman cried out, fell against a man, stumbled, and disappeared. Another revolution and the audience clutched one another.

"Pull it out!"

"Oh, I can't watch!"

He lifted the blade. The people sighed and brought their hands together.

From here he continued with his act: hammering a nail up one nostril, spitting fireballs above the crowd, and lastly swallowing a sword once more, though this time, the blade first wetted with fuel and set aflame. At the end of his shift, he gave his last and final nod of appreciation for applause and headed for the stairs while Wells urged them on, *more, louder*, for Lucky's death-defying feats! Give him a hand folks! Give him two!

Morgan stepped into Midway Alley—*the space between Stage East and West where performers rest and prepare between acts—* when Dawn pushed aside a banner on his left.

"Hey! See Johnny while you was out there?"

A faint sheen of sweat dotted her brow. Cheeks pink above a black beaded veil. She opened the clasped fan in her hand and waved furiously. Beard hairs stuck to her throat.

He shook his head, packing a bag.

Swords, cans of kerosene and lighter fluid. One for blasting, the other for mouth stunts. A torch, matches, a box of nails, and a hammer.

An eight ball, three more swords, varying lengths and widths of needles, razor blades, rags, gauze, and a saw blade awaited their fellows fresh off the stage. A dangerous crew of metal and pain.

Morgan had not yet decided what to do with the saw blade. One consideration: *a bed of saws.*

"Damn it," she sighed. "Ya sure? Cause he ain't at Shadow."

Another shake as he lingered on the drawstrings, an evasion from eye contact.

"Varlyn said he's supposed ta be workin' on Carrie. Ain't there neither…" Dawn grunted, mumbling, *"Better not be at the Kootch."*

Morgan waited with the bag slung over his shoulder.

Should he respond? He didn't know what to say.

Sorry?

I hope not?

Damn that man for not being easier to find!

He had no clue what she wanted to hear. *If* she wanted anything.

"Headin' to the backyard?"

He nodded.

All the easier to avoid others in his caravan. He could remain inconspicuous, and out of the way.

"I hate ta ask ya, but I lost my help along the way, could ya stop by Carrie? See if he's workin' on it—*like he's supposed ta."* Her eyes made to roll, stopped, "Oh, and tell 'im I'm lookin' fer 'im. Serene's tank's leakin' again," *he didn't need to know this,* but she continued, "And he's fixin' it hisself! The others—don't want 'em *lookin'* at it!"

"'Em," meaning the roustabouts. More importantly, the greenies. In no regard should any newcomer work on such an important task. Rather stick to hauling, cleaning, other low-end maintenance. *If a monkey can do it, so can a newbie,* long-time troupers often jest.

Morgan inhaled. *He could talk to Johnny if he had to.* Has in the past when his caravan required repairs.

He won't be there anyway. Probably back at the Shadow right now.

Probably, not *definitely.*

Please be at the Shadow.

Only a quick look, and when he's *not* there. Not at Carrie, not surrounded by impatient crowds, Morgan could hurry to the backyard.

He nodded.

"Thank you, darlin'." The fan shut with a clack. "I'm headin' back to the big wheel. If he ain't there... *guess I'm checkin' the fuckin' Kootch."*

With that, she disappeared the way she came.

Morgan sidestepped behind the banners across from the Ten-In-One bally. Varlyn juggled. His mother Patricia tossed fruit from the edge of the stage, upping the count of items from three, to six, to nine.

The Kootch tent stood on the far left of the Ten. He could make out the shimmer of either Daze or Vie's costume. The dancers were twins, Morgan couldn't be sure from such a distance whom was who. Hilly was nowhere to be seen.

Avoiding patrons, he continued to the right, ducking his head and tightening his hold on the bag. Pointed bits and box corners prodded his back.

Almost there. Then to the seclusion of the wagon. Where he could be alone, no one entering without a given invitation. Free to fall into bed, unwind, clean swords and needles. Disappear in mindless tasks until bedtime. And tomorrow, he would perform, and do it all over again.

"*Hustle up Johnny,* these nice folks are waiting," a dark-haired man gave a wink to the group standing outside the fenced-in area. His mouth propped open with a smile.

A lion's mane of hair parted in a voluminous heap to the right, a tidal wave of feathery layers reaching mid-spine. Lengths of ticket stubs sprouted from a jacket pocket. Rings clotted each hand, silver and gold and jewels crowned every knuckle. Slimmer bands of metal and stone wrapped the upper segment of index, middle, and ring finger.

Morgan didn't know the newcomer's name.

Dawn spotted the man on a street corner back in California. Stalled the procession of cars, trucks, and wagons, and waved him over for a chat. In only a few passed words, a nod, and a handshake, he hopped aboard.

"If you'd shut it, I could get her goin'. Just give me a fu-" Johnny bit his tongue, considering the children over his sweaty and grease-smeared shoulder. A scratch, pink and fading, stretched from the center of his back. "Give me a minute alright? That hunky-dory with you?"

The ride jock rose bedecked hands defensively. "Alright, alright, don't get sore. I'm sure the children don't mind if they miss out on riding Carrie tonight. They can come back when we swing around *next year...* right kids?"

The children called out no, and booed.

Johnny tossed a wrench into his kit in exchange for a screwdriver. "*We're open tomorrow ya idgit...* " he mumbled. "Why ya razzin' me anyhow? I ain't the one broke down my ride first week I run her solo."

"Better fixing my ride than having me on your crew."

"No, no. Yer a hard worker... just ain't a good one."

The newcomer chuckled.

"*Hey there.* You come for a ride too?" His attention fully diverted from hassling Johnny to the man approaching. Familiar paths carved lines in his cheeks, the teeth in his smile bold and naked without concealment. Too welcoming. Too eager.

Morgan gulped, averting his gaze further from the newbie, inching closer. Bypassing a fence meant not to be crossed.

He wasn't supposed to be here. Not at the carousel. This wasn't his job. He should be outside the fence. Not near the platform. They wonder why he is allowed so close without a ticket. Why? Why does he get to do this? What makes him so special?

Don't lift your head, not toward the line, they're staring.

Forcibly raising his voice, loud enough, *he hoped,* for Johnny to hear, "D-dawn is looking for you."

"Oh yeah?" a glance.

Morgan breathed in relief, *he heard me.* He would not have to repeat himself. *The anguish. The embarrassment of repeating oneself. Over, and over. Never loud enough... Or are they ever listening to begin with?*

"*Someone's in trouble,*" the jockey murmured in sing-song.

Johnny grunted, tightening a screw. "What for?"

"Serene's tank-" all he could say.

"*Hel!* Again?!"

A stiff nod, though Johnny did not see it.

"Well..." arms rested across his thighs, he sighed, "that tank's gonna have ta wait till mornin', so Dawn'll have ta live with it. I got Shadow ta run, Star's got a busted seat..." he stopped to judge his handiwork. Satisfied, "Evro see if Carrie'll start up."

The Jockey, Evro, brushed by Morgan as he stepped off the platform, jacket tails flopping against his thighs as he walked. An orange scarf coiled under the loops of leather pants, knotted at the hip, flowing with the swift movement of his leg. No shirt under the jacket. Only a crystal pendant descending from a thin gold chain. The man's boots ended above the knee, heavy with leather, collapsing in thick folds at the calf and ankle.

The outfit he wore held a passing similarity to Morgan's. Leather pants, dress jacket with tails, and boots hugging tight to his calves. Though Morgan wore no sash around his waist and the fabric of the coat was of plain black linen with no adornments of any kind.

This man's jacket was brown suede, and flashy. *The whole ensemble too attention-grabbing for Morgan's tastes.* Gold buttons with celestial etchings, a border of beige satin along the jacket cuffs, tails, and collar. Laces crisscrossed the side of his legs to the hip, large brass buckles clinked at his ankles.

He must have requested the changes from Sherilyn.

A plethora of old dress jackets went unused in storage, though none quite like this. More flamboyant and brightly colored surely, but not these details.

Johnny crouched at the column, a colorfully painted panel lay on its side near his feet. Large cogs, chains, and rotating mechanisms, *nothing Morgan understood*, hid within its center.

"Come on baby girl, start for Papa," Evro started the ride's engine, took hold of the starting gear, and pulled back.

Lights blinked and brightened. Music began to play. A tinkling melody sure to lure in children and adults alike.

Morgan considered it quite somber for an amusement ride. Slow, sinister in the way it built, and lagged, enticed, and filled the heart with dread. High pitches, followed by low, lower, lower, building, depleting. A toy whose key needs another turn before it stops marching or clapping its hands.

Nevertheless, the platform began to move, slow at first, then gained speed. The horses galloped, once more able to run free.

The patrons cheered and hurried to the front of the line.

"Thank you, Johnny," Evro crooned.

"Yeah, yeah," he held up the panel and slid it back into place. Each one painted with a scene from a fairy tale. This image depicted a beautiful young woman with roses and diamonds floating free from red parted lips. An angry, frightened girl behind her coughed-up toads and snakes. "Get back ta jockeyin', I gotta get goin'."

"Yes sir!" he said, before yelling to the crowd, "Let's all give a round of thanks to Johnny! Carrie's hero, she's patched up and raring to go!"

Light applause, and earnest thanks from eager children.

"Thank you!"

"Thank you, Johnny!"

"Yeah…" the mechanic waved away the claps, his mouth tight to one side with a smile.

The ride stopped, and while Johnny crossed the platform Evro began ushering children on board, taking tickets and helping them onto their chosen steed.

What are you naming her? Is that what he asked the children?
Which one do you like? He's a beauty, good choice.

"So is Dawn still lookin' fer me?" Johnny asked Morgan.

He shrugged, shifting the weight of his bag from one shoulder to the other. Eyes down he replied, "She said she was going back to Shadow."

Though she may be searching the Kootch tent at this very moment.

Judging by those scratches, and the pale blonde strand of hair stuck to the front of Johnny's shirt, Dawn's suspicions were spot on. The wheelman's hair was light brown, maybe even dark blonde, not nearly that light, or long enough.

"*Well... guess I'm in fer an earful,*" he grumbled. "See ya later Lucky," he pat his shoulder and headed to the Shadow's Eye.

Morgan stiffened at the touch. Johnny did not see the reaction. How the sword swallower's shoulder recoiled protectively against the contact. The *panic* of contact, the withheld breath.

"So... you want that ride now?"

Morgan turned at the voice.

The carousel jockey stood behind him, lips cocked in a half smile. The ride spun slowly, music playing, tarnished mirror panels glinting reflections of light in all directions. The ground and every person in the ride's vicinity cast in ever-moving shooting stars.

He shook his head, face down, avoiding the man's dark eyes.

Scheming. Watchful.

Are they? He seemed nice to the children.

Was that his voice? Could have been parents. Some stood on the platform. Smiling, holding a pole as the ride turned and their child giggled gleefully. Whipping reigns, hopping in the saddle.

What does he want? Why is he still talking to me?

The newcomer back peddled to the rotating stampede of horses. Still smiling, never taking his eyes off Morgan. "Let me know when you do. I'll be here." As the ride turned, he took hold of a pole and stepped aboard in one swift movement.

Before the carousel could bring Evro back around Morgan made for the backyard, clutching the straps of his bag. Flush creeping over his body and heart pounding in tune with the calliope.

SIDES OF A COIN
∽ BILLY & MORTY ∾

"Now, I want you to promise me you will be good. Be brave, be kind. Even when someone is mean to you. Even if they hurt your feelings. Promise me, Billy. You're my good boy. You will be good, and listen to the nice lady, she… she will take care of you now."

Mama's gaze met the woman in the corner.

She nodded, tears sparkling in her eyes. Hugging her own son by the arm so tight she may choose to never let him go.

"And do what makes you happy. This is a terrible world we live in. Hold on to what makes you smile. Be happy, and remember, your Mama loves you. I will always love you. Goodbye, my sweet baby."

Mama hugged with one arm, kissing her son's right cheek, his forehead, and hair. As much of his face as she could before going into one of her fits.

Blood spotted her hanky. Brown with old stains that wouldn't be washed away. Coughing, she watched her sons leave. Tears bulged from her eyes, mixing with the blood trickling from her mouth. She waved, clutching a hand to her chest. Not because her lungs hurt, but because her heart did.

Billy knew this because so did his.

He couldn't stop crying, even on the car ride back to the carnival.

He sat between the Boss Lady, Dawn, and the big beast man, Vincent, who drove. Bawling into his hands, then into the lady's shoulder when she pulled him to her. Like a mama would. Just like a mama.

Where were his manners when they arrived?

None too polite at all! *Not in his mind anyway.* The staring, the questions, the reactions.

Especially those for Vincent.

In the popular new horror film, *The Lion Man,* Cyrus Abbot— *played by the incomparable Leonard Frank*—goes on a hunting trip in Africa. In the middle of the night, he is attacked and nearly killed by an animal, a *real* wild lion. Months later, back home in New York and fully mended he realizes his newfound insatiable appetite for meat. Rare and bloody, he can't get enough! One day, as he's cutting into a fresh slab of steak, blood dripping down his fork, he looks out his window at the fiery orange sky as the sun sets, and begins his transformation into *The Lion Man!* A beast covered in hair, a mane sprouting off of his head and neck, claws growing where fingernails once were. He ravages the streets at night, mauling civilians left and right until the climax, when the woman he loves puts him down with his favorite hunting rifle.

Billy gasped as the visiting stranger pulled away the black hood.

It's Cyrus Abbot! The Lion Man, the Beast who ravaged New York!

Run! His instincts insisted.

Instead, Billy knocked a hip against the hall table, halting an escape. Cornered, he put on a twitch of a smile and motioned the man an invitation to enter.

"Thank you," he led his mother by the hand. *"You have a lovely home,"* the lion smiled, taking in the photographs, and doilies, and knick-knacks Mama carefully arranged in their cozy farmhouse.

Billy never saw someone like him in his life. Didn't know one could exist outside of horror flicks. So tall, and covered in hair, he really did look like a beast. The lion monster from the film! *At first anyway.* Now he seems so gentle. *A kitten.*

Vincent wasn't the only one to receive such rudeness. He stared at the lady's beard.

He knew it wasn't polite of him. If his mama hadn't been sick, she would have scolded him and told him to apologize. *She didn't.* So, he stared.

Magazines say ladies shouldn't have face hair. A hair or two on the chin may be plucked without much concern. If the upper lip or jaw line fills out in a moustache or beard it is a sign of unhealthiness. Hirsutism it is called, a diagnosis which will change a woman's status from Normal to Sick.

Hiding such symptoms from a doctor may be punishable by a fine or jail time.

Naturally occurring leg hair and underarm hair are not usually cause for HSA, or Health Status Adjustment, but Normal women *are* encouraged to remove it. Hairiness in a woman is unhygienic. *A lady must be smooth and clean.*

Billy didn't understand those articles. If hair is dirty, why don't men shave their bodies? Why only women? Why can men have hair?

Even under the visiting woman's veil, he noticed whiskers and couldn't stop looking while she talked to his mama. Not hearing the discussion, not a word. Their deal of Billy and his brother leaving with Dawn and her son. Leaving home to work in a carnival. Live there, travel. Leave home. Forever. They wouldn't come back. This wasn't for the day, or a weekend stay. Not a holiday vacation. But permanent.

Billy stared, tempted to tug the circlet of auburn from the tip. Wondering if it would spring back to shape.

Dawn smiled through the rudeness. Real nice, like his mama when she caught him watching her make dinner, or when she did needlepoint in front of the window. With the sun hitting high on her cheeks and lighting up her hair like gold. So pretty back then, before she got sick.

Only a little cough at first, then the wheezing, coughing until out of breath. One day she noticed the blood, but ignored it. Until it happened again. More and more frequent. Her chest started to ache. Her lungs, she said, felt full of water. So full up she couldn't take in any air. Drowning in her own chest.

Later, *every* breath became a struggle. She'd brace herself sometimes, holding chair arms, or fisting bed sheets, holding her son's hand, summoning the strength. Face going red, then purple before at last swallowing a bit of air.

Billy didn't want to leave her. But she wanted him to go. She didn't want him to watch her that way anymore. And she didn't want *them* to take her sons away. *The doctors.* She feared Billy and his brother getting locked up in a room for the rest of their life. She wished for her boys a chance at happiness, of *freedom.*

Isn't that what I have already? He wondered. *With her?* Why would it be different… *without her…*

She knew the carnival would be in town soon.

This time of year, she brought home flyers so Billy could put them up in his room with the rest of his newspaper clippings and magazine pages.

His brother didn't like his collection. Made fun of his twin's daydreams of dining with starlets and playing billiards with playboys. Said it would never happen. They would scream looking at him.

No woman would dare touch you, no man would allow it. Might infect *her.*

He's all I got now.

Their father took off before they were born, and Mama... well, he hoped she'd be watching over them now—*maybe she turned into one of those angels like in his book of mythical creatures.*

That's what Dawn explained to him on his second day away from home. When he begged her to take him back. He wanted his mama. Missed her so much.

She said his mama would be with him always now. Wherever he went, it didn't matter.

She croaked, his brother spat, frustrated with Billy's shaking head, not comprehending the stranger's words. Refusing to believe.

Even at the carnival, she could still be alive at home. Still alive. Not gone.

I'm so sorry Honey, Dawn hugged him. Patted his back for a good hour.

Mama is gone. More beautiful than ever and just as lovely as those days sitting in the sun, humming as she embroidered flowers onto scarves and her sons' initials onto handkerchiefs.

What the fuck can I do with this? He says. *Nothing!*

Someday, he might want it. He will miss her and want to hold the stitching against his cheek, rub it between his fingers.

Their mother made those things for her sons. Whether or not of any use to his brother, *that* is why he should want them. Because she made them. For her sons. Because she loved her children. As much as anyone *can* love Morty, she tried her best.

Both handkerchiefs lined Billy's front pockets, folded into triangles. Right, his own, left his brothers. The comfort of home, when needed, or a smile from a good memory.

Get a load of this fuckin' rube. Morty brought Billy back to the present.

Should I call for help? he hesitated, looking about. Nothing seemed out of the ordinary. Same curtain. Same stage. No shouting. *Mumbling*, but no panic.

What?

You said, rube. Isn't that the safe word?

The what?

You know, the word we're supposed to yell when we need help. Isn't rube the word they told us to say?

Oh! Yeah... Never mind that, shut up and pay attention.

Billy gaped at the back of the curtain. A man stepped on stage. He banged his cane on the floorboards. *Clack, clack, clack.*

"*Now...* ladies and gentlemen, this show was not advertised on the outside. Why? Oh, I'll tell ya. What you are about to see... it is not for the faint of heart. You will never forget it, once you have seen what is behind this curtain, though you may *want to...*

"They are said to commune with each other through *thought...* Folks, I *give you...* the *Twins* of One Mind."

The man talking hooked the curtain and flung it back, exposing Billy and his brother Morty to the room.

Too bright. A young man across the tent stood on a step ladder angling a spotlight at the stage. Flooding their vision with white light. Billy could make out a circular swarm within the tent. A backlit anthill. Outlines of dark figures huddling together, leaning forward in amazement, pointing, recoiling in disgust, fleeing out the exit with hands covering mouths. He could hear these faceless shadows. Gasping, women screamed, a child began to cry.

Billy frowned, and held a hand out, hiding from the light.

His brother laughed and smacked his lips. He smiled. Billy could feel it.

Aww, I was hoping one of them would go down. Fuckers deserve a fainting spell.

Morty that's not nice, someone could hurt themselves-

Exactly! That's why it's so fuuuucking fuuuunny! Oh-oh-oh like that fucknut they buried this morning! Head smack dab on a stake and out go the lights! Moron!

It was an accident, that's what Dawn said. It-it can happen at carnivals. Accidents happen all the time she said.

Two down! More to go, I hope!

"Get a good look folks. Step on up, right up close... *if you dare,"* the man laughed. A smile faced the crowd, meanwhile, eyes checked the time.

...You'd think we'd get one of the good ones to talk for us. We're the stars! Isn't that what the old bitch said? Instead, we get him. Sipping from that flask when he thinks no one is looking... He won't be laughing when his liver starts to rot... Or he finds himself eyeball-deep on a tent stake.

Billy squirmed at the mention of eyeballs.

It's not up to us Morty, we're new here. Besides, he's not too bad. It's a big group-

-Yeah, because of us. Do you think it's the dumb bastards like him bringing in the crowds? That these dimwits hollering fairytales of beasts, and Aztecs have anything to do with the draw of the audience? It's us. The stars on the banner-

We don't have a banner Morty-

Don't interrupt me William...

Sorry.

...Anyway, it's us, little brother. The Freaks are what bring in these pukes. They're scared of us. Scared of catching what we have, but they can't help themselves. It's like they get off on being disgusted. See any knobs pokin' out down there?

Billy would look for no such things, winced at the thought. A person's privates are their own business to keep.

Morty, please stop.

Why? I'm speaking the truth, you know it.

You don't know them. Normal people aren't all *bad.*

Listen to them William. Laughing, crying, screaming. You call that good? Remember when we first got here? They all *looked at us-*

Not mean, not all of them *were mean.*

No, maybe not all of them sneered and whispered behind our backs. But they all looked. Like this crowd is paying to do now. 'Twenty-five cents folks for an extra attraction, not advertised outside, something you will never see the likes of again!' They look at us like we're monsters. Not one of them. Mortimir scoffed. *The bearded bitch said we were part of the 'family' now. What a load.*

Dawn's been good to us. Vincent-

Oh wow Billy, you can count to two, congratulations. She's only 'good' because we pay the bills. She doesn't want us running off to join another outfit, so she's got to act decent to keep us around. Hel, two people have died since we got here! She can't even keep her employees alive! Yes, she's so good William, damn good at running a death trap! And that 'Beast.' A pussy whose only way of getting near anyone is to use manners and pretty words, else they'd all run. Besides those eggheads, he's got to be the most repulsive thing here. Them and that Crab Man, and his mother. You see those hands, Billy? They touch me and my lunch is coming back up.

Stop, please stop Morty. Th-those two men were accidents. That's what she said. Accidents. Give Dawn a chance. We don't know any of these people yet... Why are you-why do you hate them?

Look at us! How do you not hate them?

He looked at his hands. Twisting and curling a handkerchief around his fingers. Tracing the raised gold stitching with his thumb. B, not a W. Always Billy, she never called him William.

I just-I think they can be good. Mama was good.

Morty went silent. *To you...*

Before he could defend Mama, the barking man blocked the light.

"Hey," he grunted, from Billy's left, "Look up damnit, the rubes wanna see it," he mumbled through a smile.

You're a rube, Morty retorted.

Billy's chin lifted. *Is rube the safe word or not?* He pondered, upset and confused.

"Other way, other way," Muckers demanded, still clenching teeth, the smile a strained grin. "Keep yer fuckin' head that way and sit still."

That's right William, let them gawk. Long as they want to. No, they aren't making fun of us. They aren't revolted by us. They aren't going to hurl up their popcorn and peanuts. Look at them, all green and pop-eyed.

She isn't.

A little girl in a pink and red dress stood at the front. He could see her now that his eyes adjusted to the glare.

She held a stuffed lamb, a prize from the shooting range. Win five and you could trade them in for a goat. Three goats, and you get a big fluffy wolf.

Her papa won it for her, he bet.

Big blue eyes wondered over the boys slowly, deliberately, curious, not scared. Tiny fingers picked at the bow around the baby sheep's neck, and pet along its head and back.

Billy always liked kids. *The idea of them, what he imagined,* back at the farm. Then knew for sure he liked them at the carnival.

Morty thinks they are irritating and gross. Billy thinks they're cute and funny. Morty thinks they shouldn't be born.

He says awful things about newborns.

What the mamas and papas *should* do with a baby. Put them in a sack and drop it in the river, or dunk it in a full tub. Leave the baby on a hill like back in the old days. On the side of the road, in the middle of the woods, or... *the one that gave Billy nightmares for weeks.* Slather on the gravy and stick them in the oven.

Morty scoffed at the child. *Yeah, well that girl will get there. Bet ya before the time it takes her to bleed, she'll already be siding with the rest of them. We're Freaks, we're wretches, we're damned creatures reminding them of when the world went to shit.*

Billy sighed. Nothing to say.

Muckers' hand fumbled in his coat pocket, rattling a chain. "Now folks, any questions for the Twins?... *If you dare,*" he chuckled, sounding like a drunken clown.

Funny because there weren't any at de la Llum.

He asked Dawn why, after their very first show. Wondered the whole while when he noticed no one wearing grease paint or floppy shoes.

She told him de la Llum wasn't a circus.

He asked of the difference, and she looked him hard in the eye.

The biggest, she said.

Carnies focus on rides and games and attractions whereas circuses are about acrobats, clowns, and animals. A circus is about the scheduled main event under the big top. Carnivals are about choice, and discovery, decisions, and fun of all kinds. Prizes, laughs, and awe. Time, time to make those choices, all the time you need.

The circus may have glitz, but the carnival has wonder, she said, *and wonder stays with you forever.*

Hooray, my favorite time of the show. Asking if we're real, can we speak, how do we eat, sleep, shit. Thrilling.

They never ask about our bathroom business. We're different, they're curious. Aren't you? About the others here?

Billy could only imagine how long it takes Vincent to brush his hair every day, *being he's got more than just what's on his head.* Or how the nice Venus girl can write with her toes. He almost went to bed without dinner their first night because he couldn't stop watching her eat. *With* hands, he still gets food stains on his shirt. She didn't spill a thing, not once. Even the soup!

Mortimir sighed. *How did* I *learn about sarcasm, and it seemed to slip on by you?*

His eyes averted.

To answer your question, no. I don't. They don't give a fig about me-us, *so why give them the time of day?*

"Anyone?" the barker's head twitched right and left. "No?" a hand cupped a waxy ear.

"What are their names?" asked a tiny voice.

The girl in the pink and red dress. Fingers curled over the top of the stage beside her chin. She tilted her head, blonde hair shiny in the light, glinting with looks passed between Morty and Billy.

"Ha ha," Muckers forced, putting on a gaping wide smile filled with yellowing teeth, and blank spaces in the back. "Well, why don't you answer the girl?" his eyes narrowed at the twins.

What's a kid even doing here this late? Morty wondered briefly, then shot the barker a glare of his own.

It is late. Muckers gets impatient near closing time. Desperate to smoke behind the tent and sip from his flask. Sometimes he's out there with other men, saying he wants to visit the 'girls' and catch a private showing of *their* 'kootches.'

Billy didn't get it, and Morty laughed when he asked what *kootches* meant.

Billy smiled, "Mmm-m-my n-name's Wi-William," he touched his chest, and motioned to his left, "and muh-my bru-other is M-Mortimir. Bu-but I cu-all him Muh-Morty," his smile grew, showing teeth. Not yellow like Muckers, Mama made sure he brushed every morning and night.

Why do you try? You sound stupider than you look. M-m-m-

muh… Ugh, you are an embarrassment. I hate being seen with you.
He frowned.

The little girl smiled, bringing back Billy's.

Caused it to broaden when she asked casually, *like they were good friends,* "Can Morty talk?"

"Nah-not to uh-others bu-but he talks to m-me."

"What does he say?" her voice sweet and high, like a little rubber duck in a tub.

"*P.T. fuckin Barnum.*" Reddened eyes rolled. "Anyone else have a question?!"

The little girl shrunk from the stage at the raised voice. A man touched her arm. She clasped a big hand.

Her papa, Billy thought.

The man scooped her up, and Billy smiled again. He hugged her, and she hugged back.

"*Well*," Muckers hurried, "if you've had your fill of the twins please head on to your right, out the tent folks, yes right there," he pointed to a man leading his wife through the open flaps, *she lurched against a handkerchief,* "and have a good night."

The way he smiled made Billy think of the snake that got into the house when they were seven. It ate three of the five chicks hatched only a few days before in the chicken coop. Mama killed it with a shovel.

"Yes, *ha ha.*"

Billy thought he might rehearse the laugh. The two ha's the same each time he did it. The very same. Like how his mama knew the words to the songs she sang at night, or the stories she'd known by heart. But their mama did it different. She didn't sound fake. She meant it, Muckers doesn't.

"Right on that way folks. Tell your friends! We'll be here til Sunday! Come back before we're gone! *Hyuh-huugh.*" A different laugh, joy dying with a groan.

Muckers kept up a wave, and gesture to the exit, wave and gesture, wave and gesture until all were gone. His snake smile overly large, and eyes to match, *scaring the crowd even more than the twins.*

As soon as the last person exited—*a teen, tossing the remaining kernels of popped corn into his mouth*—Mucker's face fell. Clown excitement, to anger.

"The fuck did ya think you were doin'?" he shouted. "When the gate closes, we're *doooone!* I don't work the pats longer than I have to, ya got it!?"

"S-s-sorr-" Billy tried to apologize, hands rising with each stutter.

"S-s-s-s-s-s-s-sorry nothin'!"

Muckers sighed*, a growl to Billy's ears*, stepping off the stage and knocking the hat into his palm.

"Best be ten on the dot tomorrow night!" he spun, eyes wide. "Even if yer in the middle of questions, answer quick or shut up. Ya think I don't have shit ta do? I ain't gettin' paid ta stand around after hours while yer stu-stu-stutterin' through jackassy answers. *Talks to you*," he grunted, shaking his head. At the curtain he spit a glob of saliva to the left and lifted his cane. Pointing right at Morty, he said, "That thing's hardly more'n a boil on yer ass. It *ain't* talkin' to ya."

But, but you aren't on my-

Can it! Morty seethed. A three-fingered hand clenched in a ball, shaking.

"*Next time* keep 'em short. Yes, no." Mucker's rubbed his mouth with the back of his hand. Disgusted, he added, "And cover that thing when we're not showin'! It makes people sick!"

...I'm going to get that man...

RUMORS

∾ ? ℰ

Here they come.

He slunk behind the greeting banner line of the Midway. Generic depictions of a fire eater and human blockhead above a larger stretch of canvas with a likeness to Lucky the sword swallower.

A pair of approaching canvasmen remained unaware of an audience of one within the shadowed Alley.

"Hey! Goin' inta town?"

"Heard from a skirt I flipped tonight the grocer down the road got himself a still in the basement. Keeps the whole town liquefied."

"Believe her?"

"Why not? He's her dear ol' daddy."

The men laughed.

The one in the shadows sneered at bumbling snorts and hoots.

"If that idgit Jeb hadn't knocked out the front'a his skull I'd be polishin' off that last bottle'a mine."

"Told ya ta send him off with somethin' else. Newbie's not worth a bottle'a hooch, even if it is Rust."

"Eh, respect for the dead and all."

"First of May don't deserve respect."

"Hel, Bert. Jeb shit in your hat or what? What'd he ever do to you?"

"Cheated me outta last month's pay playin' cards before buyin' the farm. Never gonna git it back now."

"You ask the Boss Lady? Sure she pocketed whatever scratch he left behind. Tell her he owed ya."

"Think she's gonna fall fer that? Prob'ly say I bumped 'im off myself. Been the talk goin' round since the funeral. Weren't the drink got 'im. Not no accident. Someone pushed 'im onto that stake."

One glance over the shoulder would have revealed to the

departing men a glimmer in the shadows. The sparkle of a grin reflecting carnival lights.

AFTER HOURS

∽ HILLY ∾

Three women—*desperately in need of repainting*—wiggled their bodies provocatively in the wind. A bare leg trembled, a backside shimmied left and right as a robe tumbled from naked shoulders, the other's breasts would be shaken right out of her spangled bustier if she kept at it.

The men surrounding the bally earlier tonight were gone, long before the Johnnies finished with the girls. Others, men, and women, children and parents continued to drift out of the Ten-In-One, buying one more treat from the concessions, having pitch cards signed by performers before heading toward the Gate.

"Can I shake your hand?" a little boy asked.

"Why sure ya can podna!" Varlyn's Cajun drawl enthused as he extended an arm off the edge of the stage.

The child gaped, wide-mouthed, hesitant at first, most of all thrilled as he took the man's strange hand.

Two digits, shaped like a bird of prey's talon, pinched gently from either side of the boy's fingers and shook.

Hilly exhaled a plume of smoke, smiling as the mother and son waved to the Crab Man.

"How much for a private show?"

The man wore a fedora and dark green suit, his eyes devoured the view of smooth extended legs. Tempted to lay a hand on bare crossed ankles. Maybe slide to the knee, push the slinky little nightgown up a thigh. Check if this pretty young thing remembered to put on her panties this evening.

Three children with parents in tow passed the bally. Mother sneered, drawing little hands close between she and Father. Eyes darted, sharp as a prodding knife, to assure her husband did not stare at the harlot on stage. He too twisted his mouth, head swaying with criticism.

Five dollars, the least Hilly and Daze took in trade. If the trick had the look of one with money to spare Sunny asked for twenty, sometimes thirty, testing the depth of the man's wallet before inevitably lowering to fifteen or ten.

Very well off, she decided. Diamonds set in a gold wedding band. Gold watch to match, also glittering. Tailored suit, shiny shoes, cologne.

Before Hilly could inform him of the unfortunate hour. The close of the carnival. She could see no more men tonight. So very sorry sir. If only he could come back tomorrow…

She trembled at merely the thought of pitching her voice an octave higher. Of extending a hand, running it down the tailored jacket. The wink of possibility.

"Eugene!"

"Oh! *There you are, honey!* Thank you, ma'am! I-I-"

His question…? Her answer…? Hilly did nothing to aid in the lie.

"I-I will most definitely stop for a souvenir... out front! Thank you!"

Eugene shuffled to his wife. Hat wringing in his hands.

"Why were you speaking to that woman?!"

"I was asking where I could buy souvenirs."

"Don't lie to me!"

"Susan, I am not lying!"

Susan stormed away, husband whimpering at her heels.

Even if Eugene *had* arrived in time for a *private show*, Hilly would have turned him away. Six men tonight. The last buttoned his pants, tucked in his shirt, and handed over the cash moments before she came to the bally for a smoke.

The tent began to suffocate her after Johns. Stranger's smells lingering in the air, on her sheets, and skin. She'd wiped herself down with a wet rag, every place they kissed, and touched. Arms, breasts, neck, between the legs. Soaking up coital gel. A fingertip's worth sufficed for most men, those who engage quick and finish quicker. Dollops of reapplication for those savoring the time of sexual pleasures without need of familial production.

Before leaving, she tugged off the spit, sweat, and gel-dampened sheets and puffed perfume in each corner.

She inhaled from the cigarette, and let it blow away with the wind.

"Hand over one of those would ya?"

Daze hugged the banner pole at Hilly's back with one arm, hip cocked, and hand waiting.

Like her cousin, she dressed in a robe, tied tight at the waist, most likely nothing underneath since she finished off her last John. Hilly wore a satin slip, a brassiere, and nothing more. *No panties this evening Eugene.*

Hilly gave her the metal case, Sunny's, and the little box of matches, also borrowed from Sunny.

"What did you think?" a father asked.

"That was fun! Can we come back tomorrow?"

"Well... we'll see."

"Please, Daddy!"

"Maybe."

With a cigarette between her teeth, and a flame brightening her face Daze grimaced, "Gotta get that taste of Johns outta my mouth." She exhaled blue-grey smoke, pinching a crinkly hair from the tip of her tongue. "Done for the night?" Daze asked. The edge of her robe rippled, exposing thighs and a triangle of dark hair between them.

An observant gazoonie on clean-up swept nothing but dirt.

"Yes, *thank Barnum.*"

The wind picked up speed and had dark locks in a flurry about her face. *The newbie circled back to watch Daze's robe part once more.*

So lovely to look at. Daze, and her twin Vie, such beautiful women. Petite-bodied, rich, dark chocolate curls reaching slim hips. Big brown eyes the same shade as their hair, and smiles men could not deny.

"How many you have?"

"Six." Hilly's stomach hurt.

Daze barked a laughed, "Got ya beat. Eight... *well... ten,* countin' the two rousties I tugged this mornin'... *One wouldn't quit blabbin' about Jeb dyin'.* Fool knocked his sloshed self silly on a stake, *thee end.* Ain't the first time it happened."

Hilly's brows rose, taking a breath of smoke. *How empathetic, whilst also remaining ever competitive.*

Her cousin could win this contest. Though, *seven*, she remembered. Seven men today. She nearly forgot.

Contrary to *thee end*, Daze went on, "Heard they found him with his brains splattered all over, talkin' SPLAT! Some're sayin' he were pushed, and whoever done it planted that bottle. Owed money on a card game."

"Fascinating," Hilly sighed.

The women sat in silence for the next few moments. Smoking, and watching extended family, and coworkers close up for the night.

Muckers hurried from the Annex of the Ten, knocking back a flask.

Noticing the girls he grinned, tipped his hat. *"Ladies."*

"No!" Daze called.

"Fuckin' whores," he mumbled, hooking a hard left around the tent. Eyes wide and wild, even from this distance.

Chattering floated from the Ten's entrance.

Daze called, *"Hey, handsome!"*

Vincent, *the Gentleman Beast of York*, exited, leading the triplets by the hand, on his way to the backyard. Easier to access on the far side of the Kootch, rather than avoiding guy lines between tents. Especially with little sisters in tow. Tugging and pulling and running and skipping.

"Good evening, ladies," he nodded, voice a gentle husk. Perfect for reciting poems, and passages from novels of the pre-Cure world. Hilly enjoyed it. Most women seemed to, from what she'd caught of the crowds he attracts. Panting and heaving young things, both repelled and enamored by the man's appearance. His amiable voice, his wit and charm.

Two of the girls waved, Elvi not so enthusiastically as Shilzie who chattered happily, *what Hilly believed to be a hello*, to the Kootch girls, then back to her beloved adoptive brother she continued with children's babblings. Both Nylee's hands clasped in her brother and sister's, she smiled before hiding against Vincent's arm.

Hilly waved back.

Out of earshot of the siblings, Daze asked, *"Ya think he fucks them girls?"*

"Daze! What-? No!" *A Chester? Did she really insinuate such a thing?* "Are you nuts?!"

Daze laughed, prettiness replaced by a harsh, and sour-natured personality moldering over dark eyes. Slanting lower with each snicker, the top of her nose wrinkled.

"I'm just sayin'!" she continued, holding up a hand, halting her cousin's words, "He spends an *awful* lotta time with them."

"They are his sisters!"

"Not by *blood... Come on now.* He's alone with them for *hours* without *Mama Dawn* hoverin' over his shoulder. He goes in their wagon, brings them to his. Never seen no woman on his arm… What else is he doin' with his time?"

Hilly shook her head. "He takes care of them. He *loves* those girls."

Again, a mocking laugh intersected, "Okay, okay. Hel, Hills. I'm only kiddin'."

"That's not kidding! If the others heard you!"

Carnies do not play games when it comes to messing with children, *some might say more than the rest of society.*

"That's… *disgusting,*" the word faded quietly as her lips pursed around half a cigarette.

Daze did not speak for few blessed minutes.

Hilly kept her head forward, occasionally shaking, repeating the horribly sick *'kiddin,'* accusation in her mind.

That is not something to be joked with. It would hurt Vincent so deeply if he knew someone thought he would harm those innocent little girls.

Chesters are beaten out behind the trucks or *worse,* if a carny merely *suspects* a man of watching a child with lust in his eyes.

When Hilly thought she could ignore such a *joke* from her cousin, Daze asked, "You reckon he's got a hairy pecker?"

Hilly scoffed.

"What?" she laughed. "You didn't like my other question, *so…* answer this one. And don't be actin' like you ain't thought about it neither," she pointed a red fingernail. "*Everyone does.* Man's covered in hair, why not down there?" she grinned. Giggled.

"It's not anyone's business."

Though she has *wondered in the past.*

As she did about how Francis and Zach would manage sexual relations. Would each have their own lady friend? Share? Sleep with her one at a time? At the same time? If each man had a lover, how would they go about private moments? Would a curtain be involved somehow? A risen magazine or book?

Or Sabina and her husband Rolan, obviously the couple found a way to work around the vast height difference. What with their daughter, and Sab's current pregnancy.

All of these things of course crossed her mind. Human nature is to wonder over the unknown, including intimate details of the lives of others.

The difference between Hilly and her cousin was she would never ask Vincent, Francis and Zach, or Sabina and Rolan her questions. *Or* contemplate aloud with a similarly curious accomplice.

"I'd sure like it to be mine. Wouldn't even charge him... He may look like a big ol' pussycat but he's built like one'a these damn banner poles where it counts." Her palm clapped against it, jolting Hilly's spine. A firm stroke up and down. "That's *all* I need ta know... Whether he's got hair or not, would be quenchin' my curiosity." One more lewd comment snickered beside the cigarette in plumes, "Bet it tickles somethin' fierce." Smoky laughter followed Daze to dinner.

All she needs to know. After jokingly *questioning if the man may secretly be a Chester.* Hilly scoffed.

Looks and a large package, *Daze's priorities when it comes to the worth of a man.*

Looks are only the first impression, once you have perceived a person's true nature it is only a painted face waiting to be washed away. Once clean it is either ugly and rotten as their insides, or more beautiful than ever expected.

"Hey, Girly."

Her belly warmed. *Daze who?*

"Hi Johnny," Hilly breathed, butting out the cigarette.

He wiped his fingers, one at a time on a dirty rag as he approached. His shirt, clean earlier, now smudged with oil and dirt. As were his forearms, and pant legs in hand-shaped smears.

"I reckon yer not meetin' up with me huh?"

She went to open her mouth.

"Been a half hour past closin'," he propped a hip against the bally stage.

"Has it been that long?"

Patrons continued to the Gate; puttering about the midway. Begging for one more game, one more chance to win. A man waited at the popcorn stand at this very moment.

"Yup," he nodded, "Pats sure don't wanna budge tonight."

"I didn't keep you waiting, did I?"

"No, no. Let's see… I counted up tonight's take," he extended a finger with each task. "Patched up Star's seat, checked in on Serene's tank, *gonna have ta head to town for glass,*" he informed with a cocked brow. "Then *uh,*" he thought, stuffing the rag into a back pocket and clasped his hands, "did a little jig for the Family, little *chor-e-o-graphed* number I came up with, down on the Midway, but… *nah,* wasn't findin' ways ta waste time waitin' for ya at all."

Hilly laughed, covering her mouth, hiding the enormity of her smile. "Now that'd be something I'd pay two bits to see."

"Two bits," he grumbled, "A man of *my* fine skill. No less than a sawbuck. *Maybe…* even a *c-note.*"

"Ohh, I should inform Dawn of your talent. Our show would be off the circuit, and onto the New York stages in no time."

"Wouldn't that be a sight? Prob'ly shit myself, puttin' me in front of a crowd."

She giggled, "It's not that bad."

"Hmm," he disagreed.

Their laughter and jests quieted when canvas rumpled nearby. A young man, the last to leave the Ten-In-One. He twisted a handkerchief in his hands and kept his head low. Hair in tangles, like spider legs poking out of his skull, tapping at narrow shoulders. He glanced at the couple who laughed and smiled. Solemn at first, eyes distant. Soon the expression brightened, he offered a grin and raised a hand.

When Hilly and Johnny returned the same, he followed the path Muckers took moments ago. Ready to eat dinner with the rest of the family.

"Have you ever talked to him-*them*?" Hilly asked, unsure how to phrase it. Was he, *he?* Or them?

Francis and Zach were de la Llum's only other conjoined twins, connected by a strip of flesh five inches long and one inch in width, below their—*Francis's left*, and *Zach's right*—chest. Same stature, both could speak and move. *They* were a them, individual but connected. A living, thinking pair.

"*Nah*, not much. Keeps to hisself mostly. Seems like a good kid."

"Is his brother a gaff, or is he the real deal?"

Has to be real. She'd never seen something so believable if it wasn't.

"Real as me or you. Saw him move first day Dawn brought his brother by to say hello. Kids got a real bad stutter." The last an afterthought.

"Poor thing," she murmured.

Hilly heard of his predicament. A dying mother with a last-ditch hope to find a home for her son, *sons.*

Who knows where they might have ended up otherwise. Locked in a hospital ward. An asylum. The streets. *Awful.*

"*Well*," he pushed off the bally to face her, "since you ain't imbibin' me with hooch," a big hand extended, "How's about I walk you to supper instead?"

Smiling, Hilly took Johnny's hand and headed for the cookhouse.

RUN IN WITH THE DEVIL
∽ MORGAN ◞

Garbage crinkled, scraped, and swept into bins up and down the midway. Greasy napkins, paper cones with sweet crystalline ends, corndog sticks, chicken bones, popcorn, and candy wrappers.

Concession wagon shutters latched shut, the ovens within off and cooling after a long afternoon. Oil sizzled, lazily attacking detached breading at the bottom of iron skillets. Unsold candy floss shriveled, hardening in malformed sugary mounds. Popcorn and pretzels grew stale, the leftovers taking one of two paths before opening time tomorrow: tossed or eaten.

If the carnies did not go straight to bed, or to town, searching out covert purveyors of hooch and tobacco—*not lawfully illegal, but morally, for the long-term effects causing Sickness*—they could be found at the cookhouse.

Morgan did not partake in dinner. Not quite yet. Conversation and food would keep the others busy and out of the backyard for near an hour by his previous observations. He took the opportunity to head for the showers.

Cleanliness is Healthiness, a grim recollection from juvenile teachings.

Going a single day without showering once, if not twice, left Morgan itching in his own skin. Unclean. Filthy. Somehow, immoral.

If it were not for the others, he would bathe two, three, even four times a day. *Like Mother ordered.*

Why did it have to stick? Why did she remain in his mind? Scolding. Ordering. *Dirty, you are dirty!* He must cleanse himself. Scrub away the Sickness. *Filth! Do not come near me until you've washed! Get in the bath! Now!*

All quiet in the backyard.

Laughter and voices floated on grill smoke. Dawn's joyous

cackling above them all. Soon would come the melodious Serene, singing a siren's song to the carny folk. Entrancing the crew, as she does the patties. After, the prose of Vincent's favorite playwrights, perhaps his gentle beastly voice joining the mermaid's refrain.

Morgan wore today's show clothes. Others arrive at the showers draped in towels, robes, or nothing at all. Towel hung over a shoulder or folded in crooked arms. Breasts and buttocks bouncing and cocks swinging freely, uninhibited.

He couldn't, *wouldn't. The stares.*

If the tubs were not such a hassle—*and the thought of sitting in one did not cause the air in his lungs to evaporate from fear of baths past*—he would use them for the added privacy. After fear came the hassle: transporting buckets, emptying dirtied water, cleaning the tub afterward.

Scrub the tub when yer done! Dawn's rule, *scrub the tub!*

Too much time. More chances to be caught. Over and done quick. The faster he bathed, the less likely he would be seen. The sooner he could get back to his caravan.

Or, he could go with the tried-and-true method used by the oldest members of the troupe, who had not yet leapt into this advancement of showering on a lot: wash with a rag from a bucket of water.

No, never that. *The thought of bathing in his own waste got Morgan's stomach roiling.*

Three showers hid behind a tent stationed at the back of the lot. Aptly named the *wash tent.*

A wooden platform, six inches off the ground, high enough to keep the bather's feet away from splashes of mud down below. A fence of two-by-fours supported piping leading to shower heads. Knobs stuck out like fists between slats, small shelves discolored by sun exposure, water damage, and soap scum jutted below.

More piping ran to the new addition of a hot water tank on the back of the water truck.

Wooden partitions segregated each shower a month ago, until a roustie—*Blake*—backed the water truck into the wash tent while heading into town for a refill. The rear end knocked the walls flat, ripping out nails and sending splinters in all directions like buckshot. Luckily no one showered at the time. Though Angus and Boris were nearly hit.

In place of sturdy solid walls and doors with latches were poles, rope, and sheets until new partitions could be built. Not a top priority to the crew, much to Morgan's disappointment.

He set a bar of soap and bottle of shampoo on the shelf beneath the first shower and hung a towel over the fence.

The creaking platform settled beneath his weight. Holding a breath, he listened, hands hovering within billowing sheets. The family chatted.

"Would you like more beans?"

"No, I couldn't."

"I think you should."

"No, I insist."

"How about more bread?"

"Why, yes, more bread."

"Butter?"

"Indeed."

Francis and Zach.

No song, or reciting.

Plenty of time, he sighed.

Naked, wetting his bare body, and rubbing soap between flattened hands there came the sound of a splash. Morgan froze, gripping the slippery bar against his collarbone. A sudsy trail sloughed down his chest and abdomen.

"Well fuck me!" exclaimed a voice. Lower, *"Damnit."*

The footsteps kicked dirt. Dusty clouds and rocks announced the approach. Coming closer. *This way.* Either to the showers themselves or the water pump.

Shit. He tried to rinse off, he would take a shower in the morning. Reached for the towel.

It slid over the fence and flopped against the canvas down to the ground.

Morgan's stomach seized with pain. *No. No!*

The man took a few extra steps beyond the wash tent platform before tossing a bucket of muggy water into the dirt.

A sheen of water glistened on a chest and bare belly. The arms of the jacket tied around his waist, and the front of the man's pants until the knee were damp.

The bucket dropped. Clattering on its side, bouncing the handle against the dirt like an angry child's fists. A water-logged rag tumbled out. He wiped his chest, flicking moisture aside.

Hearing the running water for the first time he turned his head. Meeting, albeit briefly, the eyes of Morgan standing stone solid, but for a hand jutting downward.

I can't believe this. I can't. I can't. Fuck. Fuck! Sheets, the sheets are covering me… All it will take is a breeze in the right direction and everything's out there for the world to see. Check out Lucky's sword everyone! Ugh! Shut up, shut up, shut up.

"Hello again," said the man with crafty brown eyes, and impossibly thick black hair. Fluffing about his head and shoulders like the leaves of scorched Californian palm trees.

The jockey from earlier: *Evro.*

Since the start of the season, he traveled with de la Llum and Morgan and he never came into contact. Could not remember seeing him, except as an obscure figure loading children, and patties onto Carrie from a distance. Eating in the background while fixing a plate at dinner. Riding in a flatbed on the road. Playing cards or dice with the men.

Now meeting again. Talking to, or, more rather, *talked at*, by the man twice in a single day.

Morgan closed his eyes, jerked his head toward the water, mouth getting wet.

What do I do? What the fuck do I do?

He gulped, wiping at soap, and closed his eyes tighter. Both face and body running simultaneously hot and cold. The want to vomit and faint so strong he could do neither.

Desperation willed him to leave. Grab his clothes without a word, and put them on, covered in soap or not. Dirty clothes be damned. He'd wash from a bucket if he had to, deal with the sensation of washing in sullied water, unclean and itching in his own skin until a proper shower could be had.

I can't move. Can't move. Can't breathe.

More voices.

Oh no. Not more. Why? Fucking why? Tears stung his eyes.

Giggles, murmurs, so much laughter from the outhouses. Doors opened and clattered shut.

Silence. Whimpering.

"I know you want dinner sweetheart, in a moment, wait for your sisters."

Vincent and the girls.

Little feet scuffed dirt, rocks scampering with each step. The rhythm like skipping. One shuffle of foot, a pause, and another. Shuffle, pause, shuffle.

"Elvi stay here."

Skip, skip, skip. Crunching rocks, shifting dirt.

Evro tilted his head, smiling.

The boss's children, of course it would be them. Why not Dawn herself? Why not everyone?! Come one, come all!

Something inside Morgan feared the man behind him would hail their attention. Call the four over for a chat while he stood naked under the water, only a flimsy bit of cotton protecting children's eyes.

"No, no, darling," bigger feet with firmer steps.

Fuck, fuck, fuck. Morgan's legs cramped. *Can't move. Can't leave. Trapped.*

"Someone is taking a bath. Let's leave them alone," receding. *"Good girl."*

Such a small reprieve.

Latches. Mumbling.

"Wash your hands," the brother instructed.

Morgan was never so glad a barrel of water stood ready beside the outhouses.

"Ready? Let's go!" he could hear the smile in his voice.

The excitement of three sets of feet pulled their brother toward the carnival.

Thump. Thump. Boots falling. *Fabric against skin.* One leg, then the other.

The second shower head sprayed to life.

"Bright idea hitting the showers at dinnertime. Never thought of that. No line, plenty of warm water." A blurry face turned toward him, bringing handfuls of water to his chest. "Spilled a bucket of muck on myself just now."

Morgan's hand of its own accord washed the same place on his shoulder, upper arm, and chest. The other stayed between his thighs, instinctually shielding his genitals.

Once the soap is gone, dress and run for the caravan.

"A kiddie got sick on Carrie on her last turn, *down to the second.* Caught *four* horses… and *two kids* when his hotdog came back to say hello." He stuck his face under the water and shook off the wet. Drops, as well as strips of foreign locks of hair, thick as snakes, slithered over the top of the sheet and hit Morgan's arm. Paralyzing it. "Poor little fella. Crying, *sorry, sorry, sorry,*" he mimicked in a childish voice. Not at all patronizing, but sympathetic. "Gave the kid's parents tickets for the last day," he turned, tilting backward, voice straining with a bent neck. "Not sure if they're coming back but," he shrugged, "*eh.* Why not?"

That's… nice of him.

Morgan could only see the outline of the jockey's features. *Did not dare look directly.* His whole body froze at the thought. The conversation. The nakedness. His own, this man's. Unable to run, hide, turn away. *Stuck. Cornered. Trapped in his own traitorous body. Move! Run! Get dressed and go!*

From his peripheral the black circles of Evro's irises moved. Dark as the very buttons of Morgan's jacket, wandering over the lines and angles of his face. Unhidden by sideways glances. First face then body. A dart, down and back. As far as the sheet partition allowed.

The sight had him smirking. *Good? Bad? Why?!*

"It's the least Carrie and I could do since she made him sick all over."

He stopped talking. Blessed quiet.

Morgan eased enough in the silence to set aside the soap, wet his hair, and began massaging shampoo throughout. *One handed of course.*

Might as well finish. The small wan in chatter, *stares*, gave enough courage to see this shower through to the end.

As he washed bubbles from behind his ears the man beside him spoke again: "Do you dye that streak?"

He shook his head at the shower as he wiped shampoo from his hairline. Still not speaking. Couldn't.

Please leave me alone. Stop talking. Stop looking at me. Please, please. Ignore me.

"Really?"

Morgan nodded. *Grey came in at sixteen.*

He chanced a peek at the jockey.

He eyed the back of Morgan's head. Studying the hair plastered against the slope of his skull, neck, and upper back.

A handful at the center is all that remains of the red. The premature grey came from his mother. A gift. Mother to son. Something she hid from others with a dye job done out of town. The community mustn't know.

Please Barnum let that be the only thing she passed to me.

"*Ah*, so a *redhead*. I always fancied red hair... *White* too."

What's his game? What do you want from me?

"You know, you don't have to be *so* shy." Evro rubbed water up and down his arms. "You *can* finish your shower..." parted lips lingered, "with *both* hands." A head tilt toward lower extremities.

Morgan's face went hot. It burned hotter than the flaming swords in his performance. Starting high in the cheeks, blackening the bones and blistering the sides of his neck.

"I can't see anything—*not that you don't have something I don't have myself...*" he paused, arched a brow, "Or do you? This carny have one of those double-donged men like I hear they got in Portugal?"

Morgan found himself letting out a breath of laughter.

Evro smiled.

No, nothing like that.

He did not uncover himself.

"For a guy who gets on stage in front of people, you sure are a nervous Nelly. I'm yammering all to myself over here." He turned, shifting hair to one shoulder, allowing the water to hit his back.

Up there, on stage, once Morgan caught his breath. Eased his mind. Tricked it into submission. He is alone, performing, doing what he loves. The individuals become something else, one massive entity. A thing. The many become a crowd. And a crowd doesn't answer back. Not in words anyway. Gasps, *oo's* and *ahh's*, sounds of amazement or terror.

This man, this single man stood, *showered*, beside him. Not below him. Eye contact, face to face. Looking directly at Morgan, not *what* he does, at the sword or torch in his hand. Spoke to him, not reacting to a performance.

An exceptional difference.

"Wouldn't guess it from your show."

"What?"

He does speak! Ladies and gentlemen gather around for a once-in-a-lifetime show!

A brief hold for surprise. "I said you wouldn't guess you were such a nervous guy from watching your show. You're great at handling a crowd."

My show? "You-you've seen my show?"

Only in regards to his craft did Morgan find the will and courage to speak.

Did he enjoy it? What act does he like best? Which did he watch? The Human Voodoo Doll? Bonfire? The Furnace?

"Oh, *sure*. Sometimes I let Carrie go for a couple minutes longer to catch who's up on the... what's the stage you're on?" black slashes quirked above the jockey's obscure dark eyes.

"The Midway," he said tentatively, with some courage adding, "I-I'm on Midway East."

"*Carny speak*," he said amused. "Haven't got the gist of it yet, but anyhoo. I let Carrie go for a good long whirl so I can watch the show with the crowd. You wouldn't think it, but it's not a bad view from there. Though, I've got to squint to make out your needle act. But the reactions," he laughed, "that's the best."

Morgan's mouth tugged at the corners.

"The sword swallowing," he hissed in empathetic pain, "Doesn't that hurt?"

He shook his head.

The act of repeatedly gagging oneself to suppress the gag reflex had been tedious and uncomfortable in the beginning. Leaving his throat raw from coughing and stomach acid burns. Well worth it now to have the skill to perform such a task on stage. One continuing to amaze audiences around the country. *Thousands of years' worth of entertainment in sword swallowing. Here's hoping for thousands more.*

"And you truly cut yourself," not a question.

He'd reached for soap, turning the hand over instead. Showcasing scars from wrist to forearm. All done with razors. More decorated the opposite arm, his chest and belly. Inconceivable pinpricks dimpled numerous sections of his body. The underside of is his chin, caused by thin skewers jabbed through the flesh of the lower jaw, bypassing the tongue and exiting an open mouth. Forehead, eye lids, cheeks, palms, upper arms, pectorals and stomach.

He looked Morgan up and down. "You're not scared to do anything, huh?"

What a laugh.

Eye contact. Speak with more than one-word answers or partial sentences.

To remove a cupped hand from his dick and balls to finish showering. *Definitely too cowardly for that.*

He would swallow swords, one or more. Has gotten up to five, and practiced adding a sixth. He ate glass, hammered nails up his nose, and pulled them out with pliers. Swallowed billiard balls, goldfish, keys, watches, and ball bearings; all to be regurgitated. Laid on beds of nails, stepped up blade ladders, sliced open his arms, held hot coals on his tongue, spit fire, and pierced himself with needles and hooks, but could not look this man in the eye.

Couldn't walk through a crowd without dreading what others thought of him. Did not leave his wagon except to eat, perform, bathe, and visit the outhouses.

Morgan did not want *to be this way.*

He saw how others lived day to day. Playing the banjo or harmonica around fire pits. Gathering into groups to head into town. Laughing, smiling, enjoying the company of others.

Subconsciously he wanted the same. *Consciously he did not know how to get it.*

Emotional and physical comfort were unknown niceties as he grew.

To be held, embraced, or kissed. Told he was loved. *Nonexistent.*

His father worked as if it sustained his heartbeat, otherwise home in his office with doors closed. Morgan could not remember his father's voice, he spoke so little.

His mother's only goal, to prime him for his coming of age. Explaining at length the importance of carrying on the family line. Their pure ancestry. As she did, as his father had, both families, for over one-thousand years. The only son, only child of Mr. and Mrs.

Meyer of Stepton, Connecticut. He would keep alive what generations before worked so hard for. Purity. Immunity.

"*Well*," Evro sighed, turning bulbous knobs until the water ceased, "as much as I'd like to stay and chat, I've got to get some grub in my belly. *Starvin'*." He scooped up his clothes, folding wet pants around overly large boots.

With the inside of the jacket, he began drying his legs and feet.

"You heading over for supper?" Evro asked, standing with a cocked hip, a ball of damp clothing under an arm. "I hear its beans and bread again, *mmm-mmm, yuuummy*," his voice monotone with sarcasm.

A riot could start over the mention of beans these days. But they are cheap, and keep the entire carnival fed. Seconds to spare at every meal. Thirds. Fourths. Beans all night. Beans for all!

His head shook abruptly, then mumbled, with less intensity, "*No*, not right now."

"Guess I'll see you there then," he stepped under the sheet and off the platform, to retrieve the discarded bucket. On his way into camp, he stopped, turned, "I'm Evro. Don't think we were ever introduced before getting naked together."

"Morgan," he said.

"So *that's* your name," the words came soft at this accumulation of gained information. A lost item found. The seeking sought. Evro smiled, dark eyes sparkling blots of ink. Morgan's stomach cramped, *though not uncomfortably*. "See you later," his gaze danced up and down, smirk tightening before disappearing behind the tent.

FAMILY DINNER
‿ꙅ DAWN ꙅ‿

"Hogwash!"

"No, no, I'm serious. Woman had big ol'... *what do ya call 'em?* -antlers! Comin' right round the side of her head. Called her the Amazing Moose Gal, or Elk Broad, Deer Dame, somethin' like that," Sunny laughed into his coffee.

"*I'm sure,*" Vie bent over an outstretched leg to push his shoulder. "You're just foolin' us."

"*Nah*-Baby," to Sheri, "please tell these ladies your daddy *ain't* no liar."

Dawn looked to the girl beside her.

"*Well,*" the cup between pretty toes lowered, "if Daddy says he saw her, he must have."

"Ah, ya see!" Sunny carefully set the wrapped ankle of his wife on the bench to stand and plant a kiss on his daughter's golden head. "From the mouth of an angel, now how ya gonna call me a liar after that?"

"Hel Sunny, the girl'd call you Barnum himself if you asked her to," groaned Daze from the buffet.

If you could call it that. Beans, sliced bread, pork sausage, a pitcher of water, and a steaming pot of coffee and tea. A bit of milk remained in the icebox under the table. Dawn used a good deal in her tea, and she'd be having a few cups more before leaving the tent. No more orange juice, Dawn was sure of that, stuff went quick when they had it.

"Ain't nobody asked you!" he called back, lines rippling from forehead to a hairline receding at the temples.

Daze's features pinched to that of the nastiest patty, one whose parent had the gall to defy her, but she said no more.

"*Alright,*" Vie submitted, running her hand over Sunny's spiky brown hair. "If Sheri-Baby says so, guess I'll believe it."

"Well thank you. That's all I want. Little trust is all I'm askin' fer honey." Kissing his wife, he went on, "*Anyway...*" stopping, "Where was I?"

"*Antlers*," Dawn grunted, laughter caused her breasts to jiggle on the surface of an overflowing corset.

"Right. So, she's got these big ol' horns curlin' round her head."

The newest member-*members* of de la Llum sat at the last chair, two tables down, on the opposite side of Sunny and his family. Many seats at the crowded head table were open if he had a hankering for company; yet he deigned to separate himself from conversation. From anyone at all.

Strange, Dawn thought. Billy lopped toward the empty seats as an excited puppy would bringing its owner a thrown stick. Unlike a pup, he stopped, gripping the edge of his plate, glancing to his left side, *listening*, before tucking tail for the deserted tables.

Morty says, Morty thinks. She wasn't sure if she believed the boy's brother spoke, as he conveyed: *through the mind.* Sounds like a regular spook show. Great for advertising to the pats, however.

The twin moved for certain. Blinking, a twitch of the hand, pursing, curling lips, *drool.* But talk? She'd heard tales of men with parasitic twins talking in their ear when no one else heard a thing. Bunk the lot of it most instances. All for show.

Could it be true? That little muddled form spoke, thought, directed, dictated? Dawn didn't have her own twin for verification. Billy confirmed as such, and she didn't believe him the type to lie.

He's a simple boy. Naïve. A recluse until recently. Could be his imagination. One of those imaginary friend deals. Elvi and Nylee seem to play with one. Giggling at corners, pointing at empty walls, and mumbling to one another. Billy did the same. Peering to his left. Pausing during conversation for his brother's interjections.

If Mortimir *were* talking to him, what did he say to get his brother to turn around like that? To submit Billy to his wants.

Ain't like the little guy is big enough to bully his brother.

Ponderings of the newbies stifled when she noticed a pair come in through the closed tent flaps across from her.

A tanned hand thinly coated in oil popped in and curled around the canvas. Johnny appeared in the opening, Hilly stepped through, he followed. The man's eyes refused to leave her the whole while.

He marveled at the pale blonde curls stacked atop her head and cascading down her back. Watching the full hips and bottom shift from side to side under a silky robe, hiding admiring stares for an ample bosom and pretty face with quick darting eyes.

"*Boy wants milk, but he's lookin' at the wrong kinda cow*," she mumbled into her tea.

Nothing against the girl, but she's a dancer, one who dabbles in trade after the show. Those type aren't good for a healthy relationship. Only reason Sunny and Vie worked out was she quit tricking once the ring slid down her finger. *Took a big hit to the income after doing so*, something the couple often struggles with.

Besides that, sharing a girl he was sweet on wouldn't be something a man like Johnny would tolerate.

Simply a passing fancy, no feelings beyond that. *Dawn hoped.* This was the first girl he ever saw regular in all these years.

Use to do like the other men of the carny, sleep with willing townies at night and not have to worry about them tomorrow. Just what carnies hot under the collar *and* in their drawers do. Weren't much the types looking for attachments. A quick pump and away they go.

These two could have their time alone in Hilly's tent, but he couldn't be looking for anything more from a girl like her. He'd end up hurting himself. And boy did Dawn know, he'd been through plenty of that in his life. *Only a kid back then, poor thing.*

The pair stood at the buffet, holding plates and utensils whilst ignoring the food. Hilly inspected his filthy shirt, motioning to the handprints marking up his chest, belly, and pant legs. Commenting—*Dawn presumed about the filth.* Maybe threw in a quip concerning pungent aromas—*Dawn would've.*

He must have said something funny 'cause the girl laughed and bit her lip.

Dawn shook her head, certain she knew the trick to the man's disappearing act earlier today. No smoke and mirrors or sleight of hand, he slipped in the warm place between that girl's knees when no one was looking.

"Rocky! Hey, Rocky! Come'ere!"

No one but the man called by name paid the barker any mind. *Carny folk tend to ignore their type.* Hollering and yelling, on the job or off.

The strongman set down his plate and shuffled over. Stopping short to smile and raise a hand, "Good evenin', Miss Sherilyn."

"Good evenin', Rocky," teeth glistened between her lips.

Sheri's father jumped to his feet and hurried behind the man who dwarfed him by eight inches.

"Believe me now. This gal was a biggun', 'bout as big as our boy here. But with… *ya know*," cupped hands bulged over his chest, demonstrating tits.

Sheri giggled.

"Picture it now," long thin arms hovered on either side of Rocky's ears, sprouting out into the air. "I'm sayin' monstrous big! Longer than my own arm. She'd take down this whole damn tent turnin' her head."

"I'd believe ya Sunny darlin', but you about spun all my yarn," Dawn chuckled, beard tickling her throat.

"Save it for the pats honey," Vie smiled over her shoulder.

"*Ehh* with the both of ya," he batted a fist their way and patted Rocky's back, exposition over, letting him return to supper. "My little girl believes me," he kissed her forehead and hugged her close. "That's all that matters."

"Sure I do, Daddy."

Vie shook her head. "Baby you're far too sweet to your papa, makes him think he can get away with anything."

"And that's the way I like her," another kiss, "*Ack!* See that?" he retracted his lip, showcasing yellow back teeth, "Got me another tooth needs yankin'."

"*No*," Dawn disagreed. "Sweet as the girl is, yer teeth need pullin' 'cause'a all that damn sugar ya dump in yer coffee. Or should I be sayin', all that coffee ya spoon into yer sugar?"

"Yeah, that's right! I'm a man likes my sugar bitter… Miss *seven spoons*," he took his cup and swallowed a mouthful. "*Dee-licious.*"

Touché good sir. "Ain't it just?" She took her own sip. Black tea, creamy with milk, and sweetened with seven spoons of sugar.

Dawn gulped and waved over the newest group to enter the cook tent.

Carnivàle de la Llum's family of dwarves, and the resident

giantess. *The World Famous Samson Clan! The Biggest Little Family in the Whole U.S.A.!*

"Sabina, how ya doin' darlin'?" She took the hand of Sabina and Rolan's toddler between her fingers.

Helda, the tiniest little mouse, considering her mama stood at seven foot two. Her daddy three foot six. Grandmother Lavi only three feet, and two aunts Grace and Joy, thirty inches and twenty-four inches respectively. Dawn thought for certain this little girl would take after her petite aunts.

The show-woman in her knew it would be great for sales. The smaller the better. The woman in her, *the mother*, thought the baby's size as all the more cuddly.

"Fine. No nausea, same as Heldie," an overlarge, though purely feminine hand curved to the bulge of a small belly. "Think this time it will be a big one. Not even two months and I'm showing."

"*Aw*," Dawn cupped the giantess's belly and rubbed. "Hopin' fer a *big* little brother ain't ya Helda?"

"Yes!" she squeaked, little hands clapping together. "Big, big brother!"

The mite-sized girl's parents smiled, as did Dawn and the rest of the table.

"Enjoy yer supper sweet pea," Dawn kissed the teeny fingers.

"*Kay!*" she called as her mama and family carried on.

New footsteps, giggling.

My babies.

"Hello, Mother," Vincent kissed Dawn's smile plumped cheek. Six arms wrapped around her all at once. The coziest trap, a welcoming spider web.

"Where've y'all been? Thought ya woulda' been here sooner," she kissed the top of each girls' shaven head between words, smoothing and patting backs. Elvi and Nylee cooed in little murmurs. Shilzie smiled big, letting out singular happy laughs.

"Only a stop at the restroom," he said, pulling out the first three chairs at Dawn's right. He would sit in the fourth, beside him would be Shilzie, then Nylee and Elvi.

"Ah, say no more. Even proper gals like us gotta squat at the powder room once in a while." Dawn smiled at the girls as they took their places. Unfolding napkins atop laps, as Vincent taught them.

He headed over to ready his and the triplets' plates.

Bless that boy. The world couldn't ask for a finer gentleman. Dawn couldn't wish for a more perfect son.

Neither could Tod. He doted on the boy. Flooded him with gifts and toys at every chance. Books the favored reward. Crates worth brought from runs into town. New, old, free, bought, found.

Deservingly so. If he were a brat, he would have got no presents at all till the attitude changed. *Not their boy.* Quiet, well-mannered. *Please* and *thank you* for every adult, not only reserved for getting on the good side of his parents.

Barnum, she sighed, looking after her son, *she missed that man so much.*

Vincent couldn't be more like Tod if he faked it. All of his best qualities rolled into one. Intelligent, generous, kind beyond measure. Vincent did, however, lack all things that made Tod a true carny.

Forever respectable, but her husband knew how to make a buck, *honest or not*. How to sell a lie as the truth, and the best way to con an idgit with a wad of bills. *Only those with too much to spare, or an unfavorable disposition deserving a little recompense in the form of thievery.*

It's fine, she thought, if her son lacked such a philosophy. Not in the boy's nature. Tod knew it, and never meant to teach him the ways passed down showman to showman. Vincent became the man Tod intended from the jump, a true gentleman.

If only the girls could have met him.

"You are not having dinner?" Vincent set plates in front of his sisters.

The boy catered better than a four-armed waiter during the *Goodwellness* dinner rush.

Busy time for restaurants. Who wants to cook on a holiday with the convenience of a diner around the next corner?

"Nah darlin', fine with my tea."

The golden hairs across his forehead furrowed, noting the difference in mood. *Thinking of Father*. He hated to see her lonely when surrounded.

"I had a big lunch," she assured. "*Don't worry 'bout me*. Sit an' fill yer belly."

He did, taking his place beside Shilzie.

"Hiiiii!" An enthusiastic greeting from the buffet. Evro. Kneeling, *"Hey itty bitty!"* he tickled Helda's chin.

She giggled and with the impatience of youth, asked with outstretched hands opening and closing rapidly in anticipation. "Candy?!"

"Only if it's okay with Mama," he glanced up, *way up*, at the tall woman. "Is it okay, Mama?"

Unable to say no to her child, who nearly stumbled backward to beg with big blue eyes, Sabina submitted, *"Yes*, but you can't eat it now. *After supper."*

Now or later, candy is all she understood. Helda hopped, holding a single ring-clad finger of the jockey's hand for stability—*all she could grasp in dolly fingers*—while the other fished into a pants pocket and brought out a handful of colorfully wrapped candies.

He chuckled as she huddled the goodies up against her belly, marveling at the colors cupped in her hands. Like she'd caught a rainbow.

"Thank you thank you!"

Evro ruffled her fluffy curly hair as he stood, and watched with a grin, as she hopped away like a little bunny, following her family to the dinner table.

"You my boy," Johnny clapped a hand on the fellow jockey's shoulder, "are a troublemaker if I ever did see one. Girl's gonna keep them folks up all night and here ya are grinnin' over what you done."

"Yeah, I know it," damned proud of himself. *"She's so cute I can't help it*," he said through smiling teeth. "Just want to put her in my pocket and carry her around with me. Drop in a caramel every once in a while," his hand smooth sailed through the air, "Be all set."

Johnny laughed and moved on.

About to pass the table, and distracted by Hilly's shifting behind, he did not realize his mistake until Dawn took hold of a wrist and dragged him to a stop. A child ready for a deserved spanking.

The pretty dancer slowed her gait, glancing between the two. To the boss lady whose auburn brows rose impatiently, then took her plate to a free table in the corner.

Yeah, you keep goin' girl. Turn my switch on you next!
"What?"
"You avoidin' me?"

"No," he scoffed.

"Ya, sure? Seems like. Check the Eye, yer gone. Ask one fella where ya are, you ain't there, then another, yer gone again. Tellin' me that's a big ol' coinkydink?"

"I ain't tellin' nothin'. Can't be in one place, and everywhere all at the same time ya know."

Hilly and Johnny exchanged glances. Unmeaning to catch one another's peeking. Little shit-eating smirks formed when peepers met. A disgusting mating dance.

"*Mmm-hmm," pay attention!* She squeezed his wrist, the hairs bunched up in the creases of her fingers. "Ya fix that tank yet?"

"Gave it a gander. Gonna have ta go into town, fer glass…" his mind stalled looking at the girl, the exposed leg, the smooth thigh crossing one over the other, and the little nightgown hiking up, "…uh, other stuff. And things."

Dawn snorted, "While yer stockin' up on *stuff an' things*. I got a grocery list for ya. Milk, eggs, bacon if they got it, the usual. Hopin' there'll be packages at the post." The corner of his mouth curved upward. Dawn yanked his bristly wrist back to attention. "Ya hearin' me?"

"Yeah, yeah, I got it. Milk, eggs, bacon, packages." She released him. "Make sure you got everyone's lists together *before* I leave this time. I ain't makin' two trips again 'cause someone needs shoe polish… *Sunny!*"

"Hey now, what'd I do?!"

Morgan timidly passed through the tarp as Johnny returned to his pretty little infatuation.

Dawn waved.

Silver dollars shone dully in darkened sockets. Head down, damp hair concealing his face, he lifted a hand.

Evro waited at the buffet for Otis to hand over a fresh pot of tea. In the meantime, his focus landed on the resident sword swallower.

More than usual, the white-haired young man seemed ready to scurry into the nearest dark corner.

Why's that I wonder? Dawn thought, watching close as he edged to the food, tugging a plate with his fingertips, eyes low, avoiding the jockey.

Somethin' is going on here.

He took two slices of bread, a few spoonfuls of beans. Stopped his hand before reaching the fork on the sausage tray.

Evro watched. Smiling.

What is goin' on between those two?

Far as she knew, they never spoke to one another.

Evro worked the carousel, a quick promotion for a greenie, and Morgan hopped on and off the Midway all day, either on break, in his wagon, or on stage.

With Morgan's desperate craving for solitude, how could the two meet? Well… she sent him to Carrie today, in search of Johnny. Could have passed words then.

No. Not Morgan. Don't talk to no one unless it's a last resort. Boy would soon bleed to death rather than ask for a bandage to stanch the flow.

The pause went on. As if the decision to fork a sausage onto his plate were as hard as adding another sword down a throat full up of steel.

The dark-haired young man idly pecked the tips of a fork into the mashed beans on his plate. Skewering two charred sausages, he gave them a slow wag, gaining full attention of Morgan, and brought them to his lips. Biting off one tip, then the other. His lips curled into a small smile as he chewed.

Dawn could physically see the heaviness of the sword swallower's exhale. A whoosh caving in his chest, bowing his back as he took hold of the plate with both hands and hurried out of the tent.

Good thing no one came in, he may well have knocked them flat.

Well, how about that? Dawn found herself intrigued. *What exactly conspired between such an unlikely pair? Something salacious perhaps? Interesting. And good fer Lucky if that's the case…* She smiled and took a sip.

Pit. Pit. Pit-patter. Pit-pit-patter. Pitter-patter-pit-pit-patter.

"Oh, ya hear that Shilz? Rain's started up for ya."

Girl loves the rain, no matter if bad weather proves bothersome for the business, she loves it so. Watching for hours as a little one. Smelling the air with a smile, holding out her hand to catch the sky's tears. *Happy tears*, what Dawn told the girls.

She'd put a wet palm to her cheek or hold it out to whomever stood nearby dabbing it, pointing, as if marveling at nature's spectacle. The clouds opening up to drizzle upon the world wondrous as any sideshow act.

Shilzie sat silent, hands dropped at her sides, and mouth lax around over bitten teeth. Staring beside the chest of her brother, through his arms and hands manipulating a napkin and silverware.

Dawn followed her daughter's gaze to Billy and Mortimir. A small group waited behind the twins, plates as empty as their bellies. *Old timers and performers get first dibs on hot grub.* These boys were especially late coming off of clean-up duty. Rodney, Timmy, Blake, Clancy, Benny; less than five years experience between them.

Rodney spoke idly with Benny—*sure am hungry, love the way Otis gets the sausage good and crisp on the outside but it stays juicy on the inside mmm-mmm sure is good*—nothing particularly fascinating. Timmy picked the seat of his coveralls before taking a whiff of his fingers. Clancy grimaced at his fellow greenie's lack of manners. Blake munched his bottom lip—*save room for supper kid*—and dirtied his pale blonde hair with an oily finger after applying an itch to the temple.

Billy watched rousties and performers enter and leave, sit, stand, chat, laugh. Trailed Varlyn's wheelchair tracks in the dirt as his mother pushed, and the overlapping fan-shaped footfalls of Serene as she maneuvered behind on crutches.

Billy did not see Shilzie as he chewed beans spread over bread. Mortimir did. Slow blinking eyes aimed blankly down the length of the three tables. Shiny parted lips tugging and twitching without vocalizing.

"Shilzie?"

Vincent placed a hand on his sister's back. "Sweetheart?"

"Ba mah."

"What was that?" so quiet Vincent had to lean in to hear.

"Ba mah."

Billy's twin blinked narrow eyes and clenched his fist.

"Ba mah... Ba mah."

VOICES

∽ SHILZIE ∾

Rain tapped the curved roof. *Excuse me, excuse me, sir. Sir! Do you hear me?* Tap, tapping for attention. *Sir!* Shrugged off in beaded strands, thick as rope.

Shilzie would sit in front of an open door or parted canvas, Lionel in her arms, a quilt around her shoulders to watch. Imagining aerialists climbing the water ropes to the top and diving. Hands together, legs straight. Splashing into puddles below. Walking along these translucent bubbling wires at impossible angles on the tips of pointed toes. They would jump, cartwheel, dance, twirl.

Her water walkers did not perform tonight.

She stood in front of the caravan's Dutch door. Top half squealing to a rest against the wall. The flesh of her neck, scalp, and arms prickled with gooseflesh. The pink bow adorning a small tail of hair drooped like a wilted tulip. Wet clothes attracted the breeze, but she paid the cold no mind. She watched and listened.

The carnival dimmed after the rain arrived. Carnies rushed into camp after supper. Sheltering heads with the back of shirts or jackets. Newspapers, hats, folded arms.

Only a few solitary lanterns burned in the cook tent; strands of lighted bulbs put to bed for the night. Otis remained, packing up salvageable leftovers and washing dishes.

Look at them.

Freaks.

Worthless filthy fucking Freaks.

Disgusting.

The doctors should have crushed their skulls as they fell out of their mother's cunts! Get it over with at the beginning. They'd be better for it.

"*Mmm,*" she frowned, wrapping thin arms around a tiny midsection.

The twins, *such bad thoughts*.

Shilzie had not known what, or who spoke at first. Only fragments, whispers swelling in and out of her ears. The twisting volume knob on a gramophone, blaring and scratchy, low and distant.

She searched for the voice, unable to find lips matching the words.

Wretches. Monsters. Filth.

Vincent, her sisters, and Mama did not hear these words. No reaction. Her mama did not seek out the speaker. She would have plenty to say if she *had* heard! She hates words like that. Hurtful, and untrue.

Y'all're like anyone else, only born a little different, like how one lady has red hair and another black, some're born with claws, covered in hair, short or tall. Don't make you any different on the inside. Folks is folks no matter the packaging.

The *voice* did not hold the same sentiments for Freaks as Mama does.

What are you looking at? Keep your eyes on me much longer and I'll pop you in a boiling pot and watch as you scream! You think you are better than me? Look at you. Claw hands, bet you can't hold your own cock to piss! Have to be wheeled around by your Freak mother like a fucking infant in a shitty diaper. Better off dead. All of you.

I hate this fucking place! I am not one of you!

"Hand me that towel there." Dawn's voice startled the little girl from thought. She jumped, heels slipping out and back into wet shoes. Water collected in the toes, socks squelched and squished.

"Thank you, son." Dawn sat on the couch drying and changing Elvi and Nylee into pajamas. They laughed as she covered their heads and tousled their faces and hair, rubbing all the way down bare arms and torsos, getting the feet last. Dry down to the very last toe.

Vincent bypassed the bunks for the dresser, returning seconds later with two nightgowns the color of daffodils, and one in rose pink. One of Shilzie's favorite colors. Baby blue the other.

I'll pop you in a boiling pot and watch as you scream!

He wouldn't really do it…

"Shilzie darlin' come 'ere, gonna catch yerself a chill."

She shuffled to her mother, throwing caution over a shoulder. Expecting a face to peer in after her. A pale face in the dark. Sneering and wet. Floating bodiless in the night. Spittle oozing from the corner of smirking lips.

Imagined footsteps came up the stairs. Fast, pattering, the latch clacking and hinges squeaking. Coming toward her as fast as the rain. *Pit-pit-patter!*

You looking at me? Fucking monster…

"*Mmm*," she hurried, huddling to Vincent's side as he set down the folded gowns. Blonde hair stuck in messy tufts across his brow and cheeks. Long waves hung from his chin and down his back and chest in clumps, shirt sopping wet and clinging to the warmth of his body. A sodden jacket crumbled inside the door, soaked through from an attempt to cover the heads of his mother and sisters.

"What's wrong sweetheart?" he asked wrapping a damp arm around frail shivering shoulders.

Her eyes stayed with the door, vigilant.

"Been actin' strange since supper…"

What's wrong Shilzie?

It's just the rain.

You love rain.

Brrr, it's cold!

What are you looking at?

Is Vincent going to read to us now?

Shilzie's brother touched her forehead with a smooth palm. "She warm?"

"No... Perhaps she is only tired. It has been a long day."

"*Hmm*, maybe," Dawn didn't seem convinced. "She'll feel lots better after she's dry an' tucked in bed. Won't ya darlin'?"

Shilzie looked at her mother, unsmiling, frightened.

Hey there... the distorted voice became pleased, gentling, *what are* you *looking at? You looking at me? Wanna come over here by me? We could have a little chat. Just you and me. Right up close, we can share our secrets. I'll whisper in your ear. We'll be real good friends after that. And we can play. Lots of fun games. Like the one where I pop off your beady head and kick it around the tent. Maybe your sisters can play catch. Would that be fun? Would you like that?*

"Come here darlin' girl," she preceded to dry, and change a third daughter into a nightgown. Vincent closed the door.

Lock it! Please!

He didn't.

Lionel, Shilzie's stuffed lion, lay on his belly, arms outstretched across the table where he'd been left before showtime.

She wanted him badly. To squeeze and hug.

No. He needs to stay put. He will keep anyone from getting in. That's why Vincent didn't lock the door, he knows Lionel will stand guard.

Elvi and Nylee giggled by the bookcase, playing with rag dolls and pointing at the books.

It's in a big one!

No, a small one!

It has a lady on the cover!

They all have ladies!

Shilzie, which one was it?

We want Vincent to finish the story!

He said he would!

Ask him to finish it Shilzie!

I want to know what happens!

"*Ah*," Dawn smiled, straightening the fresh bow in her daughter's hair, "There we are, all better now."

It sounded like a question to Shilzie.

Swallowing her fear, for the sake of her brother and mother's worries, she lifted her chin and smiled.

"That'sa girl," she pressed a kiss to her forehead and stood, taking the wet clothes and towels to the hamper.

"Feeling better, love?"

Shilzie walked into his embrace. Damp or not, she didn't care if she wetted her dry nightgown, she wanted to be held.

Vincent was like one of the knights in the fairytales. When he hugged her, his armor kept away everything bad and harmful. He would never let anyone hurt her. Or Elvi and Nylee, or their mama. In her eyes he is the biggest and the strongest in all the carnival, promoted on his banner or not.

Returning with a stool, a brush, and a fresh pile of towels Dawn plopped down the seat, dropped the towels, and pointed, "Pop a squat son, it's yer turn."

"*Mother-*"

"Yer drippin' wet an' gonna snarl all over if ya don't get dried off. Now, strip that shirt and sit."

He sighed.

"Oh, I know, I know. *I can do it myself, ya don't have ta do it, I'm a grown man Mother...* Am I right?"

Vincent smirked and sat dutifully, as asked.

"Yeah, I thought as much. Here," a towel fell over his shoulder, "dry yer front."

She tossed the shirt to the corner with the wet coat.

"Got any letters need sendin'? Johnny's swingin' by the post tomorrow."

"Yes."

"How'd I guess?"

Found it!

That's the one!

This has the story!

Told you it has a lady on it!

The identical girls shuffled to their brother with the thick volume caged in outstretched hands.

"What's this?" he asked, feeling the book before peering under the towel ruffling through his hair. "Oh yes, the story. Thank you, my Dears. Where were we," he cracked the book open to the paper marker.

The triplets made it for his birthday back in January. Dawn helped, but the girls drew the pictures.

Elvi and Nylee scribbled portraits of themselves, arms up with glee in a meadow of flowers. Smiling faces replaced the flora's pollen centers. On the flipside Shilzie drew Vincent as she saw him: a knight. *Though*—because she thought he deserved one—she added a king's crown atop his fluffy head.

"What story?" Dawn asked.

"*'The Lady and her Noble Beast.'*"

"Yer daddy read that one ta me eons ago. Said it were based on a true story. Some king're somethin'."

"It is," Vincent confirmed, securing the marker between pages at the back of the book. "*Ah.* The Lady has just sat down for her evening meal."

Elvi and Nylee scurried to the couch, sitting on the edge and leaning in close, dolls hugged to their chests, eyes bulging in anticipation.

Shilzie sat at Vincent's feet, looping an arm around a wet shin, and let her head rest against his thigh. Her eyes closed when a hand settled on the side of her face, gently petting. She sighed at the warmth. Her fears diminished, worrisome words of a mean man replaced by her brother's voice:

"Do enjoy the feast lain before you this eventide," said the Beast, "And do find joy in this home, for everything here is for you. I would be most upset if you were unhappy."

"You are kind," the Lady said. "Be most assured I am pleased by your gentle heart. In that, I no longer see your ugliness."

"Yes," answered the Beast, "my heart is kind, yet I am a monster."

"Many men are monsters, more monstrous than you appear," the Lady said, "And I would choose you, rather than those with handsome faces masking dark, deceitful, and wicked hearts."

If only everyone thought like that, Shilzie heard from still, red-painted lips. *If only...* Dawn thought, brushing and drying.

If only, Shilzie agreed. *But monsters can* also *mask wicked hearts.*

FOILED

~ ? ~

Wonder how easy one of them would be? One? Why not all three?

About as easy as snuffing out the drunk, he thought.

Easy as taking candy from a baby some might say.

No, that is unusually cruel to compare a helpless baby to these things. *Pinheads.*

Three born in a single go. What sort of slimy reeking crevice gaped between the legs of the woman who birthed them? What ghoulish mutation haunts that damned woman's womb? Three Freaks. A litter of imbeciles.

Killing them would be easy—*his second test run.*

Smothering is the simplest and surest way to be rid of the trio. Quiet, little effort required. Slicing or jabbing throats will also make quick work of the job. Messy, but what does he care?

The heads are so small. Attached to thin necks, hardly wider than a grown man's wrist. Could a pin's head twist off as a cap from a jar? What about imploding between his mitts if squeezed hard enough?

Should I pull something this big now? he wavered. *Patient, I should remain patient… but it will be so easy.*

A scream dashed away the shadow's plans; it receded into the moist darkness beneath the belly of the dripping caravan.

"Shilzie," the boss's son emerged from his warm, lantern-lit abode next door.

"Vinnie?" the boss's voice. "What's goin' on?"

"Shilzie must have had a nightmare. Go on to bed, I've got her."

"Ya sure, Darlin'?"

Nods must have been exchanged, for a door opened when another closed.

"Vinza! Vinza, Vinza, ba mah! Ba maaah," cried the hideous

child in an equally sickening babble. "Ba mah unnur behd!"

"No, no, no. There is no bad man. No bad man."

Boards creaked over a bad man's head.

He didn't get you tonight.

But he'll be back.

Until then, *I'll be seein' you in your nightmares little girl.*

On the Road to
Summerhill, Louisiana

ROAD BLOCKED
❧ BILLY & MORTY ❧

"Bailey's balls on a griddle, it's hot out here!"

Sure is, Billy thought, wiping sweat on his shirt sleeve.

A dark-haired dancing girl frantically waved air at her face, pacing outside the car beside Morty and Billy.

The blonde one's crossed legs hung out the open door of the driver's seat, she fanned herself with a magazine.

I read that one! It's got a real good article about Helga Steele.

She the vamp that shows her tits all the time?

Uh... I guess. I dunno. She was in Terror Manor. Remember she played two roles-

Was she naked in it?

...No.

Then why *should I care?*

Billy's excitement tapered, looking again to the black car.

The other dancer—twin to the pacer—sat in the backseat doing the same as her cousin, but with a record. She waved the square cover between herself and the girl with no arms.

The dancer's stepdaughter, *from what Billy overheard.*

I wish I knew their names, he sighed.

He tried real hard to learn everyone's names. Their jobs at the carnival. Relations to one another. *There are just so many!* More and more each day it seems.

There are even children *living* at the carnival! More than the triplets and the tiny Samson girl. Billy hadn't realized this for weeks! At least four of them he's counted so far, how could he miss such a thing?!

I'm never gonna remember all those names.

Three nameless men sat in the shade of a big truck parked behind the dancers; all laughed at the twin's language, *and* the bickering she did with her sister's husband.

More trucks and cars towing wagons lined up beyond the big one. Six led the way from where he and his brother sat on the side of the road.

Seemed from Billy's vantage most everyone stood or sat in the shade the vehicles provided.

A leg swung slowly from the low window of a grey wagon. The smallest of the caravans. Dawn's being the biggest, followed by her children. Even Billy and Morty's was bigger than the one down the road.

Billy couldn't make out face.

What's he fiddling with on his lap?

His pecker? Morty suggested.

Looks like he's shining a knife.

So, not his pecker?

Billy shrugged. Too far away to know for certain.

The dancer got going again. Growling to the sky: "What do I gotta do to get outta here?! Let the Ringling's pull a train? *It's so fuckin' hot!"*

Why would some men want to lug around a train? Wouldn't a train be too heavy? Sure would take more than five-there's five of them, right? *Is one of them Barnum? Or is he separate? Would he pull the train? What about Bailey? That's the other man, right? Would him and Barnum do it together?*

Morty laughed so hard he shook.

"Barnum knows that woman!" the man with the dancers yelled, whipping off his cap, face red from the sun. "Now stop remindin' us! Sit down and shut it!"

"*Sunny*," his wife tiredly scolded. They'd been going at it for the last half hour.

"You ain't my daddy *or* my husband, so what makes ya think I'm gonna listen ta you? Huh?!"

Sunny swatted his hand in her direction like she was nothing but a fly and squatted against the car to get some shade.

I highly doubt you know your *daddy, lady,* Morty countered.

Neither did they, but Billy didn't bring it up.

"How much longer is this going to take?" asked the twin in the car.

"*Don't know*," said Sunny, wiping his face with a yellow

handkerchief. "Sit tight hon, we'll be movin' on soon."

"Can't we go on ahead? So's at least we can wait in our tents?" the twin hurried her pace, flipping a fan so fast Billy could hear the wind coming off it.

And who do you expect to set it up, princess? Going to let the canvasmen pull a train on you too?

Billy added a smile to the sun drawn in the dirt between his legs, then began work on the moon. Next would be a star.

"Hey, Hills… you lay with the *big man* in charge. Why not *uh,*" a click of tongue and a wink, "*ask him* if he can hurry things up a bit. *Make it worth his while.*"

Hills, *probably a nickname*, let out a little sigh, "That's not going to get the truck fixed any faster."

"Couldn't hurt."

A laugh fell from Sunny's mouth, "Sister, with how ol' Johnny goes at it, you'd be waitin' longer."

Was that a compliment? Morty wondered, Billy could feel his brother's hairless brows narrow over his nose.

The twin eyed her brother-in-law and glanced down the line of cars with a raised brow. A slow smile worked its way up the cheek facing away from her family.

"Let him work," *Hills,* ignored them both, "Johnny will figure it out." Now she looked up the road, along trucks, cars, bigger trucks, caravans, even bigger trucks.

Ahead of their own, a wagon read on its side in a swirl of text *'The Gentleman Beast of York.'* Above the banner a young man had been painted—*younger than Billy and Morty were now*—covered in hair and wearing old fashioned clothes. He gazed into the pages of an open book. Vincent's wagon.

The next one was blank on its wood-paneled sides, *all but for the outline of a banner in faded white, no words.* The triplet girls live inside.

Saw them go in this morning with their brother. After stopping, the giant lady and her little daughter visited. They hadn't left yet.

The first wagon said: *'The World's Only Bearded Snake Charmer, the Whiskered Beauty Dawn de Barcsy.'*

Entwined in the painted banner coiled a snake whose mesmerized gaze held steadfast on a young woman with hairs growing from her chin. She wore a corset, and a short skirt dripping with beads. Her outfit reminded Billy of the ladies in movies about Egypt and Arabia. They belong to *harems* in these pictures—he didn't know exactly what the word meant. Seemed like it involved lots of dancing and wiggly movements. And grapes, and fans made of feathers.

The same type of snake in the portrait's hands encircled one painted leg.

Does Dawn have a tattoo?... Gee, it really looks like her. But younger.

Real pretty, still pretty, but in that way older ladies are pretty, which is different than younger ladies. Billy wasn't sure how to describe it... the feeling he gets looking at a young lady.

Wakey, wakey hissed the snakey, Morty snickered, *or in your case, inchworm.*

Billy's face got hot, realizing the slight tingle, a stirring in his trousers as he examined the painting. In particular, the chest of the mural.

In need of distraction, he looked further down, and saw the other boss, *at least that's what rank he'd placed on the man through observation.*

He runs the Eli wheel—Billy had been corrected when calling it a Ferris wheel; little did he know there was a difference between the two—and fixes things, but he also tells the men what to do. Johnny was the first person Morty and him met when they got to the carnival.

One of the only names he could remember.

The same name as Bruce Clarke's character in the *Rebellion Trilogy.*

John 'Johnny' James.

Johnny—*the carnival's Johnny*, not Bruce Clarke—had been putting together his ride as Vincent parked out back.

The Shadow's Eye, or the *Big Wheel—what some of the workers call it.*

Tightening screws on seats the first time the boys passed under the carnival's arched entrance.

Real welcoming. Shook Billy's hand and said, *"Good ta meet ya boys."*

Morty didn't like that. Said his hands were filthy with dirt and grease. Said he smelled like he looked. Said he shouldn't have touched them. Could have washed his hands first… *He did wipe them on a rag.*

The dancer looked a long time down the line, she eventually stopped fanning herself and started to smile.

She looks like a movie starlet.

Blonde-headed, not golden like Mama. Pale, almost white. A long mishmash of curls and waves. Pinned on top of her head with a sparkling comb, some spirals hung loose down her back and at her temple. She wasn't real thin like the other dancers, but *voluptuous*, like he'd seen described in magazines about the most beautiful actresses.

A figure best for birthing Healthy offspring, as stated by doctors and other experts. *Billy and Morty's mother was of a similar build until she got Sick.*

Humph, Morty scoffed, *guess the whore wants some cock.*

Billy's brows came together.

What? Why? She's just smiling at him.

Look at her, she's a whore, that's all whore's want. Doesn't matter whose it is. Could be the gas station attendant, cook in a diner, traveling salesman, any stranger, any *man will do.*

She doesn't look like a- like a lady like that.

He assumed. If the word meant what he thought it did, then this lady seemed the opposite. Real pretty and nice. Waved back to him if he offered the greeting in the cook tent, or when leaving the Ten after the show ended.

Well, she is. They all are—well, not sure about the Freak girl. Who knows, maybe they sell her after the show to sickos who get off on that kind of thing… Ugh, who would want to fuck a Freak?! No hands, what good is that? Guess she could use her feet, a grunt of disgust trailed his words.

I think they're pretty. Billy spoke of the three dancers *and* the armless lady.

Come on William…

Why not? They got real nice smiles.

Smiles, Morty mocked. *Why not, you ask? Because they are whores. Whores don't deserve respect from people like us. From anyone. They're almost as bad as the monsters. Spreading their legs, spreading filth and Sickness all around the country. Makes me puke thinking about all the cock they've taken in their lives.*

Mama would have been so disappointed to know he talked about ladies like that.

"Oh Barnum, finally."

Every person within earshot lifted their heads at Sunny's words, attention drawn toward the approaching vehicle.

Vincent stepped out first, clad in a heavy cloak. The hood flipped back, slipped down his shoulders, and slung onto the driver's seat.

How can he stand to wear the thing? Must be hot even on a cold day.

The lion man removed leather gloves and opened the door for his mama. Gloves joining the cloak, he retrieved a can of water from the flatbed.

"So, we set?" Johnny asked Dawn, taking the can from Vincent. His voice carried down the line of cars.

"I offered that bastard the whole nut at jump, plus a percentage off the gate, and ya know what he says?"

Johnny gave his boss a once over. "By the jolly-dolly skip in yer step, I'd guess, no."

"He says no!" she enforced. "Somethin' 'bout a group'a *worried* mothers. Scared we're lookin' ta take all their money, that we'll make some kinda impression on the little ones." Her fist came down on the hood of the truck, "Barnum's ass! *They don't want a pack a' Freaks comin' through town!*"

A crowd swarmed like ants descending on sugar with the return of Dawn and Vincent. Uneasy, calling out worries and complaints, questioning. Angry and frustrated and tired.

"We're not setting up?"

"Where are we supposed to stay?"

"We can't keep going on the road."

"We need to stop."

Billy stood, wiping dirt off his behind, and kept to the side of the pack. Just to listen. He didn't have anything to say. Dawn knew what to do. She's in charge, she would keep everything under control.

Dawn's hands clamped a corseted waist, looking to Johnny. He tilted his head toward the crowd and went back to the truck engine.

Talking without speaking, *like he and Morty*.

Billy and his mama did that sometimes. Like when Morty got in a nasty mood, and she'd put her hand on Billy's cheek and look in his eyes.

I know, Baby, she'd say with pretty blues.

She knew how Morty reacted to things, how he'd yell and cry when he wouldn't get his way. Their mama always said to let him do it, let him scream if he had to. Eventually, he would stop. Orneriness lulling to calm through spent energy of tears, screaming, and flailing arm.

She taught Billy to focus on her singing when the yelling got too loud, too hard to bear.

Look at me, look at Mama.

To think of the lullaby. The one she wrote on the night they were born and sang every night since; *before she got too Sick to sing without coughing*.

Billy knew every word by heart. Would forget his own name before his mama's lullaby:

> *My sweet boys*
> *dream sweetly boys.*
> *Sleep soundly and safe,*
> *in my heart,*
> *you'll always stay.*
>
> *Dream of the stars, boys.*
> *Dream of the moon, boys.*
> *Dream of me, boys,*
> *'cause I will dream of you.*
>
> *Oh my sweet boys,*
> *dream sweetly boys.*
> *Sleep soundly and safe,*
> *in my heart,*
> *you'll always stay.*
>
> *Dream in the sun, boys.*
> *Dream in the clouds, boys.*

Dream with me, boys
and I will dream with you.

"Settle down. Seems there's been a change'a plans. We ain't stoppin' in Summerhill. 'Stead we're gonna camp out here for the night, git some rest, and git the trucks in order. We'll head on to Bastropa tomorrow. Won't take but a few hours then we'll be settin' up as usual."

"Ya heard the Boss Lady," Johnny called, wiping hands on a rag. "Boys get settin' up the cook tent, unload the grill and tables, gonna be dark soon and we got hungry people ta feed. Rest of you chip in rollin' out pallets, or make room in yer trucks, everyone's gonna need somewhere ta sleep tonight."

The crowd dispersed, getting to work as Johnny ordered. Billy stood stagnant, unsure what to do. He tucked in his arms and pressed against the wagons to make room.

Men glared, their lips snarled or twisted in disgust when spotting Morty peeking from behind Billy's ear.

Go sit down... Lookit, you're pissing them off. Get the fuck outta the way.

Billy moved against the crowd. Evading shoulders, spit projectiles, and outward-angled feet.

Dawn spoke to Vincent beside the truck. Her voice couldn't be heard over trafficking feet and mumblings. She felt her son's glistening forehead, concerned. He smiled, shook his head, and took her hand to hold between his own.

Wow, his fingers have hair growing on them! Billy hadn't noticed before.

She motioned to the wagons, he nodded, and went to the triplets' trailer.

"D-," he attempted, but she disappeared to the other side.

Aw, too slow...

"Whatcha need boys?" Johnny unscrewed the cap of the canister Dawn and Vincent brought back.

You to stay out of our business.

"I-I-I ju-ust w-wanted ta-to kn-ow if I-I-I, *w-we* cuh-ould help."

He looked them over for a moment. "Come here. Help me lift this thing. Be good fer ya ta learn a thing or two about these trucks."

Billy smiled, and stood next to Johnny, putting one hand underneath the can, and the other around its curved front.

"Now see we don't have ta worry about the engines gettin' hot like this up north, but down south it's good ta pull over once in a while and give it a drink."

He laughed, imagining the engine's mouth opening wide for a guzzle of this cool water when the can tipped to spilling.

Johnny smirked from the corner of Billy's eye.

"Radiator's cooled some since we stopped, but can't hurt ta water it down and let her rest tonight."

Light steam billowed as the water poured. When it subsided, they eased the can back.

"That should do it. If not…"

Billy looked at him.

"Let's just say that'll do it, huh pal? Leave *ifs* for the mornin'," he patted the young boy's back.

"Did you find out what's wrong with her?" The blonde dancer's arm rested on the warm metal of the hood, pink fingernails clicked against it.

"Old girl had a bit of the vapors is all. A drink should fix her up."

She gave a small laugh. It sounded as pretty as she looked.

Johnny watched her. She looked at him. They both smiled.

These two gonna fuck right here, or wait till we leave?

"You met Billy and Morty?"

"No. I haven't," she turned to the boys. Eyes on the both of them, Billy, then Morty… she didn't frown, didn't turn away, *didn't avoid Morty at all*. Her smile got bigger. Teeth straight and pearly white, lips the same pink as her fingernails. "I'm Hilly, it's nice to finally meet you two."

She's…

Billy took her hand when she lifted it. His fingers twitching. He'd never shook a lady's hand before. Well, *Dawn's*, and he'd held Mama's hand, but that was different. She was his mama, and Dawn is a lot like a mama—*is* Mama to her *own* kids—this lady, *Hilly*… is a *lady*.

"N-n-na-na-nice to m-mm-meet you."

Should I kiss her hand? Men do that in the movies. No. No, no,

I couldn't do that.

Billy let her hand go. Smooth as fresh butter, and white like milk. She smelled of sweet cream. The kind Mama would whip with a whisk and put on pies for dessert.

"Johnny teaching you two to be de la Llum's next mechanics?" she asked, glancing at Johnny.

"Like *I'd* give away my secrets," he said over his shoulder, storing the can in the back of the lead truck.

Could *I learn? Will I have to?*

No answer from his brother.

"How do you two like the carny life so far?" Hilly smiled at the boys. It hadn't gone away as Billy spoke, or when Morty's arm jumped during the handshake.

People tend to turn green at his movements. If he wet his lips or fisted a hand. *Or* nothing.

Not her.

"I-I-I-I-I," Billy closed his eyes, the word stuck to his tongue. "I-I like it," he grinned. Bigger at seeing Hilly *still* smiling. Not frowning, or glancing about, uncomfortable with the stuttering. She waited patiently, listening. "Th-th-ther-there's *lots* of pu-people. I-I-I-It's ga-gonna take a lu-long t-t-time to reme-ember all the na-names."

"Don't worry about it. I've been here for seven years, and I still get folks mixed up. You'll meet us all soon enough."

...smiling...

"Don't help that rousties come an' go with the seasons," Johnny added, now clutching a jug of water under each arm, and one by the handle in each fist.

"Need a hand?"

"*Nah.* I *like* breakin' my fingers. Feels good."

Hilly laughed and took one of the jugs. It weighed heavy in her bare white arms. Short fluttering sleeves capped her shoulders. Wrinkly and rippling like the petals of a carnation. Buttons lined the front of the dress down the center, all the way until the hem. The first few left unbuttoned, exposing enough of her chest that it made Billy remember the painted Dawn on the wagon. He looked away when he realized he stared... *again.*

"Ca-can I h-help?"

"Sure kid," he turned to the side, offering the jug in his left hand. "Take that to the cook tent would ya? Gonna pass these to the rest of 'em. *Help me with that?"* he asked Hilly. The louder, grating voice he uses when addressing the men now a calm rumble.

She nodded, and they began to walk.

"It was nice meeting you Billy, Morty," she called over her shoulder, pale hair dancing across her face and swaying with her steps.

...at...

Billy sighed, watching the first stop at Hilly's car, where she handed off the jug to Sunny. They continued on. Their heads turned toward each other, Hilly gazing up at Johnny, and him down, talking. Her smile never lessened, only seemed to get bright as a beacon the further they got. Slow steps matched, no rush down the road. Her hands clasped at the small of her back. The sway of their paths closed in on one another until their arms brushed.

...me?... She... didn't...

Billy looked at the jug and took it to the cook tent as Johnny asked.

SLEEP

∿ ? ๛

A shadow loomed long across yellowed grass. Exaggerated limbs became skeletal, insect-like with pendulous balled fists. Arms hung at the shadow's sides, feet planted firmly, squared with the shoulders, head cocked, watching, listening.

The perfect view of the *family,* Carnivàle de la Llum. Home to a lot of mangy Freaks, criminals, and killers. Trash the rest of the world doesn't want.

The grunts, *the worker bees*, slept under the stars tonight, while the deformed ones sleep sound and comfortable in wagons. Tucked into their beds, under warm covers, shielded from curious and blood-hungry pests.

Dozing bodies instinctively slapped at the bites, grumbling and turning. Limp arms dragging and legs kicking blankets. Snores intermingled into one droning sound, a chugging train in the distance.

Harmonizing alongside the bodily melody of slumber, the night buzzed with cicadas, chirped with grasshoppers. In a drying bit of marsh over a slope of hill, frogs croaked. Stopping and starting, silencing the night at every disturbance.

Animals surely; seeking out the next meal. Predators perhaps. Wild dogs. Snouts in the air, smelling the food cooked only hours ago. Meat. Charred. Burnt black in some places. That scent dissipated now, leaving only fresh, rare flesh, laid out in the grass. Easy pickings. So many flavors.

The shadow surveyed the appetizers lying side by side in neat rows like sausages on a grill. The only thing needed was a match and the sleepy piggies would start cooking.

He felt for a light, finding nothing.

The Freaks would burn. In time, the Freaks *will* burn.

ABASHT THE DEVIL STOOD
∽ MORGAN ∾

Hoooooooonk, honk-honk hooonk honk-honk hooonk hoooooooooonk.

Varlyn—perched driver's side in George's truck—scooted sideways, shut the door, and placed palms flat to his lap. His mother, at the front left fender, found reason to turn away from the road. Arms crossed, hands tucked in.

Vincent called the triplets to the back of a nearby caravan and lifted the edges of his cloak until the material draped along the tops of three tiny heads.

Zach and Francis took two steps to the right, placing the trunk of a sapling directly between their shoulders. From the road, it looked as if two men relieved themselves side by side. Unaware of the bit of flesh binding the pair together.

Others squatted beside bushes, *if not already doing so during this unscheduled restroom break*. Took coverage behind box trucks and wagons, turned up collars, rolled up windows.

"Why with the honking?"

Morgan gulped at the carousel jockey—previously a car behind, laughing with the driver. He stepped nearer Morgan's stationary wagon as a towner drove past.

Sharp, bright eyes surrounded with sagging, wrinkling skin studied both men closely beneath the brim of a baseball cap. Wide and scouring for persons of interest in this traveling carnival, searching for *Freaks*. A free show on the drive home.

Morgan stood the sword on his lap against the wall and draped a rag over the sill he sat on. Not of a window, having no glass or frame. A shelf once used to display wares, or a countertop from which to pass coin in exchange for such wares.

Its planked shutter propped open with metal bars, casting much-appreciated shade on the jockey below.

The Baron's grandfather and great-uncle traveled Europe in the carriage selling medicinal tonics as *'de Barcsy Brothers Miracle Cures and Tonics'*.

Piss and ink, turpentine and peppers, animal fat and camphor, nothing what would do customers any good by ingesting. However, the de Barcsy's were known for their charm and sold out at every stop.

When found out as frauds, the brothers undoubtedly talked their way out of criminal charges—*and more than one threat of hanging.*

It amazed Morgan to contemplate de la Llum's roots. The Baron's family peddling cures for one's Health. That the Normal, so conscious of disease and the prospect of bringing a Freak into the world, or having no Healthy or living children at all, would choose to believe in this bottled cure, this liquid boost of strength, vigor, and protection from all ailments. That it would have no ramifications. Ramifications the world as a whole battled against for the last thousand years, since the last *Miracle Cure* arose.

It cemented proof for Morgan that the human race could remember, as well as it forgets, picking and choosing what suits best at hand. Caring for their wellbeing so highly above anyone or anything else, that they would risk it all to live *forever*.

No one lives forever.

No matter if bundling up against the cold, or eating vegetables when mother says so, none of it retains youth, none of it creates immunities to inevitable aging or Sickness.

A pain nibbled in the pit of Morgan's stomach once the old man and his rickety truck were out of sight, and his focus had no choice but to return to the man below.

Biting into the meat; heat rising in Morgan's cheeks before hightailing it.

If I answer, maybe he will leave.

He inhaled slowly through his nose and replied, quietly, but brusquely. "So the performers can hide themselves."

Hadn't the jockey heard this signal before? For months he's traveled with the carnival, he *must* have noticed.

Too busy chatting away and biting sausages.

Arms crossed over his belly, hoping the pressure would ease the upset tension as thoughts, and questions of that night returned.

Had anyone seen him run? How foolish he'd looked? Witnessed what the jockey did to send him off in a rush? What did they think?

...He seemed so pleasant at the showers.

Naked: kind. Clothed: crude. No sense to it.

"You didn't," *Evro* said, brow quirked.

"No not... not me," for a moment he forgave the man's transgressions.

No, not me... *the* Freaks *have to hide themselves*, he did not want to say, no matter the truth in the harsh words.

"Oh... *oh!"* he understood, realizing the windows of the *Biggest Little Family* wagon ahead clapped shut. *"That's a shame,"* his voice gentled, frowning, *"They shouldn't have to hide..."*

Morgan agreed.

But Normies don't see it that way, he thought.

Did you know doctors use to brand them, Morgan? The Sick, with an S on the forehead. So they couldn't hide. The Freaks were done away with at birth. Life was better back then. Safer. Smarter. Sickos get off so easy now. And why?... Why?

"So, this is your place?" Evro changed subjects. "Nice. Cozy."

"Thanks," Morgan said, chin tucked against his chest, avoiding the man's observation of his home's exterior and interior.

An empty driver's seat out front. The modified wagon tongue attached to the back of a truck heaped with canvas. Strapped beneath the cab during travel were the absentee stairs with which to enter the domicile.

Inside: a single bed, a trunk at its foot, end table, and shelves parallel to the open door.

Unintentionally appropriate of a carnival wagon, stripes lined horizontally—*rather than the vertical of canvas*—corner to corner on each blank windowless wall. Pale markings detailing width and position of previously hung shelves, on which stored phony cures eighty-some years ago.

Clothes folded neatly on the lower shelves in separate piles: shirts, pants, jackets, socks, undershorts, towels, wash rags. On the floor: three pair of boots, two for the show, one for every day.

A small crate containing items regarding personal hygiene sat at hand beside the clothes; e*ase of convenience when heading out the door.* Shampoo, toothpaste and brush, hair brush, scissors, gauze, rubbing alcohol, straight razor, shaving cream, bar soap, clothing detergent.

Show supplies staked their claim on the upper shelves. Cans of fuel, metal rods, hanks of wicking cord, rags, boxes of needles, razorblades, and matches. The high-lipped shelves held every item in place, kept every sliding box from tumbling even on the harshest roadway.

A sack, stained, punctured, and badly repaired with uneven stitches, slumped at Morgan's side, full of further tools of his trade.

Six swords displayed on the wall alongside the bed. A small end table wedged against the bedside, on which sat a bowl with a black goldfish swimming within.

Again, the horns. *Hooooooonk, honk-honk hooonk honk-honk hooonk hooooooooonk.*

"What's your fishy's name?" Evro asked, ignoring the sound.

"Fin-... *Fineas.*"

"That after the Barnum fellow?"

He nodded, though neglected to divulge the spelling difference. A childish play on the name, but it made Morgan want to smile.

"*Ah.*" He looked across the wagon at the fish circling the bowl, sucking in flakes of food left over from his morning feeding. "Never saw a black one before. Thought they only came in gold-*well, orange.*"

Morgan shook his head, "No, they can be black." *Why he enlightened him on the various hues of goldfish? Hel if he knew.* "White, yellow, red, spotted, multi-colored... We get them for prizes sometimes..." the words faded.

Evro was attentive, listening. Eye contact the whole while.

Smiling as he bit down. Exhaling when his eyes closed.

Face smoldering, Morgan turned away, watched another car. This time a child's face pressed to the glass, nose round and piggish, hands flat, eyes absurdly large.

"You use him in your show? Swallow and... ya know," he lurched forward, expelling a false retch onto the road.

A nod.

The jockey shivered. "I'd be too scared I couldn't get the little guy back up. You are a braver man than I, Morgan."

A tremor racked the sword swallower's spine. The first time the jockey said his name. *Only in passing.* One word of many in a sentence. But his timbre softened around the syllables. *Gentle.* Almost cradling the letters.

A stupid thought. Ridiculous. He hadn't said his name any differently than the others.

Biting, grinning, laughing, staring, watching.

Barnum help him, how humiliating.

The lace of his guts knotted tighter. Granny knots, fisherman's knots, the hangman's noose, remembering the jockey's eyes on the bare and damp skin between the undone upper buttons of his shirt. *Warm and moist from the shower.* Placing the tip of one sausage link between his teeth. Capturing his unwitting stare and forcing it to watch as he bit down. One, then another.

I should have waited longer. I thought I gave it enough time. Enough so he would get his food and go. I didn't want to see him again. Not after that.

The entire evening became all the more embarrassing the longer he thought about it. The shower, the cook tent, running to hide in the caravan.

Something he should be used to. Formative school years were blurs of inadequacies, of being an outcast amongst peers, and tortured mercilessly for it. Taunted as a child, a teen, even as an adult shame seeks him out to once more peer in his eyes, peeling back the lids to feel every painful second.

"I'm sorry for the other night… At supper." A short pause, *as if Morgan needed a moment to remember.*

Of course, he knew what supper. A masochistic mind relives the scene at night, over and over until its host hides his face in a pillow, guts aching with humiliation. Telling the memories to stop, over and over. *Shut up, shut up, shut up, stop!*

"I was fooling, I didn't mean to embarrass you. *Really.*"

There it is again, but this time he knew for certain. Softness in his voice. A warmth to the words, strange as it seemed.

He dared to look—*really look*—for a moment, then he would lower his gaze.

Yes. The words showed there. Dark, chocolaty eyes genuinely meant all he spoke.

Morgan shrugged, as if the *'fooling'* were nothing, mindlessly picking at a splinter of wood.

The shelf needs sanding and repainting. He has gotten plenty of holes poked into his legs from sitting here. *Not that the pain bothered him.*

"I'm sorry."

An apology? Had his caravan wheeled into the unknown?

A part of him wanted to believe it. But people are cruel. People torment others in so many ways. Teasing, harassing, beating. They lie.

Morgan understood such logic from a very young age. Witnessed his mother spit on more than one *monster* on the streets outside their Stepton community. And did anyone flinch? Anyone step in and stop her, reprimand her, say anything in defense of the poor hapless man or woman wiping bubbly saliva from their cheek, between the eyes, or sprayed across the mouth. No. Because those who are Freaks, who are a modicum different from Normal, on the outskirts of acceptable, deserve all they get.

So, did he trust this man? Should he accept the apology or take it with a grain or two of salt and be weary of what he said next?

The man *had* smiled, biting into the sausage. Grinning, setting the grilled tip between his teeth. Morgan thought he recalled laughter as he ran from the tent. *Had he?* Had this man worn the biting smile as he scurried away, near flinging the dinner plate into the air, and toppling a tent on the way to the caravan line?

Morgan supposed he would learn soon enough. No avoiding him, unless he quit. *No chance.* They travel together, live on the same lot, retrieve food from the same tent, are within physical reach.

"Not the worst that's happened to me," he mumbled, carving a crease into grey wood with the edge of a jagged thumbnail.

He could still hear his mother's voice. *Mother knows what's best for you. I am the only one you can trust. The only one.* He shivered.

"Sorry." The jockey frowned.

Morgan's stomach loosened, one knot undone.

"Wasn't you. Don't be sorry."

He closed his eyes, swallowed. Shame rolled down his throat. *Mother.*

"Can't be sorry for everyone, but I am for what I did. Really, fooling is all I meant. Sausage links only look like *one* thing," a weak laugh came at the end. "And I had two of 'em. Double dong? Get it?"

A huff, almost a laugh, parted his lips, "I guess."

Morgan did not look up at the faint sound of Evro's lips parting. Nothing, until a gentle, "I was hoping to give you a laugh. You're... so serious when I see you around. Seemed like you could use a good chuckle."

Maybe he did. Morgan didn't feel it a necessity, not when he wanted nothing more than to be alone, ignored, once the carnival closed for the night. He would rather no one think about him than say a single word in his direction. If the words held the possibility of pain, he was better off without them.

"With all the yammering I do, *you'd expect* I'd catch on that not everyone appreciates the gutter-minded yarns that get me fitting to burst."

Morgan felt like such a fool. Listening to this man apologize. Nothing he said had been malicious, or even mean.

For Barnum's sake, it was done at the buffet of all places.

No one but the two men stood in line. Otis, with his back turned, and the rest of the carnival busy with meals and conversations. No one noticed Morgan anyway. Not most of the time. Only if crossing paths, usually by accidental circumstance, *having* to pass with no alternative. Only then did one see him, speak to him, acknowledge him.

He thought of himself as a shadow, *only noticeable when looking down.*

They *were* naked together minutes before.

Though Morgan made no attempt to look—not even at his silhouette through the sheet.

And of all foods, *sausages* were on the menu that night. Kind of funny now that he thought about it.

Evro put a hand on the bit of wall separating the door and window shelf. Muscle bunched in the bicep of the lean arm. A shard of crystal hung from a gold chain, he pinched it, slipping the loop across links. It caught the light as clouds shifted and sent spots of white across his chest.

"Forgive me?"

Somehow Morgan didn't feel himself shrink beneath the dark

gaze. Maybe because the man was serious.

Doubts, those voices aiming to eat their host body alive from the inside out arose.

Why should *I trust you?* he wondered. *He isn't serious.*

The man is a stranger. Barely traveled with de la Llum longer than the here-today-gone-tomorrow teenage roustabouts who run back to mommy and daddy before thirty miles pass.

One nod.

Evro laughed a little, "I'm sure you're sick to death of me yapping by now but... I want to get to know you."

"Why?" Morgan said earnestly. What could possibly interest this man?

"You..." he squinted, searching for the word in the sky, "*intrigue* me."

Again, why? Morgan thought. He felt he had no more appeal than a wet rag on his best day... though, he did put on a good show. He would give himself due credit, he worked hard at his craft, and he felt it became apparent during a performance.

"You're quiet around the lot, but on stage, you light up. *And not because of the fire,*" he smiled. "I'd like to chat again sometime. *If you don't mind.*"

A whistle preceded: "Load up! Headin' out!"

Evro sighed, "Guess we're getting back on the road," he patted the wall and made to turn.

Morgan exhaled, "W-wait," he hesitated, and Evro stopped. Sharp, neat brows rose over soft dark eyes. Expectant. Waiting.

"I-" struggling against usual judgment, *people hate, tease, and torment*, he took a chance, "I-I don't mind."

The smile that erupted on the jockey's face could not be misconstrued as anything else, other than pure joy. "Well," the grin grew, "talk to you later Morgan," he nodded, and sauntered away.

CHAPTER 16

GAZOONIE

∿ ? ℘

The stumbling pack of carnies poured from the billiard hall.

By night, an illicit establishment offering scarcely legal beverages; brewed below in the basement. Stairway door hidden by a false wall camouflaged with cue racks and décor along the seams—*should the unhealthy quenchers of thirst suddenly be deemed illegal as well as immoral.* Invading officers in search of contraband will leave the premises in a slump, for no bust has been made.

From darkness, this group of oblivious old-time crewmen and newcomers were observed.

What would a naturist deem the collective noun for a group of carnies? the watcher wondered. For, there is a kettle of vultures, a shiver of sharks, a *murder* of crows.

A swindle? A hustle? A racket of carnies?

Or maybe a curse?

No, that is a herd of Freaks. A curse... of Freaks.

A single member broke from the safety of the racket.

A straggler—*vulnerable to predators when alone.*

"Where ya goin', Timmy? Lot's this way, ya boob!"

"Can't hold it! Gotta take a leak, I'll catch up!"

The others never entertained the thought of waiting. In few steps, the hustle took a right. Migrating west to roost in their nesting tents for the remaining twilight hours.

Timmy entered the first alleyway beside the booze hall. Eying a drainage pipe crawling up the wall. Not enough coverage. Nor a stack of crates. He settled on a dumpster veiled in shadow, *obscuring a shadow.*

Good enough place to piss as any, his shrug suggested. Secluded, private. But for the figure he did not see hunkered and waiting. Did not hear it slipping deeper into oily blackness. A courtesy so the young man may have space to do his business.

He hid his crotch beside the oversized bin and procured his penis for leakage.

Stinking yellow piss sprayed the crusty sleeves of a discarded jacket. Flattened and slimy, repeatedly crushed by refuse leaking cans.

The other in the dark skirted two cans full up with empty containers, broken bottles, and rotten food.

Timmy zipped up after a shake and wiggle to rid the last golden drop from the head of his prick.

Sensing he was not alone he turned, gasped, "Jeez! You scared the Hel outta me! Thanks for waiting-"

Gratitude became confusion. Further decaying to another deeper emotion: betrayal.

His throat bobbed, gasping and sputtering. A wet snort honked in his nose as he grimaced, struggling to suck in a breath against the sudden deluge of blood painting his esophageal walls. One hand tentatively tapped the butt end of a pocketknife and a crimson blade tip with the other.

Anytime, the wielder of steel thought and retook possession of his borrowed property.

Air hissed in, blood gushed out. Poor Timmy fell down, down, down.

Better throw out the trash and catch up to the swindle.

Timmy will not be missed.

Carnies never take notice when a *gazoonie* goes missing.

Bastropa, Louisiana

TUNES OF THE BALLYHOO

∾ HILLY ∾

The day before opening night. If something were to go wrong for de la Llum, this is the day it would happen. No mishaps, and the show is sure to go on without a hitch for the duration of the stay. If only a single incident occurs, no matter how insignificant, they could count on many more before the next jump.

There *had* been a problem today. *Several.* It all began with the discovery of burst soda pops in the back of Russ's truck. Followed by stuffed prizes involuntarily sopping up the mess.

As set up began, two crates of brand-new bulbs dropped and shattered, ropes frayed, and now the Kootch tent center poles were found broken. Snapped in two across the ground with deflated canvas splayed out beneath it. Coils of rope, side poles, and stakes piled behind the bally, waiting until rigging could continue.

You dumb shit! Angus bellowed, unpacking the back of the truck.

Rodney, a greenie from Colorado, tensed, near tears under the shouts of the senior worker.

"What'd ya do?! How'd ya snap the damn things in half?!"

"I'm sorry! I-I didn't mean to!"

"Fuckin' idiot!"

"Ooo," the others taunted.

One voice ascended, *"Johnny hears about this and you're outta here. Gonna leave you on the side of the road with no ride back to mama."*

Wide-eyed, *"Please, please don't tell him! I can fix it!"*

"Snottin' and sorries ain't gonna fix shit! Get the fuck outta my sight!"

Rodney hurried away, blending with the crew working midway detail.

Johnny had *not* scolded him upon finding out.

A young boy, new, only an accident. Though he did send him over to dig the latrine.

While the men came up with replacements for the damaged poles, the dancers lounged on the lonely bally stage.

"You want sparkles, yes?"

"Yeah, ya know those little dangly spangly things?" Daze twiddled her fingers. "Like on the mirror number you did for Hills."

"Oh, yes! Those would be pretty," Lavi said. Decades lived in the States put a slight damper on an accent of Germanic origin.

She scribbled a note on the drawing pad beside a sketch. A quickly done mockup of a tiny pair of panties with dangling strands of paillettes in descending lengths to the knee, and two strings of beads curving around each hip securing the front to the back. Enough to cover the wearer's crotch and not much else. No top had been decided on, if *any* were to accompany it.

"The same for Vie?"

"Prob'ly. Ain't we always dressed the same?" Hilly's cousin said, a thin coating of disdain painted the reply. Not for Lavi, but the fact that Daze and her sister not only were identical physically, but there was no distinguishing the twins in costume. Same color, same style, every brassiere, every g-string, every stitch the same. Unless deduced by freckle placements, the two women were interchangeable. Neither more special than the other.

It's a perfect gimmick, Dawn exclaimed of the dancers, *a man can only dream fer two women at once, let alone twins.*

One night, panties-deep in a bottle of cheap hooch, Daze confessed to Hilly, *she* wants the limelight. She wants to be the most beautiful woman on stage. All eyes, attention, the yelling, all for her. *Can't have that with a doppelganger at my hip every day of my life.*

"Okay," Lavi smiled, writing again. "And for Hilly? You want new costume?"

"No, thanks. Sheri's going to mend a few old things for me."

"Not that awful pink number I hope?"

A long, slinky, chiffon nightgown with a sheer lace bust, and slits riding up to the hip bone on either side. Simple as it is, Daze turns green whenever Hilly wore it.

She nodded, hiding a smile.

"Wish you'd throw it away," her swinging heels thumped the

front panels. "Can't possibly fit you anymore."

"Sure does."

Daze scoffed.

Lavi giggled into her hand briskly, collected herself, and asked, "You come in for fitting in the morning, yes?"

"Fine by me."

"Okay. I will see you later girls, bye bye."

"Alright, bye now."

"Bye Lavi," Hilly waved, squinting at the light to watch her leave. Hips swayed with the gorgeous little woman's walk.

"You have any smokes?"

"No. Sunny might."

"*Old bastard better*," Daze scooted off the bally and dusted off her dress. "Want me to bring one back for ya?"

"No." She wanted to lay in the sun for a while. Bask in the warmth. Let the heat-soaked boards soothe her aching lower back.

Dirt and pebbles crunched under Daze's shoes, becoming lost in the bustle of the carnival.

The boys hammered spikes at all corners of the lot, *plinks* punctured the air rapid fire. Quick synced hits, one after another, from groups of three to five men driving four feet of wood deep in seconds. Canvas unrolled. Rope tightened, scraping leather gloves as the rousties hauled tents into the air. Trucks backed up, aiding in the rise of center poles. Nails drove into loose planks. Balloons inflated straight across from Hilly's feet. One popped and two women laughed. Crates tinkled with glass in the arms of passersby. Conversations everywhere among workers and performers.

Feet stomped up the other side of the bally stage, shaking her.

A grunt, and a hammer dragged off the boards, boots turned and down the steps he went.

Alone once more, Hilly closed her eyes, began to hum. Sing:

"*Love me love me*"

On the way to the lot, her favorite song played on the radio. *"Dance With Me Tonight,"* by Sherry Vena. A lovely song with the power to sway the listener.

It had been stuck in her head for hours:

"Love only, all of me"

Softer footfalls than before shifted the wood below.
Another roustie.

Humming continued between softly sung lyrics. Unconsciously the words exited the side of her mouth, mimicking the way Sherry sang. Pursing her mouth to the right, smiling at the left, brows lifting and lowering, showing every emotion felt while singing the song for the man she loved:

> *"Hold me hold me,*
> *Kiss me slowly,*
> *One look at you and I've fallen madly!"*

Wood slid against wood, and the bright behind her lids went dark. The boards waned beneath her back.

"That ain't a half bad Sherry."

Hilly's eyes opened to the underside of an old umbrella. Alternating red and yellow fabric, but for patches too light or dark to match. Edges cracked, dried by unforgiving sunlight, ripped and fraying, strings swirling frantically in the breeze. The wooden pole and stand grey with weather wear—once white—judging from peeling paint.

"Ever think of singin' for the show?" Johnny smirked, positioning the umbrella so the maximum area of shadow fell across the dancer.

"What are you doing?" she grinned, sitting up on her elbows.

Purposefully ignoring such flattery.

A good Sherry. Singing in a show. Never! No one could compare to that luscious voice. Hilly carried a tune well enough, she thought. Next to Sherry, *any* woman became as melodious as squeaky screws in a ride seat.

"Thought ya could use some shade. Found it in the old baggage trailer," his chin nodded up at the umbrella. "Use ta have tables fer the grab joints."

"Before my time?"

"Long before."

"You didn't have to go through all of the trouble," Hilly said, watching Johnny's forearms flex as he secured the umbrella firmly into its base. "Besides, the sun feels nice today."

"Yeah, well you don't need ta be sittin' in no sun. Yer white as a sheet, be a strawberry in no time," he eyed the base, pushed the weathered pole, and nodded when it didn't sway.

"All red and covered in seeds?"

He squinted, biting one side of his lip. Trying not to smile, "A *tomato* then, ya know what I mean."

She laughed, laying back against the stage.

"So, how you doin' today, Girly?"

"Fine. Relaxing, imitating Sherry, and catching up on my reading."

"*Dark Shadow,* huh," he squatted, examining the novel. "What made ya pick a spookster title like that?"

"It had Shadow in it. Made me think of the Eye." It *had* brought to mind de la Llum's big wheel. That thought naturally turned to the wheelman kneeling beside her.

He smirked and flipped through the pages, "Doubt this is about no big wheel." His brows rose, "Big *somethin',* but not no wheel."

"Read something you like?" she grinned, amused he'd skimmed over an intimate moment between the dark, exciting, mysterious stranger and the lovely maiden.

"*Nah,*" he set the book down, pulled out a rag, and wiped at chipped paint sticking to his palms. "Got my own, don't need ta read about no other fellas."

She laughed again, and he soon joined. Unable to help himself as he watched her. The way her eyes glinted, her smile.

Praises be to Barnum, she is beautiful, Johnny thought.

Wore her hair down today. Not pinned or held with ornamented combs as she often did on a working day. Loose and framing her head and shoulders in platinum spirals. The bright day made her pale blue eyes almost white, ghostly, and ethereal.

"Let me see that," she sat up and held out a hand.

"This old thing? What for?" Despite questioning, he set the wrinkled bit of cloth in her clean white palm.

Washed this morning and barely used, he still felt it too dirty to touch such delicate hands as hers.

"You've got a smudge." She led his prickly chin forward with the tip of her finger and wiped the side of his jaw. Paint chips and grease.

She smelled lovely, sweet and clean, like cream. The lotion she rubs into her arms and legs after a bath. *Skin soft as the silk underthings beneath her clothes.*

"There." She sighed, looking him over. "So. How has *your* day been?"

He squeezed the rag. "Oh, swell! Blake near dropped a wrench on my head checkin' the Eye's spokes."

"*Oh*," she sympathized, "You didn't get hurt, did you?"

"*Nah.* Landed in the seat behind me. Scared my britches off, but," he shrugged, "*coulda' been worse.*"

She frowned. The roustabouts' jobs are dangerous. Anything could happen. A tent collapsing, a ride could come up missing a bolt and topple right over. An overheating engine or generator catching fire. The men have to be careful. Vigilant. Safe.

"Well, I'm glad you are alright," her hand clutched his fingers. Rough to the touch, calloused, and worn.

Johnny's mouth quirked at her concern.

"Hey, you two!"

"Hi Sunny," she sighed. Hand covering a rapidly beating heart at such a start.

"*Sunny*," Johnny regarded, standing to adjust the umbrella. *Again. Unnecessarily.*

"What're *you* all up to?" Sunny lowered the green hatbox in his hand to the ground, *Sheri's.* Sewing supplies: scissors, thread, needles, thimbles. With elbows rested on the bally, her cousin-in-law grinned like the fool his wife often *lovingly* labels him as.

"Nothing," she answered, smiled, "Talking."

"Didn't seem like nothin'," he chuckled drunkenly, though stone sober.

"Then what'd it *seem* like Sunny?" Johnny asked.

"Seemed like you were settin' up that there umbrella," he pointed, biting back a grin. "Tell ya what, I'll leave," his hands flew up, "Ya'll can get back to yer *nothin'. Bye* Hills," he winked, picked up the hatbox, and dawdled toward the dress tent, swinging the box and throwing greetings left and right.

"So…" Johnny began slowly as Sunny disappeared. Pushing the rag into his back pocket he asked, "What're you up to tonight?"

She shrugged. "Night before opening," he offered a hand as she stood, retrieving *Dark Shadow* as well, "Nothing extravagant. Straightening up my tent."

Once up, of course. A very important step.

"I were only askin' 'cause *uh*-" he rubbed the back of his neck, avoiding her eyes.

A knowing smile lifted her lips. *He wants to see me tonight.*

"I were wonderin' if I could," the briefest pause. Keeping his nerve, "Stop by?"

She wouldn't mind that at all but, "Johnny I-"

"If yer busy-"

"It's not that, *um*," she bit her lip and turned the book in her hands slowly, end over end until upside down. *How could she put this mildly.* "It's not a good *time*… for me."

"Doesn't have ta be real late."

"No, I mean, it's a bad time of the *month*…" she let that hang in the air, raising her brows, hoping he would catch on the longer she looked into his eyes.

He should, it wasn't the first time she'd had to turn him away.

His brow started low, slowly climbed upward. "Oh-*oh*," his laugh nervous, "Well uh," he cleared his throat, "Sorry, I shouldn't'a asked. I-"

"It's okay," she shrugged.

Like every woman, she wished she wasn't on her monthly with all of its inconveniences. Though womanly obligation did have a few perks when it came to her job. Time off from stripping. She still danced some. Topless, with high waist undergarments or cinchers to hide the menstrual belt. Mostly she stuck to advertising on the bally in a skimpy dress, showing off leg and a preview of breasts. She did get out of blow-offs for the whole week, as well as no Johns.

The best part.

"I got plenty ta keep me busy anyhow. Gotta get the lot straight before tomorrow afternoon or Dawn'll pickle my head and show it off in the Ten."

"No, she'd never. This place would fall apart without you."

"Nah," his hand swatted the praise. "Could pick up any rube

from'a steel mill or oil rig who'd do my job well enough or better."

The thought made her sad. As sad as she would be if her cousins, Sheri, or Sunny left without her. It made her stomach ache to think of a day when she did not see him.

"No one could replace you around here."

"Ya really think so?"

"I do."

Can't you see I am your biggest fan, Mr. Rollercoaster Man?

CHAPTER 18

TWO BITS

∾ BILLY & MORTY ல

Knock. Knock, knockknock, knock. Knock. Knock.

"What is it?"

Billy's new boss sat at a little cluttered desk. Columns lined the pages of a red ledger at the center of messy stacks of paper. From the door he couldn't read anything, only guess the scribbles as numbers beside words. A total underlined at the bottom.

On the floor, a big black metal chest yawned open. Old, with scuffs on the corners, flecked with rust, and dented all over.

Crossways over the corner closest to Dawn was a rectangular tin with its hinged lid hanging backward. Full of folded bills and scattered coins. On the money box's side was a faint cartoon of a blond boy: eyes closed, cheeks full, and smirking with chocolate smudged around his mouth.

In the trunk, Billy noticed a top hat, top side down, filled with loose trinkets, most of them jewelry. Bundled clothes, and one of those furry little fancy blankets ladies drape over their shoulders tucked against the sides and corners of the chest. *To keep everything from sliding around during travel,* he bet.

A leather strapped scrapbook stood flush against the side, newspaper clippings poked out of the top. Folded pages, single columns, photos. The spine of the album split down the middle it held so many articles.

What's it say? Does that newspaper say murder? Morty asked.

'Murder! Couple Found Dead!'

'Carnival Catastrophe!'

'Six Men Missing!'

Interesting...

Billy caught a partial heading of *The Texas Star*: *Parents Killed in-.*

Before he could eye-snoop further, Dawn took the money tin,

closed it atop her desk, and shut the lid of the chest with a bare foot.

The end of a tail curled above red-painted toes. A snake's tail.

She does *have a tattoo like the picture on her wagon!*

With the black box shut, she sorted keys around a ring and secured two locks on its front. The tin box went into the bottom desk drawer, also locked up.

The jangling ring went right back to her skirt pocket.

"Heya Billy-" a pause when her eyes glanced the boy's left side, "-*Morty*. How ya'll doin'?"

He smiled. "F-f-fine. Wa-what are th-those ke-keys for?" He pointed to her pocket.

There were a lot of them, and he couldn't think of what needed so much locking up around here. Most everyone slept in tents. He and Morty did at first. Not a door in sight until getting their wagon.

"Well, ya saw me lock up the till. Other's're spares fer the trucks, wagons, padlocks, an' the like. Nothin' fancy."

"*Ohhh*," he mouthed without sound.

Does she have one for ours? Do we *have a key?… I don't think we do. Oh no! Did I lose it!?*

Fucking ask her already. I want out *of here. Smells like cigarettes and old pussy.*

Billy nearly blushed at his words, well one *word, though untrue.*

The wagon didn't smell like that at all… *well*, a *little* like cigarettes.

Perched on the rim of a wooden ashtray was one of those cigarette holders ladies like to use. The other… Billy didn't know what *that* smelled like.

The blush he'd avoided crept up his neck and Morty snickered.

It *did* smell like Dawn. It *is* her wagon. Tea and clean linen, *the sheets looked fresh and tucked tight around the mattress*, and another thing, smoky sweet herbs.

Streams of light grey smoke drizzled into the air from the corner. Three long, skinny, burning sticks stuck into the open mouth of a wooden snake. Along its slithering back ash fell from orange embers. The mystery sticks smelled nice.

Incense, idiot.

In-? What'd you say? Incest?

Woah-woah! Incense! In-CENSE. Do NOT confuse those two

words ever again!

Billy shrugged, unaware as to the meaning of the other word.

"What'd ya need honey?" she asked, curious to the boy's sudden gesture of indifference, but did not question it. *Chattin' with Morty prob'ly.*

"D-d-do you kna-know ha-how to cu-c-cut hu-hair?"

"*Mmm*," her mouth shifted to one side. "Nah, ain't never had the knack. '*Cept fer beard trimmin'*. Ya'd think I'd be a damn expert seein' I got me a son covered with it. Stopped tryin' long time ago after my husband walked about lopsided one occasion too many." She sighed, "Sorry darlin'."

Billy's shoulders sank.

Morty hardly let his brother get a wink of sleep last night over this.

Kept saying, "*he can't breathe, get it off of me, it's in my mouth, my eyes, it stinks. Are you trying to kill me? You're trying to kill me!*"

He'd been washing it as best he could since their mama got sick. But Morty puts up such a fuss during baths. When Mama was better, she use to help keep the water and soap out of Morty's eyes.

"But," Dawn spoke, impeding his leave, "Sheri's a damn fine hairdresser. Ya oughta ask her. Sure she's got time ta give ya a quick cut."

Sheri? Sheri, Sheri, darn, he knew the name. Heard it recently-

The Freak without arms.

Oh! The one with the dancer ladies. One of them is her step mama and her daddy stands on the stage outside and brings in the crowds. Now he remembered. He's seen her a lot. During supper and breakfast, walking with Dawn and bringing clothes to the performers.

Does she wash them?

Does it matter?

I'm just curious.

Well, stop it.

Sure seems like it would be hard to do with no arms... Seems like anything *would be hard to do without arms. Except for walking.*

William...

"Come on," she waved them to the door, sliding into a pair of beaded slippers, "I'll take ya over to the dress tent-" Before he could ask, she explained, "-where performers git dressed and prettied up before show time."

Billy waited while Dawn locked up the trailer.

"Wa-why ha-haven't we-we b-been in th-there?"

"Well, ya don't wear a costume. Just yer regulars," she motioned over him.

True, he *would* wear the same pants and shirt he wore now during a show. Maybe lift the suspenders over his shoulders and tuck in the shirt first.

"Dress tent's where Sheri an' Lavi work on their mendin' an' sewin'. Ya see folks in somethin' fancy ya best bet our ladies're responsible. *All* my boy's things. *Oh,*" she sighed in admiration for the ladies' work. Vincent *does* dress nicely. *Fancy.* "And the Samson's. Rocky—gotta add a few inches to his trousers or else he ends up in high wats."

She laughed. Billy joined in automatically.

Morty, what are high wats?

He sighed. *Really? It's when your pants are too short, and you look like an imbecile with them up above your ankles. You know, how* you *looked during our growth spurt.* Before *Mother let out our pant legs.*

Ohh. Billy glanced down. The hem fell below the ankle, resting against the top of his shoe when his feet flattened at each step. *No high wats now.* Billy smiled.

"Come on," she waved him through the backyard.

All the grey tents back here belong to workers and game people, between which strung clotheslines with shirts, trousers, and under things hung up to dry. The fire pits weren't lit, not during daytime. Billy could tell where each one had been dug by the way tents made circles around camp.

He could see the striped back of the Ten-In-One through the cook tent, whose panels were drawn up on every side this evening.

Otis shifted pans on the burners and handed over a fresh pot of coffee to one of the men who talk to crowds.

To the right, the big purple sparkly *'swing ride'* sat motionless. He hadn't gotten a good look at this ride, but he recalled shooting stars painted up the middle, and smatterings of dots and lines all over the dark underside.

The carousel spun, he only saw its red and bronze top turning, he couldn't see the horses.

Wish I could ride it.

They're for babies. All rides are, especially *the one with* hooorsies.

Billy huffed.

The Eli wheel stared down like a giant, a colossus, up near the entrance. The *'Gate,'* Billy thought it might be called. Its shadow cast over the midway, turning like a black clock as it slowly swayed its seats up into the air, around, and back down.

The trio walked between the Ten-In-One, and where the dancer ladies' tent *would* be set up, when Dawn called, not to Billy and Morty, but to a couple on stage, "Hey!"

Johnny turned, the lady he talked to was Hilly.

Why's she talking to him? Morty grumbled. His fingers tightened, pulling a fist full of his brother's hair.

Billy didn't make a peep about the pain.

She looks pretty today.

Hair down, and fluffy in the wind. A soft pale cloud around her head.

"Yeah?"

"The Hel's the Kootch? Stage is here," her arms opened wide. *"Why's* the canvas on the ground?"

"New roustie busted the poles unpackin' the trucks." His grease-darkened hands rested on cocked hips, one leg slightly extended.

That pose, with light shining over his shoulder, reminded Billy of heroes in picture show advertisements.

Just like Johnny James!

The renegades reluctant to save the day, but always do, swigging from a bottle of alcohol on the back of a horse or smoking a cigarette from the seat of a car, showing how rebellious they can be.

Who knows what kind of Sickness those smelly things can cause.

Billy never touched one in all seventeen of his years. Never got around them until joining the carnival.

A whole lot of people here seem to like them, even if they are dangerous. *At least that's what the radio tells him.*

"You can him?"

"No... Want me to?" Unless hollering at the working men, Johnny spoke coolly. A drawl not to be rushed, yet still somehow commanding. No wonder the men listen to him so good. Billy couldn't keep his eyes off the man, and he wasn't even talking to him.

Dawn thought about it, fingers drumming hips like piano keys.

Mama loved playing the piano. Billy and Morty never had the minds for it.

"*Eh.* Lost one along the way. Keep 'im on... them replacement poles is comin' outta his wage."

"Alright then."

With a break in conversation, Billy took the moment to say, "Hu-hi Johnny," and wave.

His head leaned to the left to look at the young men over Dawn's shoulder. Half smirking he replied, "Hey boys. How ya doin' today?"

"Fu-fine." He smiled, "Ga-goin-going to gu-get our hair c-cut."

"Is that right?" the smirk grew.

As Billy nodded, Dawn cut in, remembering, "It's pay day. Handle that fer me would ya?"

"Yeah."

"Before tomorrow I'm hopin'," directed around Johnny.

The dancer glanced from her hands to Dawn. Not long enough to meet her eyes.

Did she do something wrong? Seemed scared Dawn would yell at her. *What could Hilly do that would make Dawn mad?*

"Be done by tonight," he assured.

"Best be *everythin's* up an' ready ta go before mornin' comes. Gate's openin' extra early, ten sharp." Dawn set for the dress tent. Her hand clapped down three times on wooden planks dimpled with heel marks and scuffs. "Don't let me down Johnny-boy."

Billy raised a hand to Johnny and slowed his gait around the front of the stage to wave again, this time at Hilly.

She lifted her head now that Dawn was gone, and smiled.

He was grinning when he caught up to Dawn.

Each of the three tents ahead—*not at all as big as the Ten*—was striped from top to bottom in the same graying white, and red canvas. Billy imagined the color was of a ripe apple when first put to use. Now dull and faded.

Like a blush on a corpse.

Morty… don't say stuff like that.

He laughed.

"I show ya the Single-O's yet?"

"Yu-yep. Y-yes Muh-ma'am."

She took the pair around the whole carnival on their first few days. Said the acts in the Ten and Singles rotated on the road. It gave everyone the chance for a longer act, and to be the sole star in the tent. The Ten had to be quick on account of the number of acts, with short lectures and demonstrations. In the Singles the act could go on as long as the performer wished.

Vincent read entire short stories to the crowd. Sometimes going on for an hour or more at a time. Rolan and Sabina put on a number of short plays. Grace and Joy, Rolan's sisters, perform songs on the violin and piano: with miniature instruments!

Billy wanted to see that one. He couldn't imagine the sound such a tiny piano would make.

"Evenin', boys!"

"Good evening, Madam Dawn."

"Hello, Baroness."

Baroness?

Her buried old man was called the Baron, smart guy.

Oh… What's a Baron and Baroness?

Morty groaned.

Three banners hung out front promoting: *Venus de Milo Incarnate*, *Jack and the Giantess*, and another:

> '*The Amazing Bound Brothers!*
> *See Them Jump!*
> *Spin!*
> *Kick and Flip!*
> *Two Acrobats for the Price of One!*
> *See Them Live Inside!*'

Amongst the words, caricatures of twelve-year-old versions of these men flipped themselves backward through the advertisement, kicking the bubbled words of *'Spin,' 'Kick and Flip,'* with their left feet.

The real-life identical twins dressed in matching red shorts, white socks, white sports shoes, and not a stitch more.

He couldn't help but eye the thick flexible band of flesh connecting the brothers at the chest. A wad of unbreakable taffy stretching between movements.

From standing, to touching twenty toes. Extending right legs, then the left. Twisting their torsos and lifting four arms into the air.

With echoing *'hups'* the pair arched forward and stood on four hands, lifting four legs straight into the air until white shoes pointed to the clouds.

Hands steady, forearms flexed, the twins allowed their feet to fall back, and hoisted themselves upright in a flip with a single jolt from bent arms.

Billy's jaw fell. "H-how-?"

"*Don't know.* Got more grace in two bodies than most have in one." Dawn nudged her bearded chin ahead, "Let's git along."

"*W-wo-wowie!*" Billy exclaimed under his breath, watching the men do a cartwheel before two big, round, canvas bodies blocked his view.

"*Fee, Fie, Fo, Fum!*" came a woman's voice from the right.

"Rolan an' Sabina rehearsin'," Dawn tossed over her shoulder. Expecting he would ask.

She really is like a mama.

"Here we are."

An armless girl patching the seat of a man's trousers with her toes was not the first thing Billy saw upon entering the square tent. And it wasn't a tiny woman standing on the table, measuring cloth against a dummy twice her size. Or even the armless girl's papa rooting through a hatbox with thimbles stuck on the ends of each finger. It was the racks and racks of clothing that seemed to go on for miles, like pavement on a city street.

Men's attire, hats, and shoes separated off to the left, women on the right. Either *and* neither cluttered a space in between. Suits constructed of feathers and fur hung in the center space alongside matching caps with long feathers streaming from their bespangled centers. Masks with animal ears and faces strapped to blank mannequin heads on the floor beside pairs of shoes made to look like bird feet, and paws.

At the far end, on the left-hand side, were two tables with mirrors built onto the backs. Closed black cases sat on the tops beside brushes and sponges, and those poofy balls ladies use to put on powder.

A large chest bulged with folded fabrics. Feathers poked out of a burlap sack in another chest, and when Billy got closer, he saw buttons of all shapes, sizes, and colors filling its bottom.

So much to look at! So many colors. So many outfits. Some old and musky with age. Some freshly stitched and still smelling of the perfume of the women who constructed them.

Nothing but black hooded cloaks hung on a rack nearby.
They look like Vincent's.

Five, he counted. Varying in length and size. The first seemed large enough for a child, while the last would fit Vincent today. Two hangers were empty.

Something else caught Billy's eye, and Morty's too.
What the fuck is that thing?

A *loooong* green dress. Taller on the rack than Billy and Morty. Than Johnny, or even Vincent. Or the strongman who stood taller than both of them.

The tight, pole-straight, gala-worthy gown sparkled with emerald beads and sequins. Leaf-like ruffles climbed its front, sides, and back as a spiral staircase would in a mansion. Gloves hung over the hanger and would cover Billy's whole arm, overlapping onto the shoulder if he tried them on. The ends mitten-like, no fingers, in the shape of a leaf. A white cotton ball of a wig consumed a mannequin head beside green high-heel shoes. A size too big for the average man.

He couldn't imagine how Sabina, the giantess, could move in this dress. The leafy train short and not reaching high up the back of the legs.

Billy almost laughed, picturing the woman duck shuffling from the dress tent to the stage in this beanstalk gown.

What if she has to use the WC?

Guess she'd end up watering herself.

Morty and Billy shared a laugh.

"Sheri Darlin'!" Dawn called and leaned in for a hug. Morty noticed the girl's right leg lift and wrap—*like an arm should*—around Dawn's hip.

Too bad she's not wearing a skirt… eh William?

Billy shook his head, not listening, too enthralled. She held a teeny tiny needle—noticeable only for the thread snaking a path from stitches to the needle's eye—between her thimble-capped big and second toe. *Her toes!* Pinched in like fingers! With thimbles! Thimbles on her toes!

"Ya makin' me somethin' pretty?" Dawn asked affectionately of the woman standing on the tabletop.

A hand smaller than a child's waved, "No, no, not for you. This for Daze and Vie. Daze wants sparkles." The fabric had few sequins sewn into place.

She's so pretty! And her voice! A woman's voice, but the pitch tightened, uplifting to a bird's chirp.

Sure. Ehh.

Ignoring the disgruntled sound, he continued to smile open-mouthed at the lady.

"Oh, very nice. Reminds me'a that white number ya did fer Hilly."

"Yes. Daze wants one like it."

"*That so?*"

"Heya Dawn," Sheri's daddy said rifling through the green box. *He'd popped off the thimbles.*

The boss lady nodded.

"Heya Bill… Heya *Morty*." His voice rose, filling the room, near to shouting in an almost sing-song, "*How you doin' todaaay?!*"

"H-he c-can he-hear you," the corners of Billy's lips trembled atop approaching giggles.

Sunny stared, until a dull, "Sorry," and went back to the hatbox.

Is he feeble or something?

Billy shrugged.

"You two met Lavi?" Dawn asked.

He shook his head and eagerly walked to the table holding out a hand.

"N-nice to mu-meet you."

She took his top two fingers at mid-knuckle and shook.

"Is nice to meet you!" she smiled, big, and bright as the sun is gold.

So, this is who they got running the dressing room. A girl with no arms and a lady you could wrap up and gift to a kid. Seems logical. No hands and the dexterity of a dolly, I bet they stitch like the wind. Morty's eyes rolled.

"What'd ya'll need?" the armless girl asked. *Armless Wonder.* As advertised on the banner.

> '*The Armless Wonder!*
> *Watch her write, sew, eat, and drink!*
> *Using only her Toes!*
> *Venus de Milo Incarnate!*
> *Alive Inside!*'

"Billy here-" Dawn paused to add, "-*and* Morty, need their hair cut if yer not too busy."

If Dawn forgot him, Morty sure would get steamed. He hates being left out. Sometimes he ignores it; it *doesn't* bother him.

Why would I want to talk to Freaks and feebs anyway? He says.

"Ain't that luck. Just went and got my girl her toolbox." From the box, he brought up a small pair of scissors, which he snipped three times.

Snip, snip, snip. The sound seemed as loud as the metal looked sharp.

Careful old man. Morty warned gleefully. *You might cut yourself.* Billy knew his twin grinned at the shiny blades by the pull of tightening skin behind his ear. Like a school teacher tugging a bad student to the corner for punishment.

Morty used this tone before. *Often.* The time a baby bird fell from a nest in the apple tree back home. He wanted to watch as the ants covered it like overly peppered steak. *Look at them go...* he marveled, ants flooding in and out of the bloody beak.

Billy quickly showed his teeth to hide a grimace.

"Sure," her eyes squinted with her smile. "I'd be happy to."

There was a natural downward slant to them, Billy noticed. The severe U-shape of her grin sharpened a triangular jawline to a fine point.

What a pretty lady.

The smile had her entire face glowing inward out. From a lightly freckled nose, to the edges of round pink cheeks.

"Oh!" *How could he be so rude?* "I-it's n-n-nice t-to m-make yer-your ac-ac-acqua- nice to mmm-meet you!"

Billy stuck out a hand.

Sheri looked at the offered gesture of greeting. Suspended at chest height an arm's length away. She bit her lips. Snorted a giggle.

What's funny?

Wow. William. Wow.

Dawn covered her mouth with one hand. Lavi bit her lips.

Sunny took a step forward, "Little lower bud," he laughed. Gave the boy's hand a tap, lower and lower, adjusting the height.

He didn't understand, not until Sheri lifted her *left* foot—as no toes wore thimbles or held sharp needles.

Billy hopped with realization. Staring down the offending hand held out for a handshake with one who has no hands!

How could he be such a big ol' dummy!

That's easy, you are *a big ol' dummy.*

"Jee-j-jeeepers! I'm-I'm s-s-s-s-sss-sorry!"

"No harm done," Sheri shook her head, "Nice to put faces to names. We meant to come around sooner and say 'hi.'"

"That's right," her father said.

"Still wanna shake?" Neat, manicured toes wiggled.

Don't, don't, William... Morty moaned.

Billy shook the foot.

Ewww. You touched it, you touched a stranger's foot.

It's clean.

Looks *clean. No guarantees.*

Moving on from the blunder, Sheri said "Hope you won't mind takin' a seat on the floor."

Dawn dropped a pillow from a nearby chair at the armless girl's feet. The floor of the tent flanked with boards set end to end, corner to corner.

Sheri stuck the sharp end of the needle through the trousers on her lap, closing the torn fabric so as not to lose her place, and set them on the table. Folding up the legs with a quick flip of her toes and popped off the thimbles.

"Na-n-no," he shook his head adamantly, not blinking as she took the scissors from her daddy—*with her toes.*

He didn't mind at all. At home on the back porch Mama sat in her rocker and him and Morty would sit at her feet watching the clouds, birds, and Spotsy the cow trotting along the fence line munching at grass and yellow dandelions.

She'd hum as she cut, or sing if requested.

Only always.

Their lullaby of course, or Sherry Vena songs.

"Billy Baby" was Mama's favorite.

"It true we lost another roustie?" Sunny asked Dawn.

"So how you want it? A trim, or…?" Sheri trailed, watching Billy sit.

"Uh-um, na-no na-na-not a tr-im. Ma-Morty wants it shu-short."

"Yeeep. Peckerwood musta took off on us durin' the night. Didn't even hang on fer his last payment today… More fer the kitty I suppose."

There're kitties in the carnival? Where?!

No. There are no kitties ya stupe. She's talkin' about the money. Darn it!

She set the scissors on the edge of the bench. "Daddy, could you hand me that comb? It's in the little pocket—yeah that one. Thank you." The hard fingers brushed out the ends of Billy's hair from bottom to scalp. She kept extra careful on the left side so as not to scrape Morty's forehead or cheek.

Watch it, girl…

She's being careful-

I'm just sayin'. She better keep a handle on it if she's gonna snip around my face. He laughed. *Get it? HAND-le.*

"Okay, so what's Morty thinkin'? All short? Only the sides?"

"Anyone see him take off?"

"Not that I been told. His tent's cleared out of all but the canvas. Don't matter anyhow. Prob'ly take on another before we leave

town."

"Muh-ma-my mmm-Mama ya-used to cu-cut thh-the su-sssides sha-short an-and lu-leave the ta-top lu-long-longer." He grabbed a handful at the top of his head, above the forehead. "Tha-that's ha-how M-mama de-did it."

"I could do that. It's a nice look."

Billy grinned and sat facing forward, spine straight and head still.

"She finish y-oh, evenin', Dawn," a woman's voice came from the back. Canvas stirred and pushed a column of warm air throughout the tent when it fell.

"Vie." Dawn greeted.

"Sheri finish mendin' your trousers yet?"

"Almost, she's cuttin' them boys' hair real quick," Sunny said, and Billy heard the soft smack of a kiss.

Who would want to kiss him?

You know he's married. We've seen his wife.

...She must be blind. Only way I'll believe it. Woman like that... though I guess she gets her pick of men whenever she wants. Doesn't matter who she crawls back to at night when she gets her choice of dick during the day.

Does she do that? The thing with the men?

Guessing so. Doesn't matter. Still a whore. Taken enough dick and spunk for one hundred lifetimes I bet.

"Mmm," the small grimace rumbled behind Billy's lips.

Why does he have to say things like that?

It's crude, and plain gross!

"Oh! Did I cut you?" Sheri's toes—interwoven with the rounded metal of the scissors—pressed against the side of his head like a comforting hand.

"Nnn-na-nah-no," he shifted against the pillow, heels bopping the floor and hands jittering along the boards. He bumped her leg when he stuttered the lie, "N-no, ja-ju-just tha-th-thinkin'. S-sorry."

She sighed, relieved, and continued snipping. Tufts fell away in wispy rat tails and clumpy puffs like brown dust bunnies.

Bye-bye hair, Billy thought, squeezing the strands between his fingers as they fell around him.

Good riddance.

"Snip him, Baby?" Sheri's daddy asked.

"No, thought I did," she stopped. "They're fine," she snipped. *"Turn a little bit to the right. There we go."*

"Don't you worry 'bout that at all boys. My girl's got the steadiest toes between the borders."

Borders of what?

Canada and Mexico.

Oh. Billy never did so good with geography. Couldn't remember what town they were in *now*.

Bastropa... Louisiana. Morty added the state to avoid the inevitable follow-up question.

Ohhh.

"So, I heard we lost a boy the other night?" Sunny's wife, Vie, asked.

"Barnum's ass on a cracker, that all anyone talks about 'round here?"

Sheri, Lavi, and the woman at the back of the tent snickered at the exclamation. Even Morty gave a little snort before clearing his throat. *A cover-up.*

"I'll come back in a bit," another kissing sound. "Oh. Daze wanted me to give these back."

"Thank you, honey." A metallic click, *"Barnum damn that woman!* Said she could *have* a few, not *leave* me a few. Damn it. *Damn... it,*" he punctuated each word separately before sighing. A watch chain jingled as he slid the case into his pocket. "Well tell your sister *thanks* for givin' 'em back... *I suppose.* Least she didn't leave 'em on the bally like last time. Found some little patty brat usin' 'em like damn birthday candles on his candy apple. Then, *then* the damn *mother* starts yellin' at me! *I* didn't give 'em to 'im!"

"*Right.* I'll tell her all that. And I'll make sure she's good and *damned* for smokin' all your cigarettes."

"Damn right better. Bye, darlin'."

"Bye. Bye, Sheri-Baby."

"Bye, Vie."

"Wait! Where's my matches?" Sunny called.

"Damn her!" came a muffled reply.

"Damn right. Damn her double!"

Sheri edged along Billy's right ear. He held his breath, counting to ten before taking another.

Don't move William. Don't move. Morty laughed. *Careful now, she might SNIP ya. She'll SNIP ya!*

Stop it Morty, I'm not gonna jump again.

Again? I've got you more than once! Remember when you almost jammed Mother's clippers down your ear hole? More laughter, heavier and dryer than before, he gasped for breath.

It's not funny Morty. Mama thought I was gonna lose my hearing... And it hurt you too!

Not as much as you. Ohh, you cried like a little baby! Thought she was gonna have to pop a tit in your mouth to shut you up.

We were only seven, and it hurt!

Oh, get off it William! I got you, and you were a pissy baby about it.

Luckily Sheri spoke up, he didn't want to talk to his brother anymore.

"Okay, going to the other side now. Could you put your hand here?" she carefully touched a toe a few inches above Morty.

Hey! He began at her touch.

"I don't want hair gettin' in his eyes."

The severity softened, *don't be touching me with those things. Who knows what you've stepped in recently.*

Her feet looked cleaner than Billy's own hands—which previously diddled in the dirt until Morty prodded him into asking Dawn about a haircut. And before that had been lunch. He should have washed after eating—*Mama would have instructed him to do so.* He forgot after turning his plate and cup over to the dish washer.

Some older lady with long dark hair, tan skin, and lots of wrinkles across her brow, *Billy didn't know her name* yet.

He'd seen her closing up one of the concessions at night. He thought her husband might be the cook. Often bickering together behind the counter at mealtime.

Morty says that's what husbands and wives do. Bicker and make babies... *he uses a different word.*

Fuck. Bicker and fuck.

Morty and Billy were silent, Sheri continued with the haircut. Lavi moved about, stepping down onto a stool and hopping to the floor, retrieving more material and a white streamer of tape measurer. She hummed softly as she walked, would stop each climb, and start again as she compared fabrics. Sunny and Dawn discussed guards at the Kootch show. Sunny assured it never got so bad the men couldn't handle the crowd. Dawn did not sound convinced.

Begrudgingly she let off on the subject and Sunny began to ask about an all-day show. Dawn refused, set in her way that nighttime is best for girlie shows. Sunny began to protest when-

Clangclangclangclangclangclang. Bang bang bang. Honkhonk honk honkhonk!

"Heeeeeey Freaks! Freaks! Freaks!"

Clangclangclangbangbangbang. Rattling on and on during the honking and yelling. Billy could swear he saw a car's shadow through the tent.

Did canvas snag on the side mirror? He smelled gasoline. Freshly pumped into the tank. The bitter tang of hot metal, and rubbery tires.

"Sick bastards!"

"Yeah! Sickos!" a car voice agreed.

"Get out of our town!"

"Yeah, get out ya bunch of Freaks!"

Not from the racing vehicles came: *"Watch it!"*

Billy ducked, and covered himself and Morty, knocking the scissors from Sheri's toes. The sting of one hundred needle pricks ran from the crook of his thumb to the end of his pointing finger. He didn't notice the blood.

"Oh," Sheri gasped, Billy thought at the noise and hollering, but she said and did nothing else. Didn't respond any other way. No hunkering down off her stool or scooting under the table with him, which is what his body and mind told him in identical shouting orders—*meant to be followed right quick*—but he froze. Only shivered and braced himself for the car to drive through the flimsy walls.

He'd thought of it as a thick fabric, sturdy, now it might as well have been air. Easily passable by both bodies and vehicles.

"Barnum's ghost, what now?" Sunny sighed, as he walked, *walked.* "Son?"

Billy didn't hear him, didn't feel the hand on his shoulder. Felt only the bowing of the boards under Sunny's weight, the dipping of his body with the barking man's footfalls, the banging in his chest that bounced around his throat and out his ears. On the inside his guts clumped into a ball and yanked at the rest of his innards. Trying to swallow them up, but there was nowhere for them to go except to get tighter and tighter and tighter until his face felt hot, mouth went dry, and throat clenched shut. He wanted to vomit and cry, the actions fought together but must have come to a draw because neither happened.

"*Shit*, I don't know," Dawn didn't sound afraid either! Angry, annoyed, or *pissed* as Morty would say.

Shut up! Someone better shut them up!

"*Freaks, Freaks. Get out of here! Fucking Freaks!*" again came the yips as the car sped past. "*Oddiiiies! Moooonsters! Siiiickos! Freaks! Freaks! Freeeeeaks!*"

Arrrggghhh! Morty's fist trembled. Swinging, grasping at hair too short to yank.

"Billy?"

"Son, son you alright?"

Beneath the questions, the crunching gravel and disrupted dirt under speeding tires, the metallic clang, and whoops, he could still hear Lavi humming. Only for a moment it ceased, then a tiny sigh and she resumed her song.

Humming? She's humming? Why isn't she scared? Why isn't everyone under the table bracing for cover? They're going to drive through the tent any minute! They're going to hit us! Run us over flat! Flat as pancakes! As road kill!

Billy couldn't open his eyes, the cars circled behind them. The yelling waned and surged the closer and further the cars got.

"*Freaks!*" laughter, "*Freaks! Come on out! I want to see me some Freaks!*"

"Dawn! D-"

He took a chance and opened his eyes to the voice.

Johnny stood at the entrance. Alone. Hilly nowhere to be seen, and he felt immediate concern. Not just for her, but for everyone.

Sunny's wife left minutes ago. Out the back of the dress tent where cars drove now! What if she were hit?!

The twins Francis and Zach, what if they still practiced out front?

All the working men outside, others setting up booths, hanging prizes and signs with arrows pointing *'this way,' 'popcorn,' 'peanuts,' 'tickets.'*

Calm, so calm. Bored, as if he needed more excitement in his day. "Got three trucks, ten'r more little pricks bangin' pots an' pans."

"You see Vie?" Sunny interjected, his voice far from Billy's frantic chicken-running-from-a-fox fear, but serious.

"She's fine, in the Ten with Hilly."

Was Billy not supposed to be scared? What is going on? Strangers yelling about Freaks, telling the lot of them to get out of here. Shouldn't they listen? Grab their things and run?

"They armed?" Dawn stomped to the entrance, no hurry. All a nuisance to her, a fly who has gotten stuck inside the house and won't be batted away.

"None I saw."

"Anyone hurt?"

"No. Nearly ran down Blake, Irv yanked 'im outta the way." No big deal.

Am I asleep? A bizarre dream where fear is calm, and calm is fear, right is up, backwards is yellow, hopscotch is America's pastime, and cow patties are for supper on Wednesdays.

"We secured this damn lot fair an' square, not gonna git run off by a pack'a red-necked yella-bellied Normies gettin' off on shit stirrin'. *Come on!"*

They left side by side, strides strong and determined.

"Wa-wa-wh-what-what th-th-they ga-gonna d-d-do?" Billy asked Sunny, jumping at the bang of a fist on metal.

"Dawn and Johnny got this. Gotta ride it out like a storm. Right baby girl?" he kissed his daughter's hair.

Sheri nodded, concern in her eyes.

"We been through worse than this. These boys ain't even poppin' shots off like most of 'em." He looked at Morty and Billy, "Prob'ly kids thinkin' they're slick is all. Ain't serious."

"Sh-sh-sh-shooting? Ga-gu-g-g-guns?"

He nodded solemnly, hugging an arm around his daughter's shoulders. "Welcome ta the carny-biz," he grinned without humor.

Guns? People shoot guns at the carnival? Why? Why would they do that?

Didn't you hear? They hate Freaks. Want us gone because we're Sick. We'll make them Sick. We'll fuck their wives and their kids and infect them with what we are.

But, but we aren't bad. We wouldn't do that!

Not in their *minds. We're pure evil to the likes of Norms.*

A shot rang out through the carnival. Billy fell back to his side, slamming an elbow hard to keep Morty's face from smushing flat against the floor. It throbbed something fierce, his heartbeat pulsed with it. Another and another burst from guns of many types. Some shots sharp, cutting the air. Hard, soaring fast, others an explosion.

The honking stopped. Shouting from cars ended, and started in the carnival. Moving out toward the edge of the lot.

"That's right, git the fuck outta here!" he thought the voice could be Johnny's, but he couldn't be sure. Several men yelled, telling the intruders to leave, shooting their own guns into the air.

"Git the fuck off my lot!" Dawn. Billy knew for certain. The only woman's voice, and louder than all the men.

Tires ran from the shots like deer, the whir of engines going quiet.

Still the carnival folk hollered, and laughed once he could hear the townspeople no more. Then, simple as that, the crew got back to it. The plinks of hammer on nails. Boards clattering, canvas and banners hoisted.

Like nothing happened.

"Ya git them plate numbers?"

"Got two of 'em. I'll ask around, get the third."

"Good, gotta be on the lookout for 'em tomorrow night. Ya spot any faces?"

"Might know a few if I saw 'em again."

"Ask the boys about that too."

"Alright," Johnny left as Dawn entered the tent.

"And hand out them wages!" she called after him, poking her head out the canvas.

"Alright!"

She stopped after taking only one step inside. "Billy," she lifted her skirts and hurried over, "ya alright? Darlin' yer bleedin' all over like a stuck pig."

"Spooked is all," Sunny patted the young man's shoulder. "He ain't ever been through a townie welcome before."

Get up.

I can't blink.

The *darnedest* thing, Billy tried but shook instead.

"Shu-shu-should-should-d-dn't w-w-we ga-ga-go?"

Told us to leave. The people want us to go. We should go.

"*Aw,* darlin' it ain't nothin'. *Honest ta Barnum,*" dark red nails trailed through his hair. It seemed shorter. Did Sheri finish?

Get... up. You're letting them win. Get up.

"*Most the time* this happens, it's just kids. Hear their folks talkin' nonsense about people like us, carnies an'," her lips pursed in condemnation for the term, "*Freaks...* think they can make us leave, scare us. Don't really cause no harm. *Never do.*" Her eyes made a trip around her sockets like a clock.

She's lying. Billy didn't hear his brother.

She truly isn't worried? That the kids will come back? Try to chase the show off again? What if *they* bring guns next time? Those kids know the carnival people have guns. Come back prepared. Dawn thinks they *could* be back! She asked Johnny if he saw any of their faces. To be on the lookout for the trucks tomorrow!

She's l-... William... get up!

"They're too chicken shit ta do nothin' more'n bang spoons on their ma's kitchenware an' honk the horns'a their pa's trucks." Her fingers stroked his head again until his eyes closed. The gifted wetness stung.

"W-wa-wa-what if th-they-they co-me b-b-back?"

"Ain't fer you ta worry yer head about. I ain't about ta let nobody hurt my family, an' worse've tried, so *don't,*" she took his chin between thumb and fingers, "*be,*" smiling she wiggled it, "*worryin'.*"

Only when Billy nodded, and his lips twitched into an upright position did she stand, satisfied.

He did feel a *little* better by what she said. The shouting and noise rattled on in his bones. He'd never been through nothing like that before, but Dawn had. Sunny had, everyone here has been through tough times. Dawn said she has been through worse, so did Sunny, and if they weren't worried—*said Billy shouldn't*—he should do just that. *Dawn should know.* And he believed her when she said she wouldn't let nothing happen to them. She is the boss lady, and not only that, but the mama to everyone at the carnival. And mamas' don't let anything bad happen to their children.

This *mama has five dead babies under her belt.*

What?

Nothing.

"*Now*, lets git ya cleaned up. Lavi, got any bandages fer his hand?"

The tiny woman nodded, still on the tabletop—*unfazed by all the racket and gunshots.* Material in the shape of ladies under things hovered on the mannequin's lower half by pins.

She brought Dawn a roll of fabric and a bottle of medical salve from a kit stored in the drawer of a vanity table in the corner.

Not that stuff. It stings. Billy's lips tensed, then deflated.

Well if you didn't act like such a tit, we wouldn't be dealing with it now, would we? Morty scoffed. *I can't believe my own brother, cowering on the floor, shaking like a leaf. Scared of a little banging, are you? Spoons and pots. If that's all it takes, I'm surprised you could ever help Mother in the kitchen. Blubbering idiot. Scared of a bunch of Normies.* He could feel Morty's eyes shifting, arm tense, pulling at the skin of his brother's neck. *Call me a Freak, will you?*

"Sheri, wanna finish off their hair?" she held out the scissors. No blood on them.

"*Mmm-hmm.* Only a few more snips," she said softly.

Dawn inspected the sticky red hand. "*Hmm*, not as bad as I thought." Blood gone dry, turning to flakes when he rubbed his thumb against the skin.

"Just'a scratch really. More leaky than anythin' else. But that's stopped," Dawn finished wiping away the blood with a wad of gauze and grabbed for the bottle of salve offered by Lavi. "By yer sour face I guess ya know what this feels like."

He nodded.

"You boys're tough as nails! This won't be nothin' at all, right?"

Billy smiled and nodded.

"Good 'cause we're done."

His brows knit together, "D-done?"

"Yep," she patted his wrapped hand.

"I-I-I-I-I d-d-didn't even f-feel it."

She smiled. *Where do mama's get that magic power?*

"Finished." The scissors slipped off Sheri's toes onto the table. "Daddy, can you get my mirror please?"

The boys' image showed up in front of their eyes. In the round glass, Billy saw the trimmed right side of his head, and all around Morty.

No way hair could bug him anymore.

The longish locks at the front were curling up. They'd lost that once it got too long.

Someone else had done it, but this was the exact cut Mama use to give. The one she said made her boys look so handsome.

"Now that's a smart look, damn smart," Sunny complimented. "Why didn't I never think about gettin' that cut?"

Because you don't have enough hair to pull it off.

"It's very nice," Sheri said.

"So handsome," Lavi commented.

"Got us a heartbreaker right here."

Hello strangers, I remember you. Their old selves looked back from the mirror. No longer the outsiders hiding behind long dirty hair. The ones who use to live with their mama in a little farmhouse on a lonely country road in Oklahoma.

That familiar Billy and Morty sat amongst new friends. Friends who spoke like family.

For the first time in weeks Billy felt at home, and he grinned.

ROUND AND ROUND
∽ SHILZIE ∾

Run away, hurry! Don't walk! Turn that skipping into sprinting! Go, go!

Mamas and fathers strode—smiling, talking, eating popcorn by the fistful—instead of scooping up sons and daughters and hurrying to the parking lot. Down the street, for town, for home.

How do adults not feel it? The danger.

Knock it off with the smiling and laughing! Run! Take the children dancing and spinning with stuffed toys in outstretched hands and run! *Get out quick! Run away from the bad man!*

He is here. He is near. In the Ten. The backyard. The cook tent. Watching. Listening. Plotting. Boiling pots and kicking heads. Screaming. Dead babies. Boiling, dying, kicking, cursing, hating.

Shilzie shivered on Carrie's platform. Mist drifted from a hazy sky. A glittering fuzz of moisture settled on the tiny hairs of her arms and neck. Dew collected in the cleft of a bulging brow and slid down the slope of a nose too big for such a little girl.

"Are you sure you do not want to ride Falada sweetheart?" her brother asked. "Your sisters will win the race if you are not there to guide him to the finish."

His arm secured across her chest as the braided rope belts did around her sisters' waists. She clutched it with both hands.

"Okay girls, you ready to go for a ride?" Evro asked.

"Are you sure?" last chance.

Where is he? Where did he go? The Ten? Did he leave yet? He did, she was sure of it. Had to. He can't still be inside. The show is closed. What is he doing? Where is he?

"Hold on tight, *here we go*," Evro pulled the lever.

The jockey held his jacket closed with one hand. Prickles of gooseflesh ran up his bare chest and belly. Right hand gripped tight around the speed shift, pulling back, watching the riders take off from the starting line. Slowest, slowly, slow.

Elvi and Nylee laughed before the horses could take their first step. Flicking braided rope reigns against wooden necks, readying to race. Hugging the spiraled poles against their cheek, leaning into the speed.

There he is! Crawling in the mud between the wheels! He's coming!

I'm winning!

No, I am!

Briar is faster than your horse!

No, Red is faster!

What, Shilzie? He who?

Who is coming?

What wheels?

Whee! Faster, faster!

No, not *him*. A stray kitty cat.

The pale feline gnawed a chicken bone beneath Otis's concession wagon. Nibbling with nubby front teeth, ripping meat with sharp canines. Yanking, shaking, licking, sprawled on his or her belly.

Just a kitty. A pretty white kitty. Kitties aren't bad. They are soft and cuddly, and purr when they are happy.

Bad men yell, and curse. Wish hateful mean things on others. Things like dying and getting hurt. Want others to feel pain, to die! To drop hammers on feet and break bones. To slip from high places and hang from ropes and chains. Fall from rides and land on their necks. Bad men hate without reason! People different, people the same, nice or not!

"So, is she mad at me?" Evro propped an arm on a horse's rear end.

I didn't hear Evro. He got on so easily. Even with Carrie going. That means others could get on without making a noise! What if he's here?

Perching on the horses, leaping from saddle to saddle like an evil Frog Prince. Uncurling a black sticky tongue, spitting it out, wrapping around her waist, and reeling her in. The dark ooze bubbling between his lips, burning like acid. Squeezing until her head pops off.

"Shilzie," he reiterated. "Repainted Falada's eyes, didn't have the right shade of blue. Thought maybe that's why she hasn't been riding for a while."

Where is he? Scurrying up the side of the Ten? Riding Carrie with them?

The ride turned on its axis, showing her the concessions, tents, games, the midway, Star, and Shadow; black against dusk. Shadow's eye twinkled bright yellow. The slower he went the more it seemed to narrow.

"No. She has been out of sorts since Wish."

"Aww, what's wrong princess?"

Silly man, pinheads are not bright enough to explain their actions. All are dimwits. Childish until old age—*if living past thirty years.*

They surely cannot express themselves. Grunt and moan and cry. No real emotion, no thoughts. An infant without the chance of progressive intellect.

Such tiny heads contain no grasp of the world and people around them, they do not hear and see and understand. Do not know who is good and bad; the definitions are all the same.

A pinhead would run into a fire for warmth, and marvel at the flickering embers blistering their feet.

Freaks like her are no good except for popping off heads to kick and toss over goalposts for points.

Home run! Touchdown! Men on the sports radio stations say.

Feebs, imbeciles, the bad man says.

A rub on the belly calmed Shilzie some. "She spoke of a *'bad man,'* during dinner."

"A bad man? A customer? Think one said something?"

"No." *Nothing unusual.*

The townies always whisper. Disgust covered by palms or handkerchiefs.

Such an ugly little girl. That's a girl? Poor thing, should put it out of its misery. If I had a child like that, something would be done about it, I could never raise a monster.

"What about that spook show? One with Brad Foster? *Guy's cackling could give* anyone *nightmares."*

RHS's Weekend Horror Show. *Dolly's Child,* the show's most

recent premiere, starring Brad Foster and Rose Harris.

"No. The girls would have been in bed."

Could one of his stories have frightened her? he worried.

Grimm can be so gruesome.

The Juniper Tree and its villainous stepmother lopping off her stepson's head with the close of a trunk lid. *Not a bad man.*

Rapunzel's prince falling from the tower, gouging his eyes on thorns. *No bad men,* a witch caused such tragedy.

Donkeyskin, the disguised princess hiding from a covetous father seeking to wed his only daughter. A bad man indeed, but is it he who scared poor Shilzie?

Not Donkeyskin's father, the impish Rumpelstiltskin, the Devil who stole the Maiden's hands, or the ungrateful dwarf encountered by Snow White and Rose Red.

Him. *Morty.* One of them, a Freak, a new member of the family. *Not one of us! He is not like us!*

The man who isn't there. Isn't here. Anywhere. The shadow man. Watching and listening. Seething and screaming in her dreams.

Lightning eyes in the rain. Flashing white against a red sky. Thunder in his mind. Foreboding rumbling begins. Growing louder and louder. She counts until the flash of light, counting the miles until his storm is upon her. Till his steps stop, and the saliva rains on her shoulder.

"'*Bad man, bad man,*' it is all she would say that night. She has been so afraid. I do not know what to do."

Evro frowned, looking from Vincent to Shilzie. Still gripping her brother's arm, jerking at every metallic creak and hitch in tune of the swelling calliope. To her sisters, giggling and swatting one another, racing for the win.

A smirk formed. "What in the world could you be scared of?"

Shilzie lifted her gaze.

"With such a big strong brother like Vinnie to protect you. You know he won't let anyone hurt you, right sweetie?"

Vincent nodded, confirming her questioning glance.

"I'd like to see a bad man try. Your brother would throw him soaring over the midway and out the exit."

For the first time in days, Shilzie giggled.

"Gather 'round," a whistle, shrill as a nightmare concluding

scream, intercepted Shilzie's short-lived shift in mood. *"Gather 'round boys."*

The clouds are back. Not the rain Shilzie loves. Not Morty's storm. A new storm. Brewing at the horizon.

"Where they off to?" Evro's chin pointed.

When the ride came back around, and the group came into view Shilzie saw roustabouts, Johnny, Wells, and Rocky. On the outskirts of the huddle, Muckers meandered, tipping a flask into his mouth. Foggy eyes twinkled drunkenly, even from Shilzie's speedy vantage.

The group on the carousel could hear the tone, but not the words of Johnny's lowered voice.

The carnival's second-in-command held a sledgehammer below its head, patting it in the crater of his palm.

"Heading into town I suppose," her brother put on a smile. It didn't attempt to reach for his eyes.

"That… a good plan? Great turnout tonight but… we got the *pots-and-pans-salute* just yesterday."

"They will return safely," he assured. "Johnny will see to that."

A whistle from the pack leader got the men marching toward the Gate.

The young troupers followed close behind Johnny. Stub unfolded a whittling knife. Irv wrapped his knuckles in strips of cloth. Muckers wore a pair of brass knuckles under black fingerless gloves, one on each hand. Rocky had his big stalwartly fists if the need arose. *Doing so begrudgingly.*

His domineering presence a façade for those who do not know his true kindhearted nature.

Most carried concealed knives: up sleeves, in pockets, pressed against ankles within boots. Others brought baseball bats, wrenches, spare tent stakes.

Where is everyone going?
They should come on the ride with us!
Are they going to town?
For sugar?
Marianne could make a cake!
Or pie!
Or cookies!

I thought we weren't supposed to go to town after dark.
They shouldn't go!
Mama says we shouldn't go into town alone.
They will be okay, she told her sisters. Keeping them calm, unaware. *Like Vincent said, Johnny's going with them. They will be safe.*

Don't go, she called to the men.

Backs of heads, small as marbles, dissolved outside the Gate. Blonde and browns of all shades, black, grey, bald, gone, sunk in oily night outside the safety of the carnival's golden glow.

Shadow, unblinking, watched over Johnny until he and the men turned down the road, intentions aimed for driveways containing trucks. Three in particular. From there they would find young men, names, addresses.

The boys didn't come back! Leave them alone! What about Texas? Johnny, you remember! Irv, Wells, Rocky, you all know what happened!

Please Barnum, Vincent thought, hugging his sister with one arm and squeezing a spiral pole with the other until his fist trembled, *it does not have to escalate. Talking, no more. Please. Not again.*

PENANCE

ᷛᷤ **?** ᷤ

You thought you'd get away with it.

"Plea-please! Please! I-I didn't mean it! It wasn't my idea! We won't do it again!"

A knife plunged into the sweaty young man's guts. Slid out slowly, easily, inching from the skin. Lagging the longer he screamed. His arms jerked at the rope lashed to the headboard.

The teen lay in bed. Where Mommy and Daddy told him he would be safe from monsters as a little boy. As long as he kept the covers over his head, the monsters of the night could not harm him.

Shrieking, "Mom! Dad!"

Mommy and Daddy lied to their son. *As so many others have and will continue to do.* And died for it. *As so many others have and will continue to do.*

Unbeknownst to their son, his parents sprawled side by side in their beds.

Not pushed together tonight, no last obligatory-marital-fuck for them.

Arms outstretched for one another in the end. Bodies submerged in red mattresses, with matching crimson sheets and pajamas. Still gurgling on blood seeping from yawning throats.

It could be heard if one held their breath and listened closely.

You killed Mommy and Daddy. You did it. You caused all of this. You drove the truck, now I'm making it right.

The slippery pointed tip reached the winking red exit, distending taut belly flesh, and jolted forward again, angling this way and that, in and out, in and out. Fucking the wounds.

"Gaaaaahhh! Stooop, stop please, *ahh,"* he cried, "Stop pleeeease!"

The shadowed figure continued the gyrations inside the man's abdomen. *Man*, a boy really. Fourteen? Fifteen? *It does not matter.*

Bad decisions do not discriminate against age. He made his choice, and now he's owed his due. A spanking wouldn't do. No bite of a switch would teach him. This is the only way he'll learn never to do it again.

"I won't," the teenager gagged, "*I won't*," his head lolled, throat gurgling, attempting to affirm his plea. Strength depleting with the blood. With the intestines poking through shredded flesh, the weighty organs tearing free like a finger jabbing wet newspaper.

No... not anymore you won't. You won't make this mistake, not ever again.

As the boy died, the shadowy face he had yet to see came forward, painted white by the light of the moon, and caressed him. Cheek to cheek, it rubbed. Sweat, blood, and saliva slickened their skin. Moist between the two faces.

In the boy's final moments, he felt three things: panic as his heart rate slowed and body grew cold, pain from the blade in his gut tearing his bowels and glancing off his spinal column, and the tentative lick of a tongue, hot and quivering from lips to brow.

Five Weeks Later
Edgars, Mississippi

IN THE DEVIL'S SNARE
∽ MORGAN ∾

Five weeks in Louisiana. Beginning in Bastropa, traveling along the border of Texas to the toes of the foot-shaped state for the yearly stop outside Patricia and Varlyn Grady's hometown, the Floating City of New Orleans.

Home to the famous *Grady Lobster Clan*. Generations of family born with cloven hands or feet, or both. If a crustaceous man or woman graces the stage outside the southern state, one can safely presume they may have relations to the prestigious line.

After a full two weeks near the swamp and ocean encroached city built on remnants of the pre-Cure Big Easy rooftops, the troupe turned itself around, continuing north, up the opposite side of the state before hopping the fence into Mississippi.

During that time Evro somehow managed to make himself a permanent fixture in Morgan Meyer's once solitary daily routine.

Whereas the brooding performer may have chosen to eat a handful of crackers in the caravan stead of face the morning rush at breakfast, Carrie's jockey would appear, plates in hand, bright and early, ready to talk.

Instead of retreating between shows, here comes the same young man, no plate of food, but he has a smile and break time of his own. Prepared to sit out back behind Otis's concession wagon and catch popcorn tossed in the air between tales of his day, asking of Morgan's day.

How did your show go? Sorry, I missed it. Was there a big crowd? Any fainters?

Now, ducking under rope, weaving the next guy-line to step over a wooden stake with a flattened head. Mashed splitters sticking out around the circular edge like a boy's cowlick in the morning. He asked: "Do you know how long we're staying in the Miss?"

"Five still dates. Why? *Do you have somewhere else to be?*"

Morgan kept his head tilted, avoiding angled ropes holding the Ten at full mast.

Sputtering, "Well certainly! I have meetings to attend, palms to grease. Only been workin' the show into my schedule during downtime at the office."

Morgan smirked.

"Only five? We were in Louisie for that many weeks."

"Maybe more, or less." He shrugged.

Dates dropped due to retraction of permits. Towns skipped— dependent on segregation, or Sick scares. Worry of outbreaks, or plain fear getting the best of Normies. Locking down borders and allowing no strangers.

"Dawn didn't give you a route card?"

"Kindly of you to believe I know what that is."

"Right. You haven't been with it long enough for her to give you one." So many drop in and out during a season, providing one to a greenie would be a waste of paper.

"With it? That another one of those carny phrases?" Evro swung round one tether, to the next, bobbing from one side of Morgan to another. "Like clem, and ding, and gazoonie? Got called that one the other day. *Wasn't sure if I should be insulted...* put on that I was anyhoo for the Hel of it."

Another smirk.

"Should I? What is it? A gazoonie?"

"A new worker. The kind who come and go, leave when the work gets tough."

"Ah. So how long would it take to be *'with it?'"*

"If you stay on the whole year-*season."*

Again, "Ah."

"Ya ready Boo?" Patricia called.

Her son juggled three red rubber balls on the bally. *"Yup. Toss me anutha."*

The on-looking mother tossed in a blue one, then a green one, each her son caught and threw high above his head.

"A year with a carnival. I could've missed being here at all. Was working on my last few bucks for travel when Dawn scooped me up. You know that?"

"Where were you planning on going?"

"Anywhere, didn't matter. Wanted to get away from Cali for a spell."

"Is that where you're from? Originally?"

"Maybe? Here or there along the west coast. Never been sure of my birthplace. My family moved around a lot." He laughed, "*A lot. We never stayed in one place more than a week or two.*"

"Why?" He shifted the bag as it began to slide off his shoulder.

Freely he admitted, "Travelers, *Gypsies*. My mother's family came over from Romania a few generations back and my father's is from here in the States. My grandmother use to say our family was the first to refuse the Cure and be cast out back in the day. I think every Gypsy family likes to claim to be the first. *It's a prestige thing.*"

Carnies are thought of as outsiders, sympathizers for employing Sick. Beneath showfolk come Gypsies. *Flattened on the bottom are the Sick, and swimming in the blood and gore, Freaks.*

In the eyes of Normies, *some* circuits could be trusted as playing straight: no gambling, sex shows, or rigged games.

No matter the good or service, Gypsies are thieves and liars, spreaders of filth.

Peddling wares as simple as handmade clothing, and a Normie will search for the catch. Checking each fold and between each stitch. How would they be gypped by the Gypsy? Lice infested fabric? Are their mitts in my pocket when I'm not looking? Stealing my children?

Healthy individuals—babes *or* adults—are kidnapped every day and sold to those desperate enough to obtain one. To raise a child as their own, to impregnate, be impregnated. Ruthlessness is in no short amount when it comes to Health and breeding.

Stealing is in their blood, one of Morgan's mother's many warnings of the disease-infested Gyps. *Bugs roam their bodies, jump out of greasy hair. Never get too close if you meet one Morgan. Little bloodsuckers will surely pass on horrid Gypsy Sicknesses.*

Scabies, the Pox, she'd even heard tell of a contagious cancer. *Not true.*

Morgan's mother believed a simple sneeze on the street would have her laid up in her death bed if she so much as heard the sound.

He looked at him again. The jockey, the carny, the Gypsy, smile on his face watching the bally where Varlyn and Patricia practiced for show time.

If only Morgan's mother could see him now. Walking beside a Gypsy, *befriending* a Gypsy. What Morgan has made of this relationship thus far anyhow: friendship.

Chats at the buffet line. Mild at first, much the same as before. Small answers, perhaps a sentence or two if single words would not suffice. Weeks later broadening.

Evro caught him emerging as a mole from a hole, heading toward Midway East, accompanying along the way, and taking a seat backstage as Morgan prepared for his act.

Now they met after shows, Morgan might linger the last few minutes until Evro shut down Carrie and unloaded the last batch of patties. Lent a hand in wiping down the horses and sweeping the platform clean of tickets, popcorn, and loose change. *Which Evro pocketed.* Swearing he would spend it on a good cause. *Candy* the cause, though he gave it all to the triplets, Rolan and Sabina's daughter, and the workers' kids. Something Morgan couldn't refrain from admiring.

Anyone else would have kept the easy money for themselves.

This man turned the pennies into candy and gave it away to children.

Morgan nearly scoffed.

His dear mother would gasp at the man. Balk and back away with hands outstretched, deterring him away, far away. A man who gives treats to children—*half of them Sick children*—because of his heritage.

"*Oh*," immediately he wished to breathe it back in.

How should he respond? Other Immune would sneer, recoil, curse Evro, or spit on him.

He may be his mother's son, but it did not mean he inherited her hatred as well as her prematurely graying hair.

A slight laugh parted the jockey's plump, smirking mouth. "Don't worry. I won't steal a strand of your hair and put a curse on you."

"Oh, no. I didn't mean-I don't-"

Shit. Now he thinks I'm some bigoted prick.

"Pulling your leg, Morgan," he chuckled, squeezing a frigid

shoulder momentarily. "Certain I'd be running from the carnival by now with you heading a lynch mob if this news worried you."

"I wouldn't do that."

"I know," dark eyes grazed him from head to foot, "I wouldn't have told you otherwise. *I'm not stupid.*"

Now he, *de la Llum's King of joviality*, grew somber. Though only for a blink. Enough to tell Morgan that perhaps Evro dealt with misgivings in the past because of his family and heritage.

Perhaps? Most definitely.

There is not a Freak or Sick man in the world who goes without stares, or intolerance from a Healthy individual. Same for carnies and Gypsies. *Though never as bad as the Sick.* No one suffers as much hatred, and cruelty as those who do not blend with the crowd. Who wear differences on the outside where anyone looking can see.

Morgan heard Evro's voice but missed what was said. "What?"

"I said, '*nope, no curses.*' Despite media propaganda on me and mine, far fewer of us peddle in the mysticism racket as most folks may believe. Palm reading, crystal balls, star charts. Brewing Health potions, hexing one who vexes us."

Morgan did not admit he fell on the 'most folks' side of Gypsy preconceptions.

This group of people in the pre-Cure world, who would be known as Gypsies, were indeed the first to openly shun FRK-32.

Others, who would become the descendants of today's Immune, remained quiet, lied about receiving their one-time dose of the miracle Cure. *Keeping to groups of like-minded individuals, far away from the wrath of militant Cure promoters, and abrasive anti-Cure activists.*

When the truth of the Cure's side effects came to light, those who suffered from the repercussions turned on the pre-Gypsies.

These people knew what would inevitably happen, they must have known. Who would willingly dismiss the chance of ridding themselves of all sickness?

Soon, the affected not only *hated* this group, but aimed to punish them. Attacked, beat, and killed those who still retained the ability to conceive and raise Healthy children when they could not. The pre-Gypsies retreated from society, traveled, carved out hidden communes deep in the wilderness, on the fringes of the world, watching it crumble from the outside.

The insiders continued with their theories of how these people, thought of as skeptics and conspiratorial fanatics beforehand, knew what would happen. From plausible, to farfetched, which caught on as all fantastical ideals do.

Powers. Precognition, foresight, clairvoyance. Like the aged fortune tellers in films warning protagonists of great danger, promising an influx of money, great love soon to come, be on the lookout for your soul mate. All for a bit of silver crossing the palm.

These rumors were thrown about amongst the dwindling populace until rumor became truth in the minds of survivors. Tall tales turned to prejudice in today's world.

"My grandmother, however," Evro grinned, "played heavy into the all-seeing-all-knowing Gypsy gag. Worked as a Mystic for a show like this one when she was young. She taught me everything. Crystal healing, rune stones. I could even read your cards."

"Tarot cards?"

"Any other kind worth mentioning? There's *real-*" ring-decked hands gripped the air, "-power in them. The outcome *always* comes true. Swear on my life," he drew an X over the left side of his bare chest, "I did a reading for my uncle once, *meanest bastard you could know*, but he only let those nearest and dearest to him know *that* man. *The sweetie,* to everyone else. *Oh he's so charming, so intelligent, he's* this, *he's* that, the cat's meow. He could convince an Immune they were ailing from *such-and-such* disease. That's how much of a con this man was."

Impossible. The Immune can not, will not ever, get Sick

Morgan nodded, withholding a smile. *When he gets going, he really takes off. He makes it look so easy. Speaking without measuring every word before letting it drop from his lips.*

"I did a reading for him—*asking after money.* When he would strike it rich. *Get rich quick his game.* And there's a placement in the Celtic cross spread-"

Again, Morgan nodded, feigning knowledge on the subject.

"-It represents how others see you. Out of the whole deck he gets the *Devil,*" he shrugged, hands shaking. "Can't fake that!" He laughed.

Morgan scoffed in amusement. It *could,* and frequently *is,* faked or in carny-*gaffed*, but he chose to believe Evro. If his uncle was a bastard conman, and the Devil his family knew, he accepted the card drawn as an accurate representation.

Morgan knew nothing about Tarot cards, other than supposedly foretelling the future, past and present. Safe to assume what a card titled *'the Devil'* indicates.

"So, what's your card?"

"My grandmother would've said the Fool."

Morgan nearly snorted at such accuracy, but halted it with his fingers, letting a mere huff of breath escape instead.

The jockey must have noticed the near burst of laughter when one side of his mouth rose, creasing the cheek.

Continuing, "And I would agree. Lighthearted, carefree, willing to jump in headfirst without a second thought. No other way to live," he grinned, eyeing the sword swallower. "It'd be a bore without the unexpected."

Morgan couldn't agree in good standing. His life for the past several years has been scripted and followed without straying. No improvisation allowed. Wake up, eat, perform *or* travel, practice routines, maintain swords and props, bathe, and go to bed.

"What would my card be?" he asked. Curious as to how this man saw him through the eyes of a card reader. Which figure detailed his mood, his morals, his way of thinking? He doubted any card said would match his true feelings. Evro hadn't known him long enough, hadn't gotten enough out of him during mild conversations of where the show is headed next and how the carnival faired on previous trips through the area. Had the crowds been unruly during Morgan's performance? Any violent or hostile toward *the Sick* who traveled among *the Normal?*

Evro looked at the ground. Dirt, with flat and scruffy patches of golden-brown grass parched as a man lost in a desert. The left side of his mouth quirked tightly into his cheek as he considered. *Which to choose from seventy-eight options?*

"I would *like* to say your card would come from the Sword suit."

Morgan's lips twitched briefly.

"*But,*" he stalled, lingering on the word, "we'll only know for sure if you let me give you a reading. Only the cards know what a person is truly hiding away, deep inside." His voice dropped to a mock-macabre timbre, "*In the darkest shadows of the mind.*"

Morgan scoffed. An illogical nervous feeling pinched in his belly. *Not a chance inert playing cards could reveal his deepest darkest secrets.*

Evro would name a card or two that might match. And he would nod, to appease him.

Why so nervous? He didn't believe in card readings, not after witnessing the Mystics who ran with the carnival.

It is all body language. Facial cues. Changes in demeanor. Reading what a patty wants to hear by the look in their eyes, the questions asked. Breathing. Fidgeting at the mention of money or love. A hoax, Morgan knew this.

"I'm not hiding anything."

"Says the guy I had to pull teeth from to get a single peep out."

"No, you didn't," he mumbled.

"Don't see you talking to anyone else." Without allowing a counter he urged, "What are you afraid of? It's all for fun."

Morgan stopped, sighed, rubbed the back of his neck.

End of the line. Midway Stage East. Answer now, no more time to think.

The Wheel of Fortune spun off to the right, warming up for the patties lined at the Gate.

Whiiiiiiiirrrrrrr, plinkplinkplinkplinkplink.

"*Hey, Gina!*"

"*What!? What is it!?*"

"*Got change for a fiver?*"

"*Yeah, yeah.*"

A sack of coins hit the counter of the joint beside the wheel.

The bottle game. A pat is given three balls and the task of knocking over a three-bottle pyramid in one throw to win a prize.

Although, there's the chance an unsuspecting pat might throw fruitlessly at bottles weighted at the bottoms. *Only* those at the *base* of the pyramid. The con appears more legit if the top bottle falls off easy.

"*Come on*," Evro didn't hesitate to tousle and tug Morgan's jacket lapel, nearly brushing fingers across his bare chest.

Just for fun, it's just for fun. Fun. Do it. Just do it.
His stomach hurt.

"*Just for fun,*" he breathed, eyes on the sky.

"I swear, I won't reveal your deepest darkest desires, your life's destiny, or any of that other Gypsy propaganda hocus pocus. For a goof and that's it. Yes?" He dipped, bent at the knees, to look up into Morgan's downcast eyes, "Yes?"

"If I say yes, will you quit pestering?" his voice quieted when he noticed Gina and Sheila's heads turning toward the unlikely pair. The carnival hermit—*watch him combust under your stares and disappear before your very eyes folks!*—and the one Dawn might bill as the world's chattiest man-*Gypsy*. A more eye-catching word for the bill.

"Maybe," he grinned, oblivious to those outside the conversation. "Yes?"

"*Yeah,*" his head shook, loosening hair hooked over an ear, "Yes, fine."

It wouldn't be so bad. Not like he believed in them anyway. Another trick of the traveler. Gypsy or carny, both have their games.

Evro clapped, rings clicking, "I'm gonna go get 'em, see you later."

Morgan smirked as he took off. Cheek near quivering, rejecting the not often felt expression.

"Hey, where ya goin'?! Gate's openin', hun! *What is he doin' now?*" Sheila asked Gina.

Evro avoided the picket surrounding Carrie with a twist of his hips and hopped over staked ropes. "*Be right back!*"

Morgan laughed into his fingers. The sound dry, and silent.

"Lucky!"

I'm sorry! Apologize, his immediate impulse for enjoying the spectacle of a man so overjoyed.

Morgan's mother would not have stood for it. There is no time in this life for humor and frivolous things. Family and high standing in society. The community's opinion. Health, and children to carry on that Health. A *reputable* line. Continuing into the future through generations as royalty amongst mere Normies.

Only Wells. *Not her.*

He waited on stage east, checking his pocket watch. "Git up here, crowd's comin' in."

"Let's hear it for Lucky! The Man with the Devil's Lucky Streak! Let's give him a round of applause!" Wells clapped. *"Nice job kid."*

He followed the barker downstairs. At the bottom waited his bag of tricks, from which he took a canteen of water—*cold this morning, now warmed by the day's heat*—a rag, and wiped away drying trickles of blood from his forearm and hand. Three shallow straight wounds made with a razor blade. A demonstration of his tolerance to pain. *Many women disappeared into the crowd when the first drop of blood hit the stage.*

Scabbing staunched further flow, *no need for a bandage.*

Rocky would take center stage next, bending bars and lifting volunteers, two, three, or four at a time atop his shoulders and arms. He mounted the steps dressed as a barbarian today.

Leather straps wrapped bulging forearms and shins. More leather and distressed fur draped from his waist, his legs left bare underneath to show the flexing muscles of thick thighs and calves.

Other days he may dress as a Roman gladiator, a Greek god, a member of a lost Aztec tribe… in Morgan's opinion, the same outfit with a different nationality, and maybe an adornment or two. Though Morgan had to give Rocky a heap of credit. Not many men could wear a costume akin to a woman's skirt and not get heckled for it.

Who would dare? The man is big as an oak tree. *Though kind*, something not usual for strongmen. Not those Morgan heard tale, or saw for himself, in passing troupes.

Not *all* brutes. One other strongman Morgan knew, felt no need to proclaim his dominance over weaker males. He'd only met him once. Years ago when he first decided to join a professional outfit. That man introduced him to the Baroness Dawn de Barcsy, and Carnivàle de la Llum.

She'd wanted more children.

He was a disappointment; a girl would be a blessing. A little girl:

red hair, done up in pigtails, dressed in polka dot dresses on outings. Sweet and beautiful and pink-cheeked. The mothers of Stepton would writhe in envy over such a pretty little girl as Miranda Meyer's daughter.

Once of age, every family in the community would come forward with eager sons, begging for bride rights. She'd have her pick of the litter. The richest family, the best name, the most power, and she would get it, by means of her bright, Healthy little angel. Instead, she had a son.

Strange, odd, parents and teachers whispered when he was young. A *waste,* other boys mocked. Throwing food, school books, and pencils at the short, skinny boy growing into a short, skinny adolescent. A worthwhile man, Immune or not, should be physically impressive in stature, muscle, or weight. Portray dominance, someone capable of protecting his mate and offspring.

Morgan ignored the schoolyard treatment, often better than he received at home. His father ignored him, abuse taking on the form of neglect; his mother could do, and did, much worse.

For three months Morgan survived on the little money in his savings. Was never the plan to leave so suddenly. *No plan at all. Leave. One day, leave.*

A real sword gouged his funds from the very beginning. If he truly wished to become a performer, he required the tool of his trade. No longer must he slip spoons or straightened wire hangers down his throat. He had the real deal. As much of a burden it made to his wallet, Morgan could not be happier once the cold dull steel slid against his hand. The first real purchase of his life. Something *he* wanted. Not what he was told to want.

During ninety days of vagrancy, with little food and less money, only a sword and the clothes on his back, he performed.

On street corners, in the middle of markets, parking lots, from sunup until sundown. Swallowing a sword and pulling it back up. *His only accomplishment at the time.*

Few stopped to watch, fewer dropped pennies or the occasional nickel into the tin cup utilized for coffee drinking in the morning and soup eating at night.

On the fateful day, heading down the street to his most profitable corner outside a well-established General Store in the center of town, he spotted a flyer nailed to a bulletin board. Amongst the ads and news articles one bill stood out.

Loud red ink on a glaringly white sheet of paper. Hartford Traveling Circus advertised their arrival above an illustration: A tent bursting with lions, elephants, aerialists, and jugglers from a spread open entrance.

A chance to secure a spot as a real performer, one with a steady income and sustainable shelter. Food and water, shade from the sun burning his skin during the day, and a bed and blankets to battle cold rattling his bones at night. Free of the glares from vagrant Freaks and dying Norms for being Healthy. *If they knew he was Immune, he would surely be killed out of spite.* Safe from thieves threatening with a knife to the belly for a measly crust of bread or a single penny, *his life savings.*

Off he went, chanting the location in his mind, over and over.

650 Antelope, 650 Antelope.

The field on the edge of town where annual fairs are held, and local farmers sell produce and show cattle.

He kept this mantra going as he marched—blanket wrapped sword in hand—hurrying down the street, avoiding mothers and children, men restocking wares or sweeping dust from storefront stoops.

Morgan remembered the address just fine. *Where else in town would a circus set up but the fairgrounds?* Repeating the address helped ease the anxiety of prospectively speaking to a Hartford.

Legendary performers made up the illustrious Hartford family. Equestrians, strongmen, tightrope walkers. Better than the best has to offer! Not only the largest, but the longest-running traveling show in the post-Cure U.S. Perhaps the world.

A full three rings under the big top, a separate menagerie, museum, and sideshows. Games, food, prizes, rides. Aerialists, acrobats, human cannonballs, clowns, jugglers. Animal tamers of all sorts. All big cats imaginable, elephants, bears, dogs, zebra, hippos, giraffes. Any exotic beast from the seven continents could be found within Hartford canvas. Spectacles of every sort, all of the glam and awe a circus required, Hartford delivered, and more.

Legs trembling from the walk, sweat running down his spine, and stomach knotted by nerves, fear, and anticipation, he made it to

650 Antelope.

Looming in the distance in a usually barren field, surrounded by a crescent of trees was the Hartford big top. Red, yellow, and blue striped spires rose toward the sky, improbably tall, taller than any building in town and bright as could be. The only color, the only joy in a world drained of hue, and hope.

Morgan walked under the Gate arches. A great sign formed of wood letters and lights reading *'Hartford Traveling Circus.'* A smaller marquee below informed, *'since 3036.'*

Ninety years.

A roustie carrying wooden crates had the hopeful's eyes stuck like glue, let alone the jugglers passing tumblers, balls, and fruit. The contortionists climbing atop one another in twisted positions, or the lion tamer walking a mighty beast—*an impossibly large white lion*—with a mane impressive as a peacock's plume on display.

"Hey, cutie," a blonde woman cooed. "Come back tomorrow and we'll really give you something to gawk at," the woman laughed, offering a playful shimmy in his direction before continuing to a stage nearby.

Two teenage girls, twins, with dark hair and dark eyes practiced matching dance steps to a song cranking from a record player. On the edge of the stage sat a younger girl with hair so pale it was nearly white.

Two years later he wouldn't remember seeing those girls once before when they arrived at de la Llum looking for work, as *he* would be soon enough.

"S-sir," Morgan mustered of a man absorbing the shade of a blue and red tent. Through the opening came the sound, and stench of animals. An elephant trumpeted, horses snorted.

Sweat beneath the arms and around the neck stained the man's dark shirt. Heavy circles weighted his eyes. Exhausted or hung over, *possibly both.*

"Yeah?" he spat a ball of bubbly phlegm between scuffed work boots, "What ya want?"

"Could-" *ask, ask him and get it over with, you need this, you want this,* "-could you tell me where I can speak with management?" He nearly sputtered, quickly adding, "Of the circus?"

"Oh! Thought you meant of the bank we're standin' in..." he

scoffed, "Over yonder kid," he pointed to a line of three, opulently large caravans on the edge of the lot. Painted in bright solid colors of red, blue, and purple, with gold flower and swirl detailing. *Hartford Traveling Circus* emblazed each broadside along a white twisting banner.

"Thank you."

"*Mmm-hmm.* Good luck," still within earshot, he whispered, *"You'll need it."*

Out of the three imposing homes on wheels, he chose to knock on the red caravan, which upon closer inspection had painted on its back end a strongman.

Bald, sporting a curled moustache—as seemed tradition of every strongman he ever saw until this point in time. *Rocky would meet half of this archetype, days later. A bald head, but no moustache, curled or otherwise.*

The caricature beamed with a smile as he lifted the very sun from the sky. *Rollace Hartford, the Strongest Man in the Universe.*

Hesitance held him at the bottom of the steps. Strongmen are known for their tempers, especially towards those they perceive as weak.

Morgan was no strongman; of below average height, five foot six inches, and thin, no matter how much he ate. Ribs and spine noticeable when bending at just the right angle, though never jutting through the skin as a convict from open prison windows. Nowhere near skinny enough to be billed as a human skeleton in the sideshow, but he wouldn't win any arm-wrestling matches. Someone a strongman views as a weakling.

A curled knuckle rose to the door-

He's a Hartford. He's a professional. He has to be… Hope he doesn't kill me.

-and knocked.

"Yes?! Come in!"

A desk sat directly across from the entry. To the right, a wall with two swinging doors at its center. Beyond that, a small kitchen, bed, and numerous weights cluttered the floor. Photos and mementos papered the walls around the desk: family portraits, candids of roustabouts, performers, customers, flyers promoting dates long since passed, old banners, pennants, and a round bell.

Those found at the top of a Test Your Strength game. This one had a large half-circle of a dent distorting its lower edge and a partially flattened top.

"Hello! Who might you be?"

The voice seemingly amplifying off of a vibrating bass drum belonged to a man big enough to contain such resonance. He stood a few inches shy of six and a half feet tall, all of him round and bulging with muscle. Indeed bald, as the painting on the caravan suggested, with an impressive black moustache meticulously curled with wax. Skin tan, eyes bright green and sparkling.

Just what Morgan expected to see of a strongman, but his smile and gleaming eyes were not.

"I-I'm M-morgan," *does he need my last name?* "Meyer."

"Good to meet you, Morgan Meyer," the man slapped his hand into Morgan's and shook vigorously. "Rollace Hartford, *Rollo to my friends and family.*" The grin so enthusiastic it edged on terrifying. Had it not been for the kind eyes Morgan may have changed his mind about asking this man for a job. "What can I do for you, friend?"

"I-," *I'm speaking to a Hartford. Rollace Hartford of the Hartford Traveling Circus.* The *Rollace Hartford!* Morgan hunched into the pain rolling his insides into a ball. Beads of sweat wetted his shirt. The sword handle went slick and began to slip from his grip, he caught it around the covered blade. "I-"

Rollace Hartford still smiled, never letting it slacken.

"I-I'm a sword... swallower," louder than the current whisper, he asked, "I was wondering if-"

That steadfast smile withered.

"If maybe you might, if I could-," eyes jittered across the floor, not worthy to look a Hartford in the eye.

I've only just started, I don't deserve to work for Hartford. I only know one trick, any sword swallower can do that!

Rollace, *Rollo to his friends and family*, saved Morgan the trouble of fighting his nerves, and gently interrupted with a sigh, "I am sorry, son," his voice quieted as he placed meaty hands on equally meaty hips. "We have seven swallowers."

More, if he included those specializing in other feats but were known to eat steel when the occasion arose.

"*Seven?*" Morgan echoed, mouthing the word as his shoulders drooped.

"Seven," he affirmed. "I am truly sorry, but we do not have room for another."

"Could," he fought to ask, "could I show you what I can do? *I-I'm new*," he admitted, "but I'll learn." Morgan wanted to be more than a sword swallower, he believed he could learn it all, feats of pain, eating and breathing fire, driving nails up his nose, regurgitation, an all-in-one performer. "I want to do more," he gripped the sword with both hands. "Blockhead routines, fire eating, I can do it," *if you let me try, please. Please, give me a chance, please. Give me the tools and I will learn it all!*

Rollace frowned. He believed the kid. This kind of conviction would get him all he wanted in life. The circus simply didn't have the time it would take for this young man to become the performer he achieved to be. If Morgan Meyer could do everything he said, right here and now, he would have hired him, if only to save on the cost of acts. Why pay five employees when one can do every job?

Rollace Hartford sighed. *No.*

"*Thank you for your time…*"

A greenie working for the world's most famous circus. Should slather on the grease paint now, fucking hilarious.

Rollace Hartford stopped Morgan's shoulder with one curled palm. This young man wouldn't leave empty-handed. Not yet, not now, not when Rollace saw potential in this quiet, yet determined performer. It wasn't every day someone gathered the gall to ask a Hartford directly for a position. Most wavered at the Gate, never stepping beyond, too afraid to enter a lot not yet ready for the public. Scampering away at the first holler of a taunting roustie. No more than watching, wondering, hoping, or asking the first worker strolling by for a job before a swift '*nope.*'

Rollace had a plan for this boy.

Above Morgan's head was a photograph of Rollo, his siblings, and two of his dearest friends taken twenty years ago.

Men and women of early thirties, and late twenties, except for Wallenna who had been nineteen. The man dressed to impress on the far right, turned thirty-two the night before.

The finest man Rollace ever met: the Baron Tod de Barcsy.

Hugging up to the gentleman tipping a silk top hat toward the flashbulb, the finest woman he ever knew, the Baron's beautiful wife: the Baroness Dawn de Barcsy, the World's Only Bearded Snake Charmer.

"We may not be in need of a swordy, but I think you may find a home elsewhere young man," he patted the slim shoulder and approached the desk. A ledger held the names, dates, and locations of the top-performing acts on the circuit. Hartford kept a close eye on their brothers, or sisters, in the business. To better avoid competition in the same area. Not for fear of low attendance against another outfit, but for assurance of *full* attendance on a set of dates.

A motto Rollace's father lived by: *Why squash the competition when there is no competition?!*

"Ah ha!" he tapped the page, took a pen, and scratched a name, date, and location across a scrap of paper. "Here you are."

Morgan took the note:

Carnivàle de la Llum, Stamford, 19 th *& 20* th

He glanced at Rollace Hartford, brows scrunched, *what's this?*

"That my friend, is the place you belong."

He read the bold, blocky script again. Stamford wasn't far.

Morgan scarcely dared to scoot one town over from the Stepton community, *which in this case was a blessing or he may never have joined de la Llum.*

"When you get there, head to the Big Wheel out front, there ought to be a man named Johnny at the helm. Tell him you want to speak with the Baroness," he put up a hand, though Morgan made no attempt to interrupt his directions. "Now, before he can say anything, tell him Rollo sent you. He will take you to her straight away. She'll be the beauteous gal with a beard," he laughed, eyes twinkling with affection. "Tell Dawn I recommended you myself," the thick fingers of his left hand touched his swelling chest. "She's a wonderful lady, she should give you the shot you need."

Big Wheel, Johnny, Baroness, Rollo sent me, recommended me himself.

"Thank you," Morgan exhaled, gratefulness expelling with it. "Thank you so much, Mr. Hartford."

"*Ah*-Rollo, you can call me Rollo."

He nodded, clutching the paper as if it were a treasure map.

Repeating again: *Big Wheel, Johnny, Baroness, Rollo sent me, recommended me himself.*

Before Morgan could leave the red caravan—*containing the kindest person he'd ever met in his whole life thus far inside it*—Rollo stopped him with, "And Morgan Meyer, one more thing…"

Morgan stopped and looked Rollo Hartford in the eye.

"Tell Dawn she still gives me the Scaly Shakes."

He never did figure out exactly what that phrase meant.

Yet, Dawn had been delighted by the nervously mumbled message.

Clapped her hands, laughing so hard she wheezed: *"Rollace Hartford, you old goat!"*

Morgan's first shift ended; he would not perform again for another thirty minutes. He *could* go back to his caravan, or…

I could stop by Carrie.

How did this happen? Eight years without becoming close with anyone, and now in his grasp the beginnings of a friendship. How long must one talk to another, before coworker tips the scale toward friend?

He imagined such scenarios before—attempted connection with a human being—full of silence. Discomfort on both ends from lack of interaction and input, *all Morgan's doing.* Eventually, the second party excusing themselves to the restroom or a prior engagement, a lie to escape the unbearable awkwardness of dealing with a man incapable of holding a conversation.

Not with Evro.

Morgan headed into the oncoming crowd. Eye contact avoided and breath held. Several patties watched his passage, he shrugged his bag uncomfortably.

They recognize me from the Midway, that's all. That's why they are staring.

A little girl wailed, pointing at a row of slum prizes lining the shelves of a joint. Crying for a cat with button eyes as her father laid more coin in order to win the toy. She hopped, holding his pant leg, stomping her feet. He aimed the baseball toward the angled wicker basket, took a breath, and threw. It landed, bounced, nudged the rim, bounced once more, and fell out. The girl's face bloomed bright red as new tears rolled, and snot leaked from her nose.

Other than to increase Healthy numbers in the world, he didn't quite understand the want for a child. Often the tiny humans screamed. Smelly with food or any number of bodily fluids. Cried when they did not get their way, when they *did* get their way. *He didn't see the appeal.*

Kids aren't all bad. He'd seen plenty wide-eyed little boys and girls. Quiet, and respectful, cheering, and clapping during his bow.

The triplets are sweet. Rolan and Sabina's daughter a darling little thing, *with or without her stature.*

Not all behaved as the spoiled patty brats crying for toys and shrieking when their mothers deny popcorn before riding the carousel.

Of which was straight ahead-

Where's Evro?

Carrie spun, but her jockey appeared absent.

A boy in red rode a white horse as he went around. Morgan locked his eyes on the point of focus. Evro did not appear to be on the platform walking between horses, urging the riders' excitement with his infinite energy and smile. The boy went around and came back, around, and back.

A roustie manned the controls. Jimmy, or is it Steve?

The ride lagged, coming to a stop.

Clearing his throat, "Where's Evro?"

"Hey!" the replacement yelled, concerned a patty snuck around the fence. "Oh," he realized. *The sword swallower. What's his name?* "Huh? Oh, told me to watch the ride, went that way I think," the roustie slung a curved finger over his shoulder, toward the concession wagons.

Morgan nodded, leaving the man to begrudgingly help children out of harnesses and off the horses.

An intoxicating heat of smell gust around him, rushed his nostrils. Butter, oil, sugar, fried dough. The area bustled with patties indulging in corndogs, candy apples, and fried chicken. Congested lines waited for lemonade and sweet confections. Fathers and mothers, children, teenagers, and lovers linked at the arm walked away with eager mouths biting into hot dogs and pinched fingers pulling tufts of cottony candy floss.

Otis ran the main grab joint in the center with his wife Marianne during work hours, preparing the majority of food consumed by patties. To his right and left were sold simple treats, such as sweets, popcorn, peanuts, and drinks.

Candy butchers wandered the lot carrying these same items in trays hanging from their shoulders on display. An impulse buy while waiting in line at the Star or watching free shows on the Midway.

Under hypnosis to the chant of: *"Get your popcorn, get your peanuts, get your chocolate bars, get them here!"*

Flora, with the help of her young son Toby, handed over the popcorn as soon as he scooped it into sacks on the left. Ruth to the right, held out three chocolate bars to a teenage boy with one wrinkled hand, and held the other upturned, waiting for payment before giving up the goods. Her daughter Emma swirled candy floss onto paper cones behind her. No Evro.

Morgan did notice something. At first, it didn't seem out of place.

A bottle of soda, cap absent, contents half drained on the edge of Ruth's countertop. Hidden behind a sign listing the variety of confections.

Not inherently strange, it very well could belong to Ruth or her daughter.

Beside it, as Morgan stepped closer, was a half-eaten bag of popcorn and behind that, a jacket.

He made his way between the lines, drawn to the items.

Evro's, he knew before reaching to touch the satin-lined lapel.

"Need somethin', Lucky?" Ruth asked. "Line is thinnin', better tell me now."

The next Ten-In-One show must be starting soon, the only reason for a lax in customers.

"N-no. Thank you," he mumbled. Avoiding the older woman's eyes he inquired, "Was E-," he near stammered his newfound companion's name, "Evro here?"

A churning sensation began in his guts that he could not explain.

It *wasn't* because he talked to Jimmy-Steve, Ruth, or walked through crowds of eyes.

Something else, an unknown emotion.

A candy butcher with a reloaded tray stepped away from Flora's wagon: *"Popcorn, popcorn, get it while it's still hot, get your popcorn! Fresh, buttery popcorn!"*

"Asked me to watch his things for a bit-*that'll be a dime honey*-he'll be back soon."

The space between the concession wagons created short dusty alleys leading to the edge of the lot. Two stake trucks with wood-fenced flatbeds and a box truck parked end to end.

A shadow grew from behind the central truck's box. Piles of empty potato sacks, barrels, or discarded crates?

It moved.

Morgan stepped toward the obstruction, away from the concessions, from the carnival-heard—*something*.

Yes? Yeah? A positive term, he was sure. *Oh? Ow?*

Wasn't certain *what* he heard. *If* he heard over the crowds, the screaming, the laughter, the chatter, the clattering pans, bubbling oil, sizzling meat on the grill, popping corn, clinking coins, and the rustling exchange of bills.

The partial shadow shifted, bobbing as a sunflower might in the wind. Morgan angled toward the doors, more importantly staring through the cab into the driver's side mirror.

A person on the other side of the truck. Shiny loafers and—knees, boot-clad shins flat against the ground.

The sound he heard, he recognized it now, so obvious with an image to go with it. A man grunting. A tight, grating little voice panting quick, *"Yeahs,"* and groaning, hissing a final, *"Ah."*

Morgan gulped. He could not stop his feet from stepping steadily onward until a twitching hand lay against the car door, pressing above the sun, moon, and star sigil of de la Llum.

The person on his knees turned away from Morgan's vision, hunching, straightened, wiped his mouth, and stood before the patty.

The man sipped air to calm his breath, buttoning plaid dress pants.

"Can't get that from the wife," he laughed, tucking a pale pink shirt around a rotund belly.

"That's what I'm here for."

Another laugh, so satisfied with himself, *"How much do I owe you?"* A wallet spread wide to reveal a tight bellows of pale green bills.

"A dollar ought to do it, handsome," that smile. Those eyes.

"A dollar?" he crooned under a sweaty brow, *"Is that all?"* The pat brushed two bills along the much younger man's bare chest. Lust blossomed in the sweaty man's eyes, it had not been sated by the act he now paid for. Up the man's chin, he swiped the money, *"I think that performance was worthy of* at least *ten dollars."*

Morgan watched ringed fingers reach for the excessive payment, only to have it swept back, and flattened against the client's chest.

"There's more *in it for you if you're willing to do* more *business with me. My wife and kids will be busy with the Freaks for hours. So, what do you say we have a little* more *fun?"*

More.

Morgan shoved himself away from the truck. He couldn't listen any longer. Couldn't watch the way the patty grinned, or the way *he* could muster to smile back. That he could touch the man, take his money. Do those things for money. *More.*

Morgan hurried up the steps and slammed a shoulder into the door as he turned the knob. The hinges whined in protest and shut up quick when he threw the knob back into the jam. The black bag hurdled over his shoulder and hit the end of the bed, scattering contents over the floorboards. A sword scooted Fineas's bowl against the wall.

The black fish darted in sloshing water, frightened with nowhere to hide.

Morgan gasped a hot, salty breath against the pressure in his throat. He paced the small home. A sweaty hand covered his forehead that pounded with the hammer of his heart. Lungs ached for breath that seemed unwanted when each intake shoved away exhales with internal flattened hands.

I thought I could fucking trust him. No. Why could I do that? Never trusted anyone before, why start now? Why the fuck would I deserve someone like that. One person. Not even one fucking person I can talk to, who I can believe.

Morgan grimaced, clutching the back of his neck.

Figures, the first person I let get close, the first person I consider trusting.

What am I to him? A potential trick? Has he been working me? His private cow to milk for money while we're on the road? Steady income? A blind sucker up to bat for the long game until he's gotten all he wants from me? Is that it???

No one is who they say they are. Never are! Even the nicest person can be a fucking liar, a fucking deceiver who acts so fucking nice to your face then laughs at it when your back is turned. Everyone can just fuck off. Fuck this fucking world and everyone in it!

He sat with a thud, bed springs squawking, cupping his eyes, elbows digging deep into shaking knees.

Why can't people just say who they are? Why do they have to always do this? This is why I stay away. Exactly *why! They all lie, they don't care. They don't care one fucking bit. Every single person just fucking-*

"*-hurts me,*" he grimaced, relinquishing a choked sob.

The last time he felt so hurt fell on the last day at home with his parents. The last moments with his mother. Hurt, betrayed, frightened, left with no hope, no belief in human beings as a species capable of compassion, or the ability to care for one another. *Only think of themselves. What they want. What they can get. No one else matters.*

Most of all he felt afraid, afraid of always being alone.

Lonely as a child. No siblings, no friends, detached parents. During his years at de la Llum, the loneliness settled into a numb acceptance.

Changing over the last weeks into a little spark of something different. Of comfort and warmth from another person, through the spoken word. Filling that aching hollow in Morgan's chest, enough to give him hope. The most painful of all emotions.

Gone again. Raw and bleeding, and just as empty.

He cried. Cried until he wiped his eyes and spotted the tools of his craft splayed on the ground. Two swords formed an X, a third lay to the left, fallen from the table after it's assault on Fineas. A bottle of fuel with a broken neck dripped between the boards, forming a puddle beneath the caravan. The torch lay against the wall. Matches had not scattered, the box must have skittered beneath the bed.

Sniffling, he dropped his hands and noticed blood. He rolled up the sleeve.

The shallow cuts sliced into the underside of his forearm split. New blood soaked the inside of his coat. Sticky and damp, and hot. The thick nauseating scent of copper wafted from the cuff at every roll to the elbow. Red saturated the palm and fell off his fingers in fat drops.

Today's fresh wounds were not the only evidence of his feats of pain. They mirrored the same three scars on his right arm.

The only relief during that last night at home, when he feared his mother more than he ever hated her, and when he hated himself the most. When he meant to end it all.

The first time a blade slid its wicked tongue against his skin. Such sweet release. Beloved diversion.

Tears traced the healed scars, instead of the edge of a blade. Flat, cool slivers glinted in a sharp metal pool surrounding an open box.

'Romance Brand - Double Edge Razor Blades,' grey font on a pink background. 'Danger - May Cause Injury.'

The Outskirts of
Jackson, Mississippi

CHILDISH THINGS

∽ SHILZIE ∾

Preparing for the stage can be chaotic.

No matter how many years with the circuit each performance tightens the belly with anticipation. *Excitement. Worry. Fear.* Nerves zipping up and down legs into toes, and arms into fingertips.

Is my make-up right? Costume on? Hair styled? Wig pinned tight? Props ready? Music playing? Instruments tuned? Tricks rehearsed? Feats perfected? Dance steps memorized? Will I stumble up the steps? Fall off the stage? Trip on my own feet? Will the crowd boo and hiss? Cheer and clap? Yawn? Do nothing at all?

Some may feel this way; Shilzie never does. Certainly not her sisters.

The pair played beside Vincent's sofa. Elvi stacking blocks, and Nylee knocking the cubes down once her sister yelled *'Go!'* The two giggled at the gratifying clunks and started over again once the squares of painted wood scattered in a heap. A pyramid, or towers leaning precariously right or left with each addition. The same result when tipped, flicked, knocked, and how they laugh having so much fun.

Shilzie, do you want to play?

Yeah, come play!

Please!

You can stack the blocks, and we'll knock them down!

Yeah, please!

Come play!

Come play, Shilzie!

Let's see who can build the highest tower!

With a definitive bite to her lip, she shook her head. All too content. Sitting at her brother's feet, petting Lionel, whom she cradled in her lap, his golden hair flat against a tan back.

Remaining near Vincent meant protection from bad men.

One in particular, had not acted on his threats made during supper coming up on two months ago. *Not yet.*

Her brother comforted her each night since then. Staying up late, getting no sleep for himself when she couldn't shut her eyes for fear of the face.

The floating white face. Pale. Moist with rainwater. Emerging from the shadows, dripping, and grinning. An expression of haunting disdain turned to a malicious sneer within a blink. Crooked teeth peaking from a crooked smile.

There was a crooked man.

Little, uneven stones aligned on a hill.

And he had a crooked smile.

Chipped tombstones. Sharp, deadly. Glistening in her dreams, slick with saliva. Snapping, *crunch crunch crunch.*

She'd almost been bitten when the face peered over the edge of her bed, mouth agape over exposed toes, before she awoke crying.

She felt it! She did! The warmth and the wetness of his little mouth. Sucking the toes before biting down!

This little piggy, that little piggy, all little piggies.

Watching from the darkness. In the rain. Threatening without parting his lips. Only his voice.

Get it over with at the beginning. They'd be better for it.

Wretches. Monsters. Filth.

Better off dead. All of you.

Vincent hurried from one caravan over at the sound of her cries. Up with a flash to hold her hand, sing soft songs. Cradle her on the couch reading fairy tales. Catching her tears, kissing her cheek, humming against her ear. She woke many mornings still resting against his chest. Warm robe clad arms around her. Ready with a smile, asking if she slept well. He didn't dare disturb her slumber. Instead, held her all night, soothing away bad dreams with rocking, and soft pats on the back.

During those restless weeks her brother assured every whimper, each downward glance, or worried gaze over the shoulder, that no matter what troubled her so—*he didn't know, she couldn't tell, didn't want to*—all would be well. Swore on his very heart. *And Vincent never breaks a promise.*

"There is no bad man," he said. *"No bad man will harm you."*

She felt silly being so scared of what Morty—*the bad man, the crooked man, eater of piggies*—thought during dinner weeks ago. Threatening Varlyn, taunting Shilzie with horrible games of sport.

I'll pop you in a boiling pot and watch as you scream!

Just you and me. We can share our secrets.

She'd heard bad talk before. About people like her. Disgusting. Ugly. Monsters. But from him, who *is* one of *them?* One of us. The monsters.

If not with her people, where could she find safety?

Pop off your beady head and kick it around the tent. Would you like that?

So stupid. She's not a baby anymore. She shouldn't get so scared. Morty can't do any of those things to her anyway. No matter how much he says so, the meanie can't do a thing! *No feet. No legs. One arm. Attached to his brother.*

Still, she had been so scared.

A face—*no body, no brother, one arm, three fingers, tiny teeth*—floating in the dark, whispering those things. Again, and again. *Boiling pot. Pop off your beady head. Better off. Wretches.*

He can't hurt me. He can't…

Vincent cleared his throat, pen scratching parchment. He sat up straight, shoulders back, forearms resting on the edge of a mahogany desktop, knees brushing the underside.

Simultaneously readying himself for the stage and writing a letter. Or, maybe a note? A list?

Shilzie couldn't be sure. *Reading is hard.*

He wore leather boots, and black velvet trousers with silver buttons along the sides. He hadn't decided on a shirt, vest, or jacket.

Perhaps he would not wear one. Mama urged he play to the crowd bare-chested on occasion, proving to be no gaff. A regular Normie wearing a wig, with horsehair glued to his face and hands.

Shilzie couldn't figure out why, but it seemed more women attended his shows when performing this way.

His performance is no different. In both versions of his act, he explains his condition, allowing male or female volunteers on stage to attest to his condition's authenticity, and from there move on to reading, or reciting poetry from memory.

Women want to touch his chest or face. Not pulling for loosely glued hair, but petting, as if he were a kitty cat sitting on their laps. Men tug at his beard, no more, no less.

Why so many ladies? Is Vincent not interesting to men? And why less male attendance when he has no shirt? It's a shirt. Only a bit of clothing. The roustabouts work without them on hot days. Rocky never performs in one, Lucky usually doesn't either, just a jacket. The same with Evro. Why are the crowds so different when *Vincent* does it?

Odd.

Grown-ups are strange. Especially Normies. Especially Normie *ladies*. They look at her brother funny. Not in a scared way, Shilzie *knows* that look. She wasn't sure *how* the women looked at him.

Odd, different. An emotion she couldn't place. It reminded her of how the men look at the dancing girls, but again, different. *Gentler. Nicer... Sometimes.* Sometimes they think about his pants, what's in them. *Legs, obviously.* The ladies get excited, real silly from the weird thoughts.

Shilzie sighed, stroking Lionel's head, and watched her sisters some more: blocks fall, stack, clatter, giggles. After the third bout of laughter, she craned her neck back till she could see a partially upside-down Vincent.

He smiled as he wrote. Blonde hand moving in a neat looping script, filling the page. The third he'd written so far and not the last. For a moment he paused and sat back against his seat.

The blocks clattered again, setting off Nylee and Elvi in joyous hysterics, which Vincent smirked at before noticing an admirer below.

A breath of laughter left his smile, "Silly girl." Fingers tickled beneath Shilzie's chin. He reread the last sentence before returning to his sister, "Would you like to help me pick an outfit for the show?"

She nodded, eagerly hopping to her feet, and hurried to the rod suspending shirts, vests, jackets, trousers, and cloaks.

Vincent stood behind her as she slid the weighted items back and forth.

"How about this?" he asked, touching a red vest.

Head shaking, she said, "nuh." Not what she was looking for.

"A different color then?"

"Yah, nuh tha." Not that one, that wasn't it.

She flipped and flipped. Lionel's body flattened beneath her arm, paws batting as the clothing flew past.

Dark green, grey, black, white, purple, maroon. She hesitated when she found the light blue vest with the white stitched stripes but continued.

"Thees wunn."

Blue-grey, doubled-breasted, with silver buttons swirling with leafy filigree patterns. Shilzie's favorite, it made her brother's eyes bright as ocean waters. Brought out the gold of his hair, extra shiny in the light.

"This one?"

She nodded, grin nearly reaching her ears as he lifted the hanger and held it at arm's length.

"Are you sure?" the hair on his cheek shifted to one side with his smirk. "I could swear to Barnum you picked this for our *last* show," his brow rose playfully. "Shouldn't I wear something different? The red vest *is* new after all."

"Nuh, nuh, thees wunn, thees wunn," she urged adamantly, poking the vest with her finger in quick taps.

"*Yes, yes*, of course," he succumbed willingly, "Whatever you wish, my love. If this is what you think I should wear, I will."

He took a white shirt from the rack, considered taking a black jacket, and left it where it hung. The clothes lay across the bed.

Want to play?

Yeah, do you want to play?

Not right now, Shilzie faced her sisters as Vincent bent to jot a line at the bottom of his letter.

No Shilzie, not you!

Charles!

Oh, of course.

Charles usually prefers Hide and Seek to any other game. Elvi and Nylee can never seem to find him.

We're playing blocks, want to play?

The girls giggled and began stacking. Staring at the wall while speaking to their friend.

Your turn Charles! Okay, I'll knock them down for you!

I get to do it next!

You got to do it lots already!
No, I haven't!
Charles, tell her I get to go again!
Shilzie decided to let Charles handle her sisters' dispute.

Vincent sat again. A hairbrush idle on the desk corner instead of its usual place on the shelf below the mirror. The pair of scissors were still high where she and her sisters couldn't get to it. Sometimes Vincent let them use the scissors to cut shapes into paper, as long as he or Dawn supervised. *The girls were not to touch the scissors otherwise. Any sharp or dangerous item.*

I wish I could read. She thought as words formed beneath her brother's pen. Dropping eves, she thought her mama might say, or was she being a Nosy Nancy?

No, Charles!
No!
Her sisters giggled.
We're still playing blocks!
Yeah! And it's my turn!
It's mine!
Her sisters laughed.

Shilzie took the comb, thumbing the bristles before running them down her brother's long hair.

Brushing, yes, petting, yes. Braiding is discouraged. As much as it pained him to tell his sisters no.

The last time the triplets attempted to twist his hair into plaits it took him and Dawn hours to untangle the mess. So frustrated, Dawn broached the option of cutting the snarls and knots out entirely. Starting over.

It would have devastated Shilzie. The culprit who helped start such calamity. She'd only been brushing his hair, twisting strands into ropes. *That's when her sisters took notice,* wanting to recreate the beautiful style Serene so often made with her long dark hair. Only the girls had not as much paid attention to the steps as they had to the final product. Improvising, they took handfuls and tied knots, and more knots until left with no more hair to tie.

Shilzie understood her mother's exasperation. The people needed to see Vincent in all of his glory later that evening. His hair makes the show, makes him who he is.

There were other beasts: dog people, cat people, wolf men, and monkey women in the carnival's past. Vincent is special, more so than any of them combined. More than any hair-covered person to ever live, as Shilzie wholeheartedly believed. Extraordinarily lovely, like a painting. Regal with his golden hair, and clothes right out of one of his history books. With the manner and disposition of any chivalrous knight.

Shilzie set a section of brushed hair over Vincent's shoulder, moving on to another handful. Her fingers slid through the strands easily, like rippling waters reflecting yellow sunshine. The curving hairs bumped and glided against her knuckles and the webbing of each finger.

Playing with it as a baby were some of her clearest memories. Gripping tight to the waves as he carried her and her sisters until they could walk for themselves. The three spent hours running their fingers through the silky golden strands before ultimately falling asleep to his voice.

"Whas tha?" Shilzie rested her forearm on a furry shoulder to point.

"It is a letter to a friend."

Friend? Weren't all of his friends at the carnival?

Vincent smiled at her pouting lips and befuddled brow as if he could read her thoughts. "She lives in Maryland. You will meet her soon," he turned in his seat, and brushed the underside of her chin with his knuckles, "And when you do, she will be your friend as well."

She. Shilzie could see her in his eyes. Red hair, not the dark kind like Mama. A mix between an orange peel, and copper, the pennies pats flick onto platters for prizes. Light skin, like honey and cream, and eyes dark as the ink he wrote with. *Shilzie saw this woman at the carnival a year ago.*

The lady volunteered to join Vincent on stage. He gave her a flower, a white rose, and said from memory, what he told Shilzie, and her sisters was called a *Sonnet,* by William Shakespeare.

Something about roses being fair, thorns, sweet odours.

The woman didn't giggle or act the slightest bit afraid—*like some stupid ladies do,* most *aren't scared of him, but there is always one being mean and dumb*—when he took her hand and recited the sonnet.

She held the flower beneath her nose, breathing the sweet smell as she watched the triplets' brother. The petals covered the slow start of a smile, keeping it hidden from the crowd.

A lot of the men didn't like what they saw.

A Freak touching one of their women. Trying to sucker her in with his pretty words. Allowed it that once, sure a good Normie girl like her wouldn't be bamboozled by a Freak.

Shilzie hadn't realized any of this at the time. Thought it any regular show, another lady in another town, but now, now clearly it had not been so.

The woman should have left the stage after the sonnet, but Vincent leaned nearer, held her hand close to his chest. She kept still, breathing shallowly, looking up into his blue eyes as his voice lowered, reciting a poem Shilzie never heard before:

A rose's petals doth blossom
From a lover's ardent touch
Thorns on a stem wither
Upon gentle fingers grasp
Their breath entwined the sweetest bouquet
The breeze on which leaves shiver
Pluck but one petal is to decide a lover's fate
Will it last, will it fade, this love?
Does one love? Or does one not?

"My fwenn?" Shilzie asked.

"Yes, she will be your new friend, and Elvi and Nylee's. I have told her all about you and she cannot wait to meet you."

"I yur fwenn?" Shilzie worried. The fondness in Vincent's eyes when he spoke of his friend. How his expression and voice gentled in the same instant. Did he care more about her than Shilzie? Was she not his friend too?

"You are more than that sweetheart," his hand consumed her cheek, warming nearly half of her small head. A frown that was also a smile told Shilzie he understood her feelings. "You are my little sister," he pulled her into a hug, rubbing circles on her back, "The love I have for you is one that cannot be replaced."

She smiled. Grunted, as two more sets of arms squeezed.
Hugs!
We want hugs too!
Who is the friend?
I want a friend!
Charles wants to know too!

Vincent chuckled, "And of course I cannot forget my other lovely sisters," her brother's arms opened wide to pull all three against him and press a kiss to the top of each of their heads.

Elvi and Nylee squirmed and giggled at tickling whiskers.

The door opened with a mild squeak.

Blinding yellow light became a backdrop, a rippling stage curtain behind the embracing group's mother.

"My babies still here?" She stopped, cocking a hip, "Well ain't this the sweetest sight I ever saw. Where's yer Mama's hugs?"

Elvi and Nylee excitedly shuffled to their mother with arms outstretched. "Ma ma ma ma," they called.

Shilzie remained with her brother a moment longer until he stood and walked her across the caravan by the hand.

"Gettin' ready fer the show?" she asked, patting and rubbing three small backs.

"Yes, the girls are ready."

"Lecturin' with no top on?" she wondered, adding before Vincent could finish. "Sure wish ya would. Little fillies buy out tickets mighty quick when they hear tell of a handsome young man on display half nekkid." She bumped his hairy stomach with her knuckles and winked.

"*No*," he laughed. "Shilzie just chose my outfit for today."

"You do that?" she kissed her daughter. "Coverin' 'im up ta keep yer big brother all to yerself an' not lose 'im ta some silly lady? That's my smart girl."

Vincent smirked.

Shilzie and her sisters giggled.

"Oh, damnit, forgot why I come ta see ya. Law's come 'round."

"Is it serious?" Vincent didn't appear worried.

A shrug, "Gonna go have me a little chat an' find out. Thought I'd come let ya know first, in the case my mouth gits me hauled away. Bail's in the kitty, but don't spend more'n I would. Waste'a coin if ya ask me. Couple'a nights in the can don't do no harm. Better 'comadations than rousties git most days."

Shilzie's siblings laughed. She didn't, her mind wandered, traveled at the mentioning of law—a *Carny Curse*. Two men at the Gate. Tik spoke with them near the ticket booth with Varlyn and Patricia.

One of the men stood with arms limp as noodles at his sides, mouth twisted up like a used tissue. Eyes squinting at de la Llum's Crab Man and Lobster Queen.

Tik twitched, answering the older man's questions.

He don't know shit, the younger man thought.

The older of the two wants to talk to the proprietor of this operation. *A woman. A bearded woman.* About a serious issue in his town.

A man has been found dead.

And he wants to know what *she* knows about it.

DIRTY PENNIES
∾ DAWN ↝

"So whas dis about? What you tink we do?" the furious clacking of a wooden fan whip-cracked from the midway. "Oh, you in big trouble now. Boss Lady's comin' for ya." Varlyn wheeled backward, allowing space for the approaching woman.

"Dis man say sumthin' 'bout a murda," Patricia called. "Gonna blame it on us, yeah?" she asked the strangers.

Upon the carnival owner's arrival, the two men disregarded the questions and comments of Patricia and Varlyn Grady.

Dawn severely disliked the men at first sight. Normies in a position of power, armed with badges and a gun. Any reason given by this type of man would be found acceptable in court if he were to draw his weapon and fire upon every Sicko in the vicinity.

They rushed us judge!

It was in self-defense, we swear!

To protect our Health, we had to mow down the Freaks your Honor!

Blast 'em full'a holes and leave 'em in puddles!

Little as she liked it, as owner of the show it's part of the job description to be cordial to guests.

Fuck cordiality. Fuck it right in the rear.

Typical lot lice clustered beside parked cars.

Gentlemen, hearing tell from work chums about ladies offering a certain *service*, parked on the left side of the lot nearest the Kootch tent—*for less conspicuous arrival and departure.*

The remaining early birds waited in the designated parking space outside the Gate, bobbing heads side to side, watching the finishing touches before the carnival opened to the public. Impatiently eying the podium. Fists ready at the wallet for admission and tickets. Pre-mapping routes toward the big wheel, carousel, and swing ride, or down the midway to the Ten-In-One.

Food first? Rides, then food? Shows? Food? Rides? Games?

The little buggers hopped person to person, group to group, theorizing why the police arrived.

An accident the night before? A kidnapped child? Contagion from the Sick? A Freak gone missing? If so, where!? Better be on the lookout for the Freak!

"B-boss Lady," Tik's left eye twitched. Another stutterer. Unlike Billy, this man's whole body felt the effect. His knee jerked, "These men wanna t-talk ta ya."

"You're the owner of this circus, correct?"

There are many things Dawn de Barcsy doesn't like: dogs, penny-pinching patrons, birds twittering in the early morning. Another is calling a carnival a circus. That distaste only intensified when referring to *her* carnival. A personal insult, she would declare such an offensive inaccuracy.

"Of a circus? No sir. But I *am* the owner of this carnival. Carnivàle de la Llum, says so right above yer head."

"Please Ma'am I'm not here to discuss the difference between circuses and carnivals." The detective took a step forward. "Do you know what happened this morning, missus?"

"De Barcsy."

"First, I visited the scene of a murder. Second, I received a telegraph all the way from Bastropa, Louisiana." The man's slow cadence never faltered. No inflection, no indication of anger.

Intentional? Dawn suspected cunning in those spectacularly blue eyes. He knows what he says and means it.

Bastropa? Those yokels started that shit with their pans!

"The Bastropa department suspects your show may be involved in a murder case of their own. *Murders.* A fourteen-year-old and his parents. Seems he bragged to a neighbor the night before his death. He and a group of friends drove by your carnival. Guns were involved. Your people shot at the young men?"

"They was drivin' *through* the lot. Honkin' horns an' bangin' pots an' pans, threatenin' us, near runnin' us down, what do ya expect us ta do?"

He shrugged, "Report the incident to the authorities?"

Authorities, like they'd do fuck all to help Sickos in distress.

"You know how often my show gits hassled by Normies

Detective-? *Sorry, didn't catch yer name."*

"Detective Joseph Wydell."

"Detective Wydell. So often, that what them boys did ain't new ta us. Ain't clever, ain't nothin' special. 'Bout as interestin' as a skeeter bite and as big a nuisance. And what do ya do to a skeeter? Swat it till it goes away."

"Or crush it beneath your hand," gas fire blue eyes sparked under hound dog droopy lids. A gaze which says the man is tired of your shit before it has the chance to hit the bottom of the toilet. "The boy and his family were not the only bodies discovered in Bastropa. Another young man, his father, and two siblings. Found hanging in their barn. Seems like quite a coincidence the two sets of murders include young men. *The same age as the individuals who drove through your lot.* Don't you think so Mrs. de Barcsy?"

"I'm truly sorry fer the families, I am, no youngin' deserves ta die. But I don't know what ta tell ya. Didn't do nothin' in Bastropa, and we been on this lot since we got here. Haven't sent men ta town fer a bottle'a milk or even a crate'a taters."

"You know for a fact your men haven't gone into town?"

"The trucks're parked right near our beds," a half-truth, the box trucks parked behind the concessions, and beside the Single-O's to block those who wander. Looky-loos peaking in at the backyard or teen boys sneaking into the Kootch show. "Somebody woulda' heard somethin'. Woulda' heard me hollerin' clear from town if someone started a truck in the middle'a the night."

"How many do you employ Mrs. de Barcsy?" He did not specify men, women, or Health status.

"Oh, I don't know. Anywhere from eighty to a hundred're more. Depends how many youngsters stay on durin' the season."

Beneath a dark grey brush of moustache Wydell's mouth seemed to squint along with his eyes. "And you are aware of each one hundred persons' whereabouts at all times?"

"...Course not."

"So, a man, *or woman*, could have easily *walked* to town without disturbing a soul last night. The victim's home is only a mile from here."

"Not likely, but it's somethin' *could* be done. I'm tellin' ya, it ain't one'a my people." *No one would hurt those kids without her*

say so, scare 'em, sure, but not kill. Not for something like that. And there's been no reason in this burg to start knocking off Normies at midnight. *"... In fact.* If ya bothered ta read through the registry I sent ahead ta ya'll *months* ago when I booked this lot, ya'd know I employ no Sick who've had run-ins with the law. Clean records all of 'em'."

"I've read it," he mumbled, lazily tracing tent peaks and declines with tired eyes. "Four of the individuals are your adopted children. Three girls, all age twelve as of September tenth of last year, and a man, twenty-five last January twenty-sixth, born in York, England. Thirteen more are listed as performers, and various others with minor ailments and early stages of disease... and yourself."

Dawn bit the inside of pursed lips.

Wydell lifted an expectant hand. The second officer pulled a tube of thick fabric from a coat pocket. Dawn forgot about him as she and his senior spoke.

Half the detective's age; no older than Vincent if she laid down a bet.

She wondered if he were shadowing the older man, learning the ropes of detecting and locking up monsters.

"We found this beside the victim. Does it look familiar?"

The tube unfurled slowly, the width narrowing until a point. A twenty-four-inch white pennant, stained with ruddy finger smears.

Carnivàle de la Llum billowed off of a split diamond sigil, the dark top half held a crescent moon tipped on its side, frown points aiming below to its opposing light half holding a black sun with a pale star at its center.

"One'a our pennants. Came to the first show I s'pose. So did a bunch'a folks. Got anythin' better than that? 'Cause a travelin' salesman's got the same opportunity a troupe do. Or is it simpler ta pin murder on a Sicko?"

"The world is full of monsters Mrs. de Barcsy, all of them are human. And it is my job to put them away, Sick or otherwise. It makes no difference to me. As long as they can't go on hurting others."

She quieted. Surprised and wondering if he spoke true, or falsified his personal beliefs to earn her trust. Build a rapport while stealthily prying information with her none the wiser.

"We also found this." He produced a single work glove. Many of the males gathered for a listen had a pair poking from their back pockets. Wydell observed as such. "Appears your men wear similar gloves. *Anvil Corporation*," he read from the print inside the wrist, complete with anvil-shaped logo. "Don't show folks purchase canvas supplies from this company?"

"Ain't *only* show folks. Sells tools an' machinery ta factory workers, farmers, smiths. Is that all Detective? I got a show ta start."

Tick-tock show is about to begin. Pats are piling up.

"I'm sorry if I've been a bother Mrs. de Barcsy," he concentrated on rolling the pennant. "Perhaps I should come by another time, say ten o'clock tomorrow? I'll bring more officers, we could question your crew in a few short hours."

"Sounds dandy."

"However, until then I would be much obliged if your show remained closed for today. As a sign of good faith that you, and your employees, are willing to cooperate and truly have no connection to these recent crimes."

Dawn sucked her teeth. *"Why of course… Detective."*

With a tip of hat, "Have a nice day Mrs. de Barcsy. Enjoy your time in Jackson."

Sure. Fuckin'. Will.

STRENGTH OF MIND
∽ BILLY & MORTY ∾

The tent felt bigger with no sound. Too big.

No one greeted the boys in the Annex on arrival. Not the man who talks—*Muckers.* Not any of the many boys who point the spotlight. Not any customers—*patties or marks. Like the workers say. Or is someone* named *Mark?*

Morty sighed, *what time is it?*

Billy tugged a watch out by a single strap.

Six punctures total, three lopsided and stretched from use. Dark brown leather, gone hard and crusty around aged edges. No buckle side for Billy to wear properly around the wrist.

Mama gave it to Morty and him for their twelfth birthday. It belonged to Granddaddy William, Billy's namesake.

Twelve thirty.

Don't the gawkers start piling in at twelve? What the Hel is going on?

I don't know. We got here on time. Where is everybody?

Voices warped behind the rough grey canvas: Vincent reading, men bickering, the mermaid vocalizing, children laughing, women chatting quietly.

Ten shows in all on the other side. Not always the same people. Sometimes performers stand on the stage outside, showing for free. Other times doing longer *lectures* in the single tents.

Serene's permanent position seemed to be stage one. Singing songs about the ocean, Spanish ladies and men named Johnny.

Wonder what Johnny—de la Llum's Johnny—*thinks of that? Wonder if he likes it? Hearing his name in songs.*

Next to Serene, the Chupa-something—a *gaff,* Dawn said.

Billy wasn't sure what that meant.

It looked like a chicken-dog left to dry up in the sun. Jerky not meant to be eaten. *It would be gross to eat that thing.*

Then the triplet little girls, and their brother Vincent.

Billy didn't think they were *really* related. Vincent has blonde hair, and they have brown, and he's covered in it, they aren't. Come to think of it, none of Dawn's kids look like her either.

They're adopted. Idiot.

...Ohh.

Fifth came the contorshist? contaronist?

"A bender *is what we call them,"* Dawn explained, as an easier term to remember.

A lady named Olga who twists her body like a band of rubber. Can bend her leg so far behind her back she could kiss her own feet!

Lavi worked the Ten today, the little lady Billy and Morty first met in the dress tent. Her two daughters are on the *Midway*, and her son and his wife will perform outside.

There is also a *'Fish Boy.'* A doll head and arms stuck on a taxidermy trout.

One of the working men plays popular songs on his harmonica sometimes, he was here today.

Billy liked it best when he plays Frankie Cochran songs or the themes from Bruce Clarke pictures. Heroic compositions building tension while Bruce saves the day from any villain thrown at him. From crooks and mobsters to monsters, and he always sweeps the damsels off their feet.

The girl without arms, Sherilyn, took stage on the other side of the wall as well. Picking up a glass to drink from, signing autographs, things people do every day, but with her feet! A lot of folks do real simple stuff. Stuff that shouldn't be so interesting to watch, but it sure is somehow. Billy notices the same customers come through the Annex to see he and his brother more than once a day. Two or three times!

Last in the Ten side, on a green pillow on top of a wooden stand wound a pile of rope, tied with a loop on its end. Said to be one of the nooses that hung the doctors responsible for the Cure.

Billy'd seen one of the working men making this one.

Covered in motor oil to darken it, he drug the rope through the dirt, scraped it up and down with a knife until the twine went wiry, unwound some of the end, and burnt it black.

It looks old; however, plain old rope. The very same holding up the tents. The customers could gaze at the ceiling and see what it looked like before getting dirtied up.

Everyone on the other side held conversations, waiting for the carnival to open.

Billy sat quietly, hands on his lap, humming the theme of *Rebellion Part II,* until Morty told him to quit it.

A new voice entered the tent. Loud, real happy, not Muckers. *He* would yell, or sound sore even if no one caused him to be so. In a permanent state of madness and smelling of the hooch drink Billy heard people talking about.

And barrels and tubs being rusty. What does that have to do with something you drink?

It's where they make it.

In a tub?

Or a barrel.

Ew. I hope they don't wash in that tub before making it.

Probably do.

Eww.

Gives it flavor.

Ewwww.

The voice got close enough for the twins to hear, "Yeah, shows off, coppers closed us for today. *I dunno*, gonna have ta ask the Boss Lady."

Coppers? Like police?

I thought I smelled bacon.

"Hey, baby girl," much closer, "Vie's lookin' for you."

"Why?" Sherilyn wondered.

"*Ohh,* I can't tell ya."

"Come on," laughter.

"Nah, it's a surprise, now-*go* find her and find out yerself."

"*Alright*. Bye, Daddy."

"Bye, baby."

A kissing smack, more steps, and the Annex entrance flapped open.

"Hey you two," Sunny, "Guess what?" no time for a guess, "You get the day off today. Show's closed. Come on outta there." He waved them over.

"Wu-w-why are wu-we c-cl-closed?"

Does this mean we have to pack up and leave? We only got to be open for one day. Aren't we supposed to stay a week? That's what Dawn said.

Sunny shrugged, forehead wrinkling, "Couple a' coppers pulled up to the Gate and shut us down. Some kinda trouble, I guess. Nothin' I think we need ta worry over. This happens from time ta time."

Wowie.

Morty groaned deep in his throat.

First, he learns Normal people come to the carnival yelling they're going to get them—Sick folks—and chase the whole lot of them away—*sometimes with guns!* Now the police shut the show down! It's like an action picture!

Uuuugggg.

"Come on," he waved again, harder and faster, "Come on come on. I'll take ya 'round the carny. Give ya the real meat an' potatoes 'bout this place."

But it's not dinner yet...

Morty sighed.

Except for Serene, Vincent, and his three sisters the Ten was empty. The girls, two of them, yanked at each other's dolls. laughing and trying to pull away when the other would reach for a stuffed arm or leg. The third little girl stood at the foot end of Serene's tank.

Vincent rolled up his sleeves, exposing very hairy arms—*even on the underside where most men's arms are smooth*—and helped Serene out of the water.

Egh, Morty gagged. *Look at that thing! It's one giant foot! And those toes, can't even call them that, ugh, turn me away William, I can't stand to look at it.*

Billy angled his head to the left, still watching. He didn't think her feet were gross. Different. Two ankles in one. The small feet coming off of the smooth short trunk could be touching if a person didn't look close enough. Hardly an imprint separated the last three toes. Ripples of skin, nails like half-moons. The big toes—*not so big*—and second toes, peeked from the near-flat ridge as a cattail from water.

Serene thanked Vincent when she stood on her one foot… feet… foot?

Water streamed off of her outfit. Flat, shiny discs plated the tight blue skirt from waist to ankle. It really looked like scales. Black cords held up a top made up of nothing but two clam shells covering her… *bosoms*.

Whatcha looking at William? Checking out her clams are ya?
No!
Suuuure you aren't. I did. Nice little pair she's got… for a Freak.
"Do you need help down the stairs?" Vincent asked.
"No, I can make it with my crutches."
Vincent went behind the tank to get her walking sticks.
Billy's gaze wandered to the little girl.
She splashed a hand in the sloshing water of the tank. Mid-clap, she looked at the trio nearing the exit.
Her smile went to a frown.
Billy grinned and waved.
She hadn't met them yet. That's all. They were still strangers. He bet her mama and brother told her not to talk to people she didn't know, so it was okay if she was a little nervous.
Yeah, keep staring…
Huh?

"This way boys, come on!" Sunny held the canvas aside for the boys. "You ride Star yet?" he asked.

Billy shuffled to keep up with Sunny's lengthy steps, twisting his handkerchief. He wasn't sure when he pulled it out, maybe when he put back Granddaddy's watch?

"Na-na-no. Wu-we ha-ha-haven't rah-ridden any ru-rides yet."
Morty won't let me.
Damn right, I won't. We ain't kids.
Adults ride them too.
Well, they're stupider than they look… and they look plenty stupid to begin with. Any adult going round and round on one of those kiddie rides is nothing but a rube and should be locked up with

the rest of the loonies up in Briarhill… Hey, isn't that one fella holed up there? The one who killed that little girl?

Billy sighed. Shook his head. Harv Jackson. Locked up in Briarhill Asylum a few months after the release of his one and only radio hit.

"That's a shame, real good fun-*if ya ain't scared of heights a'course.* And if ya got a strong stomach," Sunny clutched his belly. "Only road it the once. Sure were fun!… *Till the end.*"

Billy looked at the massive ride as they started down the midway. Swings hung from the large top by chains.

That doesn't look safe at all! What the Hel is wrong with these people?!

It must be. Children ride it-

They'd let children ride a flaming bull into a brick wall if it made them a buck!

I don't think so.

Obviously, you haven't been paying attention around here, William. You see all those lies in the tent? The noose, the fish boy, the chupa-monster? Anything… anything to make a few extra cents. Next, you will tell me you don't think the bearded one is fleecing our wages. Sure seems short for the draw we bring. I think we ought to have a word with her about that… Let her know we don't appreciate what she's doing. That we won't stand for it.

He stopped listening to his brother and tuned back in as Sunny said, "You know Vinnie's the one who named her?"

"Ru-really?"

"Sure, sure. Yep, when he was a wee bitty thing," he held out a hand as he walked, just under waist high. "His papa read him some old story by a guy named… Talkin, Toekin, Tallkeen, *somethin'* like that, got it from there I hear."

He nodded, not recognizing any of those names.

'Cause he doesn't know what he's talking about, blabbing like usual William, ignore the dumb bastard. I sure am trying to… he grumbled, arm flexed, palm clapping his brother's neck with every step.

"How about Bruce? You meet 'im?"

"N-no."

Sunny let out a single deep chuckle.

Why is that funny?

"Oh, you are in for a *treat* my boys. You see Bruce-well, ah come on, it's somethin' ya gotta see, ta believe."

Like your marriage? That you somehow managed to get a lady into bed before *this wife? How has no one beaten him over the head yet? He won't shut up! Just shut up! Shut up!*

I like Sunny. He's nice.

Nice and stupid maybe. Nice and loud.

The three came up to the Evening Star, and jeepers, the size! If Billy had been wearing a hat it would've slipped right off his head as he looked up!

"Watch-watch this, play along boys, play along," he snickered. "Heya there, Brucie! Ya meet Billy and Morty?"

Bruce, a short man—*not short like the Samson family*—but smaller than most of the ladies on the lot.

He wore grey coveralls stained with motor oil, and a striped, tweed cap sitting askew, not quite straight over his right eyebrow.

His cheeks were round and rosy. A thick, bushy moustache the color of peach innards hid a little O of a mouth..

Ohh, fix that hat, will you? It's buggin' the Hel out of me!

But it's on his head, I can't just grab it.

It's crooked and it's driving me crazy!

"Nah, don't think I have," Bruce wiped his hands before reaching out for a shake.

Billy shook, with a smile.

Fix it, fix it!

Freckles spilled like knocked-over cinnamon down the backs of small hands and short fingers. They were red from sun exposure and smudged with dark, dried liquid and dust.

"My name is Bruce, and I'm sure," he stepped back, "you know Star." Bruce looked up at the ride, smiling big. Proud.

"Ya-yeah. Ha-haven't ga-got to rrr-ride yet."

And you won't. I told you William, no rides. Especially not with this crooked hat-wearing son of a bitch at the wheel. It's making me nutty!

"Oh, come by anytime, Star would love it."

Huh?

"As long as you treat her kindly, she'll give you a good time."

The red-faced man's smile grew the more he nodded. "She loves makin' people happy. Oh, she sure does."

Sunny took a step back from the little group, index finger sealing his lips, wrinkled like he sucked a lemon. Close to the ride now, he patted the large mechanical column. The metal *clang, clang, clanged* when the big ring on his index finger struck with each clap.

"Star's lookin' good, ya give her a new coat'a paint?"

"Now, now, Sunny, please, I've told you…"

His voice was gentle—*meek, weak, a pussy,* Morty's words of choice—but stern. Tiny eyes worried.

He reached up, standing on tiptoes to grip Sunny's wrist and bring it away from the ride.

"Star doesn't like being handled that way. Gotta treat her gentle, she *is* a lady after all." His pink hand smoothed over where Sunny clapped. Had to stand on the points of his boots to reach.

What?

Billy agreed with his brother when his brows seemed to cross at the man's reaction.

"Oh, I know. Just sayin' she's lookin' good! Oh, and new seats too?" Sunny sat in one of the hanging seats. Swinging back, kicking up his feet.

"S-sunny, you're sitting on her belt, you're gonna stretch it. You're hurting her Sunny-please," he moved Sunny up and away, inspecting the belt and metal frame for damages. From pink to red-faced, he turned, "It's nice ta meet you," he said to Billy and Morty, "But I gotta tend to Star, she needs to be put to bed for the day, just," he motioned the group away.

Lips puffing around a grin Sunny nudged the boys' shoulders to get them moving. *So Bruce could be left alone with Star.*

Is he-does he think that kiddie ride is a lady? Like, an alive lady? Morty questioned. Billy could feel that his brother's jaw hung open as much as his own.

"Shh-she?" he knew the carousel was called a girl, and the big wheel a boy, but… *not like that!*

"Yeah-Bruce is," Sunny roughed a hand up and down the back of his neck, chuckling, "he's an interestin' feller is all I'll say. He's got a real *special* relationship with his ride that no other jockey has. *Reeeeeal* special."

He stood with hands on hips watching Bruce from afar as he dusted off the abused seat, and gently folded the belt. Bruce talked to himself, *or maybe the Evening Star.* He pet the chains, gazed up the purple structure, looking over the ride's lightbulb speckled underside.

He went back to the column and—Billy wouldn't have believed it unless he saw it with his own peepers.

Bruce put both hands against the metal, leaned in, and kissed it.

Sunny exploded with giggles, grabbing his belly with both hands. *"I was hopin' he'd do that!* Oh boy. Oh Barnum, ol' Brucie, you nut!"

That's it! We're leaving tonight. A man in love with a machine is too much for me, William. This is too far!

Billy didn't want to, *it wasn't nice,* and Mama taught him better—*laughing at others isn't polite, unless they are telling a joke*—but he started to laugh.

A man in love with a ride? Who would of thunk it?!

"Git outta the way!"

A gloved hand knocked Billy's shoulder, ending the laughs and swinging him backward so hard he threw out his arms for balance.

A roustie did the pushing. A big one. Heavy around the middle and wide-shouldered. Dark grey stubble covered his jaw.

"And wear a damn ball cap! Keep that shit hid when you're outta the Ten!"

Watch who you call shit, fuckface! Morty mumbled, *I'll make you eat those words. Shit? Shit?! I'll stuff your own shit down your throat till you choke! Eat it and live with the taste forever, that'll learn you. You'll think twice before talkin' shit to me ever again!*

Billy squirmed, frowning and rubbing his sore shoulder.

"Aw, don't pay no mind, man's a lousy brute," Sunny pat the boys' shoulders. *"Pay no mind."*

Plink! Billy jumped. Sunny didn't. *Claaaaaaang!*

"Hey, boys!" a voice called as the loud noise subsided. *Johnny.* An oversized mallet with gold and brown stripes on its handle angled across his right shoulder. "Head on over here!"

A big group stood around. All working men. Some crouched, others sat on crates or overturned buckets, watching Johnny and a smaller cluster of men swing the mallet onto the lever at the bottom of *'Hercules,'* the Test Your Strength game, or *High Striker*.

A big sign at the top of the thirty-foot tower showed two muscular arms reaching out from the bell, holding the yellow letters of its name. Lightning bolts marked each unit beside numbers, starting at zero, then one-hundred, all the way to one thousand, changing in color and text as they climbed. Black, bold letters marked zero, one thousand a bright white-lavender, and spiky like an electric charge.

"Angus givin' ya trouble?"

"Ain't he always," Sunny confirmed. "Told him to-" he nudged the air in Morty's direction, "-to cover up Morty there when he ain't workin'." Sighing, "I *was* gonna say something but-he's one'a your men so-didn't think it was my place ta-ya know."

He squeezed the hammer's handle. The veins in Johnny's forearm stood out like well-fed worms in soil as he watched Angus disappear beside the Ten-In-One's Annex.

Billy thought, if he really wanted to, he might just snap it.

"He ever gives you two grief again you come find me. Alright? Should know better than ta say that kinda thing to you boys..." He stared down the midway again, brows furrowed.

My hero, Morty groaned. Billy could feel a tug behind the ear when his brother's eyes rolled around.

At least he's being nice Morty.

Mmm-hmm... Sure hung up on that nice thing, aren't you?

"Come on!" someone yelled. *"Hit the damn thing!"*

"Shut yer hole!" Johnny called back. To Billy, he asked, "You boys wanna give Hercules a try?"

"Uh," his eyes inched up the tower. "Nah-*nnn*," the height made Billy's stomach drop. The thought of hitting the lever and the puck not jumping passed zero too scary. *What if the men laughed? What if Johnny or Sunny did? Morty* would.

"Go on, give it a go." The end of the mallet stuck out of his fist. "Don't think I've seen you two try yer luck at any joint since ya joined up."

Morty won't let me play any games, he didn't say. *No rides, no games.*

"Don't got it rigged, that's saved for the marks during show hours. See?" He bopped the lever with the top side of the mallet's

head. The puck didn't move. Johnny frowned.

Someone snickered into their palm.

"Damn it, Gil," he laughed. "Git off the guy!"

The snickerer, Gil, leaned forward off a line of rope connecting Hercules to a stake in the ground.

"*Now*, it ain't rigged." This time the puck bounced up and down.

Here we go… Morty snickered, the volume growing louder and louder as his brother reached for the mallet.

"*Barnum, would you look at this?*"

"Gotta *see this.*"

The circle of men closed around the game like his fist on the mallet.

A lot heavier than he thought it would be. Johnny made it look easy, made it look light like a feather—*but his arms are bigger around than both of Billy's put together. Maybe even three or four of his arms.*

"Don't listen to them rubes." He took a step back, but not too far.

He nodded. *Jeez, the bell is a long way up. Jeez, they're watching. Jeez!*

Just hit it!

"Come on! You got this, Billy-Boy!" Sunny encouraged, clapping.

With both hands he lifted the mallet, and staggered. Eyeballed the lever, the tower, counting numbers up and up. He aimed the head's nose over where he had to strike, lifted the weight, arms shaking like leaves on a windblown sapling.

Right on the lever, swing, and bring it down as hard as I can.

The mallet rose over his head and came right back down. Panicking, Billy tried to reroute the momentum onto the center of the lever.

He missed. The puck jerked an inch high off the base.

His cheeks turned red before the men started laughing.

"Aw, that's alright," claps from one person. "Try again Bills. First swing don't count anyway." Sunny's voice was welcome in the noise of the men.

"Shut it!" Johnny ordered.

The chuckling quieted to snickers and giggles: *it didn't stop*

Morty.

Oh, William, that was pathetic. You barely hit the-did you see how it hopped- he trailed off.

"Let me show ya the trick."

Hopped like a little baby bunny, laughing, laughing, laughing.

Billy gave Johnny the mallet, hiding teary eyes.

"Gotta keep yer hands close together and step up to it while ya swing. And keep yer eye on that lever, don't look at nothin' else, got it?" He went to swing, stopped, smirked, "Picturin' the face of someone ya don't like don't hurt neither. *Hey there Angus, what ya doin' down there?"* he asked the panel.

Billy giggled.

Johnny took a step back, demonstrating, eyes on the lever, came forward, swooping the mallet up and over his head and down hard. *Plink! Claaaaang!*

The noise of the bell lingered in Billy's ears. Making fun of him, like Morty and the men did. He wouldn't hear that sound again, unless Johnny hit the lever again, or someone *else* bigger and stronger took a turn.

"Here, try again."

"Nnn-"

"No, nothin'." His rough hand took Billy's and put it on the handle. "Ya think them boys can do any better? Blake can't knock it passed four hundred. Ben and Rodney, maybe five, if ya add their scores up. Most of 'em miss the lever every time. Blamin' it on not bein' able ta *'con-cen-trate'* with the men yappin', the head's loose on the hammer, Gil's gaffed the line. It's a game kid, have a good time."

He *did* want Billy to have a good time. It made Billy think of how their mama talked when she tried teaching her sons dancing, or piano. Billy couldn't do either, felt embarrassed having her watch as he messed up. Tripping on his feet and falling, or hitting a note way off-key. Smiling and urging him to try again. To have fun even if he wasn't good at it. Do it 'cause it was fun. You don't have to be good at something to have fun doing it.

"O-okay."

He pat Billy's back and returned to his place a few steps away.

This time he did as Johnny said. Cupped his hands one above

the other, stood a few feet away from the lever. Came up to it as he lifted the mallet, keeping the lever in his sights, and brought it down.

I hit it!

The puck went up. One-hundred, two, three, three and a half. The puck stopped between three and four hundred, but he smiled all the same.

There were laughs again, not as many as before.

"Go again," Johnny urged, his smile tugging to the left.

"Good job Billy-Boy!"

Yeah 'good job' Billy-Boy, managed to hit the lever this time. Go ahead, try again, you're gonna miss now. That last one was a fluke and you know it. Go on, embarrass us again with your measly whack with your wittle hammer.

Billy swung again, hit. The puck stopped at two hundred. Laughs, harder, louder. The roustie from before, Angus, spilled coffee as he clutched his stomach.

Swing and miss. Nicking the center of the panel and sending it no more than a few inches toward the bell.

"Y'all see that one?! A whole two inches! *Hey Blake, ain't that the same size as your pecker?"* coffee sloshed, near emptying the cup.

"Hey!"

"He ain't scorin' that high."

"Hey!!!"

Laughter.

You see that?! Weak as a little girl. Go again, sweetheart. Beat that high-flying score.

The heat came back to Billy's cheeks. He swung again. Two-hundred. Muckers joined the group. Yellow teeth bright in red lips. More men, some who run the games.

All laughing, pointing, Morty joining in. The loudest of them all.

You smell that?

What? he asked weakly, trying not to let the tears roll down his cheeks.

That fishy smell… oh, wait that's you little brother. You're letting your pussy show in front of all these big strong men.

Stop it, Morty.

William's a pussy, a big crying pussy! Flappin' and drippin' in the wind while these rubes point and laugh. Come on snatch-face, you need your lover boy to come back over here and help you swing that big ol' hammer? Come on Billy-Boyo show them again how strong you are! Come on rough n' tough, do it! Show me how strong you are! Or should we leave while you're ahead and find the hairy bitch. Tell her we got a new act for her. World's Biggest Pussy! Watch it squirt tears!

Shut uuup!!!

Hard as he could, Billy swung at the lever, but it wasn't that anymore. Not bits of metal, bolts, and springs. It was his brother's face.

Nubby chin, crooked nose, squinty jerk eyes.

Saying all those things to him. All those times Morty's been mean and he couldn't do anything about it.

He slammed down the mallet, imagining it would shut him up good. Close his mouth and make him stop for once.

Claaaaaaaaaaaaaaaaaaaaaang!!!!!

Silence.

"*Ha ha haaaaa!* Yes, my boy, yes! Hot damn!" Sunny ran into Billy, tackling a hug into his side, patting his belly and back excitedly. The boy stared at the bell still vibrating at the top of the tower. "You see that, you all see that! Like ta see you boys do better! Billy-Boy got himself a ring-dinger!"

I did it. I hit… the bell. I did… it.

Morty's arm flopped.

"Helluva job, kid," Johnny roughed a hand in Billy's hair. "Showed 'em didn't ya?"

"I-I did." He grinned, "I did!"

But not the men. He stopped hearing their laughs. Their taunts.

He showed his brother. For once, he proved him wrong.

A GOOD MAN

∾ HILLY ∾

Her fingers gripped the edge of the mattress, eyes closed. Concentrating on his movement, the friction their bodies created.

She envisioned strong hands, flexed forearms pulling her lower body against his pelvis. Thick torso and hard abdomen slick with exertion. The muscles of his upper arms bulging with every push and pull. Lines of muscle highlighted by the glow of day seeping through canvas walls. Radiant yellow luminosity caressing golden tan skin.

It built within her, she panted, on the cusp. "Oh…" she let go. *"Oh Johnny!"* she cried.

He stopped mid-thrust.

"It's," out of breath, not yet finished, "it's *Donnie*… Donnie Klein…"

Hilly opened her eyes for the first time since she and the John got into bed.

She dropped one shoulder, peeking at the middle-aged man behind her. Of pasty complexion, bright pink contoured a hairy chest, narrow shoulders, and round belly. Splotches of color dabbled the sides of a skinny neck as if he'd misapplied rouge in the dark.

"Tha-that's what I said," stroking a clammy forearm, "*Donnie*," she breathed, feigning arousal.

"Oh," he grinned, proud of his manhood, and went back to pumping.

Hilly didn't have to wait long until *Donnie Klein,* finished his business, placed twenty-five dollars on the vanity—*Sunny managed to up the price from the standard fee. Mr. Klein is lawyer by trade, he can afford it*—and left.

"Everything go alright, hon?" Irv asked through canvas, approaching after Mr. Klein's leave. Previously sitting on a folding chair nearby, reading from a newspaper. Listening distress calls, should Mr. Klein get too rough.

"Yes." He finished, he paid, he went home.

"Need me for anything else?" Anything code for *anyone*. *Pre-show* Johns.

"No. Thank you, Irv."

"Anytime."

As Irving departed from his duties there came an inquiring, "Hilly?"

"Come in," she took a pink robe draped over the baseboard and pulled it on as Vie stepped through a part in the sidewall between rooms.

"Is Johnny still here?"

Her hands paused, tying a bow at the waist, "Johnny? No. He's not here." Hadn't been all day—*except in her imagination*—as much as she would have liked it.

"Weren't you just with him?"

Hilly shook her head, curls loosening from a silver comb.

"*Huh*... Call me loony," she stepped around the vanity, pulled out the stool, and sat, "but, I swear I heard you," she cleared her throat, big brown eyes coy, "*sayin'* his name... *Quite loudly.*"

Hilly's cheeks bloomed. Laughing, "No! *No,* I did *not. Donnie,* Donnie Klein was his name... He was a very... *nice* man." A nice man who looked an awful lot like someone else she knew when she closed her eyes.

That was where Donnie Klein and Johnny's similarities started and ended. *With imagination.*

"*Mmm-hmm,* nice like a certain roustabout you're always sneakin' around with?"

"We aren't-we don't *sneak.*"

He visits her *sometimes.* Yes, it is usually during after hours, when there is not another John in sight. Alone, as long as they wish. When he can take his time and enjoy that time he has. No rush. No need for urgency.

When else should he visit her tent? He can't see her during show hours whenever he wants... *not every day.* Only recently had he snuck away from work before she went on stage. Or, when *she* would propose they go back to her room between shows. A rarity. Hardly ever.

Vie nodded, agreeing, "No, you *are* right. You two don't sneak. Gallivantin' up and down the midway, real innocent-like. Sittin' on the bally, chatting over supper where everyone can see."

"So," she laughed. "We talk. Am I forbidden to talk to him?"

She put up a hand, somehow maternal after the playful teasing. "You and Johnny have been friendly lately. And you know what your mama used to say." Vie straightened, elongated her neck, lifted a brow, in the fashion of Jezzie Ettinger, and recited huskily: "*You can't catch feelings for a John. What you are feeling isn't real when you lay with them. Being intimate will do that to a woman, make her think she's in love. And they don't love you. A John will never love you. All they want is to spend time and money between your legs. Remember girls,*" she shook her finger adamantly, "*they're just another customer.*" Vie brushed a strand of curls behind her cousin's ear. In her usual tone she worried, "I don't want you gettin' hurt is all. I've seen it too many times with Daze. *Too much, too often.*"

With gentle, though unintended truculence she broached, "What about you and Sunny?"

"Sunny was never a John." Dark hair swayed as she shook her head.

"Really?" *Hilly hadn't known that.*

Sunny and Vie got together so quickly after joining de la Llum. Married within months. She assumed since the age of fourteen—*seven, seven years they have been married already*—how their relationship began. *Maybe she shouldn't have.*

"Not even once." She smoothed out her skirt, smirking. "Muckers talked for us in the beginning remember?"

Hilly groaned.

"Drunk, peeping behind the curtain. Reserved space up front by the stage for men payin' extra. Then Dawn brought Sunny over from the Single-O's." The smile on Vie's face was one of true bliss as she clutched her stomach, *as if stifling butterflies.* "He was *so* funny. I couldn't keep to my steps. He'd be over in the corner makin' faces, imitating the men in the crowd. And he *never* watched us like they did. Never stared at our tits, or tilted his head, *you know that way men do.*"

To get a better look at the rear carriage or search for a hint of hair or pink flesh beneath shifting panties.

"No, he didn't." Hilly agreed.

A professional talker—*little as someone might believe when witnessing a goofy man such as he is.*

When there's a tip to build, Sunny is the man to call on. He will do it right, or not at all.

"That's how it started. *He made me laugh.* Whether I was out front, on stage dancing, or stopping for breaks on the road. He could always make me laugh." She sighed, looked at Hilly, "And he *never* tried to get into my bed. Payin' or not. *Only* spent time together, and over that time, I…" she smiled, looking gorgeous, "fell in love with him… Our first time was our wedding night."

"Aww," Hilly couldn't help but croon, *"how romantic."*

"It was. *He's so sweet*," a light laugh, *"And* the best I've ever had."

"Really?" She had to ask, "Why?"

With delicate, consuming slowness, and in the same instant all at once, a smile formed, "Because he loves me."

Sudden tears pooled in Hilly's eyes. A desperation bloomed in her chest. Heart weeping in the presence of these genuine words, longing to experience such a love as her fortunate cousin has had over the years.

"You're lucky to have him," the lump in her throat did not affect her voice.

So pretty, so happy. "I wouldn't trade the old lug for anyone else."

They weren't perfect. No relationship is without problems, Hilly wasn't daft enough to believe in the *'ever-after'* endings of her dime novels. But what the pair did have was happiness. A light switching on or off when one or the other entered or left the room.

Sunny made Vie laugh to forget the lewd jeers of men; she, and his daughter Sheri made him tender and sweet. A give and take, truly beautiful to witness.

Hilly felt she would give anything she had, just to have the love of a good man. One who would hold her at night, wipe away her tears, protect her.

Sometimes she wondered if Johnny could be that person. He was gentle toward her in ways she didn't see him with others. Like Sunny to Vie, Johnny made Hilly laugh, and smile.

Each time those warm sensations built in her belly, her mother's voice would arise, and remind her, *he's just another customer.*

And, don't forget, *men aren't* friends *with* whores. Not friends, not lovers.

Daze wasn't the only one to be fooled by a John. Hilly caught herself dreaming of one man or another often in her teen years. Hoping he would come back another night before the carnival left forever. Hoping he would come to her, tell her all of the things she longed for. *I love you.* Visualizing in her mind, their lives together.

Her very first kiss. Lips pressed to lips. Making love for hours the night after he whisked her away from the life of hooking. Married the next day, maybe that very night. Soon after, or perhaps in a year or two, *Hilly was never certain what she wanted*, she would find out she was with child. It would be a little boy who looked like his father. Just like the man who rescued her. Loved her enough to do such a thing. To risk his future on love, for her.

Only to be left disappointed, hurt, when none of those ideals came to be.

She would find someone to love one day. She believed in it… Wanted *to believe in it.*

Men don't fall in love with whores. Can't be friends with one either.

Vie and Sunny are an oddity, one belonging on display in the Ten-In-One. A once in a lifetime sight to behold.

Maybe men only fall in love with women like Vie. Certainly not those like herself. Or it would have surely happened by now. Not once.

At present, she *did* greatly enjoy Johnny's company. Even if Vie might think the relationship a bad idea, she could still have a good time with him. No real harm in it. And if he were to continue visiting her tent at night, could she turn him away?

Just another John.

Hilly exhaled slowly.

"I'm sorry if I said something, Hills."

"No. You're right, and… *I know.*"

"Doesn't mean you can't have a good time with him," Vie's words echoed her previous thoughts. "He *is* wickedly handsome," she laughed. *He is that, but it's not the only reason Hilly enjoys his company.* "I'm gonna go check on Sheri. She took off runnin' for the dress tent after I gave her those silks we picked up. Bet there's three blouses and a dress all sewed up and ready to wear."

"Isn't she in the Ten today?"

"Cops up and shut us down for the day. *Maybe even longer than that.*"

"Why?"

"Sheri said we were closed. Didn't know nothin' more."

"Hmm." Before Vie could turn, Hilly suddenly remembered, "Did you need Johnny for something? You came in asking after him."

"Oh! Right. Daze says there's somethin' wrong with her bed. Says the rousties must have dropped it and knocked a screw loose." Vie shrugged, "Who knows? *Oh*, and the pole in her room is tilted. Always nits to pick with her," she shook her head. "Will you let him know? *Next time you see him?*" A ghost of a smile formed on her small, dark red lips. One that said she didn't have to ask, she *knew* Hilly would see him soon. Within the hour even.

"I'll tell him."

"Okay, see you at lunch."

"Bye."

Hilly lounged against her arms a moment, gazing around the tent. Pennants hung on the side wall shared with Daze.

The Famous American Circus, *Hilly's birthplace.* Lady Freida's Fabulon, Cirque de L'air, Corbin Amusements, P. T. B Carnival & Company, Hartford Traveling Circus, and de la Llum. All home, for a season, or many, throughout her life.

Vie moved about her room, shuffling papers, closing a trunk before heading out. Daze sat on her bed, the frame squeaked. Kept squeaking.

"Get yer pants off!"

"I'm tryin'."

Kissing, loud smacking ones. Once moans arose Hilly's hearing shut off all sound in that direction.

A bell dinged: *Hercules. One thousand points, we have a winner!*

The boys, enjoying the day off. They will be drunk before supper. Emptied of the last of their hooch. She hoped none would visit her tonight… *Johnny the one exception.*

You can't help yourself. Her mind returned to him so often lately. Even with a John, she thought of him. Fantasized about him, that *he* gripped her hips, sinking calloused fingers into her skin. Delving inside her. His image made her cry out in pleasure. Not the John, not what he did, not his hands, not how he worked himself inside her, not his face. His breath, his voice.

She wanted to see him.

Grinning, she jumped from bed, cleaned up, and got dressed.

Workers clustered the backyard's edges, one pair tossed a baseball, a group waited as a man hammered two tent stakes into the dirt, preparing a game of horseshoes. Hilly could hear all, if not most of the roustabouts up front, rowdy and laughing as usual. Children played nearby, no doubt at the joints or begging for a ride on the carousel.

Otis straightened up the cook tent: stacking plates, pouring stale coffee out of cups into a pile of sawdust, and scrubbing utensils left over from breakfast. Lunch steamed on the stovetop and smoked on the griddle.

Across the sea of tents, Hilly could make out someone juggling—*trying to*—in the shade of the caravans. From this distance she couldn't get a good view of a face, only a thin male form tossing balls, fumbling, and bending to retrieve them.

By telltale descriptors of dark clothing and light hair she deduced the man was Lucky.

Of the younger spectrum of troupers, only the lone sword swallower, and the towheaded roustie, Blake, has equally or fairer hair as she. Stub, Ron, and other men of a certain age cannot help their snowy heads. Most of the older ladies indebted dye to hide the grey.

Tip number four in last month's *VVV* magazine—*Vivacity, Vigor, Vitality.* Women of a certain age—*beyond reproductive years, the editors meant*—or those such as Lucky whose locks pale before true seniority, should dye hair to appear younger.

Youth is Health, and Health is beauty.

She took a right around the sleep quarters, passing between the Kootch and Ten-In-One.

On the bally, Varlyn spoke with Claude, a Single-O talker. He and Lance trade shifts between the Midway and Singles occasionally.

"Evenin', Chere," Varlyn waved.

Hilly smiled, returning the gesture.

Sweat glistened on both men's foreheads. Beading above their brows and dripping along the path from temple to cheek. Stains of moisture darkened shirt collars, pooled in elongated ovals under Claude's arms near to the waist.

She could only imagine how the rousties took to the heat. Varlyn and Claude would have spent most of the day in the shade of a tent. The rousties labor under the sun no matter the task.

Instead of taking another right up the midway, Hilly kept her path straight, heading for the concessions which appeared open, not yet shuttered after the untimely shutdown.

"Nylee, sweetheart be careful," Vincent stood beside the carousel, dressed to the nines in one of many historic show costumes. A grey-blue vest with silver buttons over a bishop-sleeved shirt ruffling at the cuff. Blotches dampened the sleeves, the densest along the underside of his forearms.

"Incoming, pretty lady!"

The jockey's warning saved Hilly from either kicking Helda onto the gravel with her shin or being knocked on her behind by Nylee.

The older girl clutched briefly at Hilly's skirt as she ran, hiding from the tiny three-year-old in clumsy pursuit. Short chubby legs wobbled as any toddlers would, these especially small, nearer in length to a one-year-old babe. She also held the skirt, peering from one side to another at Nylee, giggling raptly between breaths.

"Heldie, come here honey," Rolan, her daddy, called with a wave.

At his scratchy voice, she screamed out joyously and ran into open arms.

Elvi had not been far behind the initial chase, and instead of tagging her identical sister, deeming her *it*, she danced circles around Hilly before panting and grinning her way back to the carousel.

Hilly laughed watching their play.

Vincent approached, ready to corral his sisters back to the enclosure of the ride.

"I apologize. *Girls, you should be more careful.*" The tone neither stern, nor scolding their behavior. Hilly didn't think the older brother capable of such a thing.

She held up a hand at the unnecessary words, "It's fine."

His eyes were grateful for the understanding. That Hilly, a *Normal* woman, did not shriek when the *Sick* children ran at her, touched her. Most might have fainted. Fell to their knees in horror.

They are little girls. Innocent children.

Behind Vincent, Hilly noticed the third of the trio of sisters sitting atop a white horse on the carousel. The reigns thumped softly, urging the still animal to go faster.

She lifted her head, eyes bright, teeth gleaming out of an overlarge grin. One so big it seemed to consume the small face. She waved.

Hilly returned it, and continued forth.

"Where are you going looking so nice on our day off?"

The jockey's dark eyes made an appreciative pass over her figure. Observatory rather than sexual. No ocular hands palmed her ass or breasts, testing for ripeness before purchase.

"Nowhere," she shrugged innocently.

"To see a *man*, perhaps?" by man, he meant Johnny. *Even a greenie knows.*

Was she truly so transparent?

"*Maybe.*" Yes.

"Have fun."

Hilly tried not to smile too enthusiastically. He *could* be busy. A closed carnival did not necessarily connote spare time.

Doesn't mean a man won't get thirsty doing it, she reasoned.

"Ruth?" Hilly called, peering over the high concession counter.

"Yeah?" the older woman adjusted thick glasses, "What can I do for ya, honey?"

"Can I get two sodas please?"

"Sure thing."

When she turned for the ice box Hilly realized her pockets were empty. "Ruth, I'll be right back-"

"Forget your money?"

Hilly could only give a single nod.

"Take 'em, dear. It's a hot one today." One wrinkled lid winked over a brown eye with the beginnings of a cataract.

She smiled, "Thank you."

With a chilled glass neck in each hand, she headed for the Gate. More specifically the wheel next to it.

Four of twelve seats had been removed. Those remaining swung on the bottom half of the circular framework—common procedure when not in use, or overnight, *most importantly during harsh winds.* Seven would be taken off in that case, the ride is less likely to tip when not so top heavy.

Elevated voices climbed atop one another for dominance, rising over music playing from a portable radio positioned on a toolbox.

Not all rousties accounted for after all. Napping, gone to town, waiting in line for lunch.

Few stood, most sat on overturned crates and barrels.

"Still can't believe he hit it," one said in awe, looking over his shoulder.

"How's it feel? Freak beat your high score."

No response, Hilly suspected a sneer.

Sunny took a sip from his flask and offered it to—*for a moment she did not recognize who*, until his head angled to the left, exposing a second set of eyes, nose, and lips. Billy and Morty.

Billy adamantly shook his head no at the tipped decanter and waved it away with both hands. Nose bunched at the smell. The duo shared a laugh, Morty stared far and away, until fixing on Hilly, which she did not notice. Too focused on biting back a smile when Johnny spotted her.

"Oh, I love this song!" Blake near shouted in delight, whirling in the crowd to turn up the volume.

A nasal vocalist whined the words:

>   'Oh my honey, she drives me cray-zee

Oh my girl, she's got me wiiiiild
Oh my darling, she's a beauty
Oh that hearty girl is mine!

Yeah, you got me in a . . . whirl girl
Got my arms in a biiiind
Got my sleeves wrapped up . . . tight girl
Oh my girl you got me wiiiiild'

"Surprised they still play this shit. Guy stole the title from Babyface himself, Frankie *Barnum Damned* Cochran!"

'Oh you drive me craaaaay-zee
Got me runnin' all the time
Got me bouncin' off the walls girl
Got me so mad I cannot hide-

That you're my one and only
You're my baby
You're my honey

You're the one I . . . call for
You're the one I . . . scream for
You're the one I call at night!'

"N-n-no. He-he-he w-went to ca-court, a-and huh-had to c-ch-change it." Billy corrected.
He knows his stuff, Hilly admired.

'Yeah, you got me in a . . . whirl girl
Got my arms in a biiiind
Got my sleeves wrapped up . . . tight girl
Oh my girl you got me wiiiiild

Yeah my baby
Yeah my honey
Got me bouncin'

Off the walls girl
Can't control me
Can't constrict me
'Cause I love my girl
That girl is miiiiine!'

"No, he didn't! It's right there in the song!"

Billy nodded arguably, "Th-the s-song is cu-called 'Cu-c-crazy fu-for mmm-my ga-girl, *tha-that g-girl is mm-mine.*'"

"My point! He stole it!"

"B-but it-it's in par-parenthe-ses. Th-that's a-a-allowed."

The roustie glared, jaw set askew. "... I'm goin' ta lunch."

'People tell me
That I'm crazy
That I'm zany
And I'm loopy
I'm not loony
That girl is miiiiine

No, no, no
That
Girl
Is
Miiiiiine!'

When Harvey 'Harv' Jackson's one and only hit—*before being wrapped in the jacket he so vibrantly sang of*—tapered off, the broadcast went into a commercial for *'Hughes Brand Shoe Polish.'*

Frankie sang the copyrighted Hughes Brand jingle, *"That Girl is Mine,"* beneath the announcer's voice:

'Fine as a fettle
Fit as a fiddle
My baby is in tip-top shape
From her head, down to her pretty little feet
Oh, that girl is mine!

doo do do do do doo do do'

"Sorry Frankie," *click*, Johnny switched off the knob.

"I like that song," Blake mumbled, lower lip stuck halfway out. "Don't git why so many don't like it."

"He didn't write the damn thing!" Sunny informed loudly.

"... He didn't?"

"No," came from all around the young man.

"Dumb shit," Angus grunted.

Blake frowned. "Well, I didn't know! *Jeez*. Sorry! I *still* like it though," he added, snatching the hat off his head and heading to the backyard. Lunch, *or* to escape the accusing stares of senior cohorts.

Men whistled at the incoming female.

"Here comes your biggest fan, Mr. Rollercoaster Man," one snickered. *It may have been Sunny.*

"Hu-h-hi H-hilly!" Billy waved shyly.

She sent him a smile.

Extending a still cool, and sweating bottle, "I thought you might be thirsty."

Hoots of, *"Oooooo!"*

"You bet he is!"

"Ya feelin' a little doll dizzy Johnny?"

"I sure am! Wooo!"

"Shut it!" Gently, "That's mighty fine of you." Johnny popped off the lid with his thumb. "Thanks, Girly," he smiled, taking a swig of the drink, leaving the bottle nearly half empty.

"And you didn't bring me one? Your *very own* cousin-in-law, your *family*. I'm crushed." Sunny feigned clutching his chest, "Simply crushed, right in the ol' ticker."

"Here," she laughed, offering the second bottle.

"No, no. Don't want no *pity* soda-pop. You know what? I'll just have to get me my own. Thank *yoooou* very much," spinning on his heel, he swooped an arm around Billy's shoulders, turning the boy. "Come on, Billy-Buddy, I can see when I'm unwanted. What do ya say we beat the crowd and get ourselves some grub before it's gone?"

The young man nodded, following along, first waving to Hilly and Johnny. Several others followed. Hilly granted full attention to the roustie in front of her before witnessing every man leave.

"So, ya heard about closin' huh? And first thing you do is bring me somethin' ta drink?" His eyes seemed to smirk.

"It's hot out. I thought you might need something to cool you off."

"That I do," he wiped the back of his neck with a rag and took another drink. "Real nice of you ta think of me."

Hilly's lips parted.

Angus stood from a crate, knees cracking. "What about me? I don't get nothin' on a hot day?"

Her soda remained unopened. Tempted to hand it over, if only to quiet the man taking slow creeping steps.

"Why don't you be a good little lady and go get me one of them pops."

"Get it yerself," Johnny grumbled, looking down at him, fingers tapping on the bottle. Audibly thumping the glass.

"Nah. It's a dame's duty ta run off and fetch for a man, always has been. Same as a bitchly dog," he stated. Directly to Hilly, "But I guess you ain't no *ordinary* little lady." Thick, sun-burnt lips peeled apart, eyes deadpan and cold. "Here," he pulled a dollar bill from his pocket, holding it between index and middle finger, "get me somethin' ta drink. I'll even let ya keep the spare scratch."

Johnny noted Hilly's shrunken stance, unease causing her shoulders to slouch and arms to cross.

Shoving off of the big wheel's tower, *"Angus."*

"That not enough?" A step closer, another dollar, two flapped in his tweezed grasp. "What? My money not *good enough* for you?"

"Leave her be."

"How about I give you a little more, then you can spread them snow-white cheeks for me instead?"

"That's enough!"

"Oh, it's enough? Enough for me ta fuck her till her ass leaks? If you say so *bossman,* let's go, *Girly!"*

Angus reached for her arm with such haste he knocked the intersecting soda bottle, and sent it soaring from Johnny's rising hand.

Glass crashed onto the seat parked over the loading line, littering sparkling shards and brown liquid in the shape of an erupting star.

Fast as the bottle's flight, Johnny took the large man by the neck and flattened his body to the ground.

Hilly clutched her breast. The soda struck beside her foot.

"Now you listen ta me you sonofabitch! Yer gonna find somethin' ta busy yourself with *right* now, *far* away from here, or you're gonna pack yer shit, and blow." Angus's eyes went white around pinpricks of color, spittle stretched between gasping and grimacing lips. "But there's one thing yer gonna do for certain. You ain't *never* talkin' ta her like that again." His tight hand thrust Angus's neck forward to whisper, *"You understandin' me?"*

"Johnny, please," she implored, eying the back end. *For Dawn.* She didn't want him getting in trouble over this. Not because of her.

He turned Angus loose.

"Go on, git!"

Angus's boots scuffed saw-dusted earth as he scampered to his feet and took off.

At the midway he puffed his chest, coughing and rubbing his throat, "Yer-yer gonna regret that!"

"Git!"

He disappeared in the direction of the Single-O's.

Breathing hard, Johnny glanced over his shoulder. Gaze and timber both lowering, "You alright?"

"Y-yes."

"Shouldn't'a talked that way to you." Finally, he met her eyes, "Sorry if…" disconnecting again, "if I scared you or anythin'."

"No, I'm fine."

No trembling, no fear of him, startled, but fine. Satisfied with what he saw in her eyes he took a glance at her hands: no bottle. A puddle formed beneath her right foot. *"Ah Hel,"* he took those few steps to the wet, rocking seat, and sighed. "I'm sorry Girly, made a mess all over," he said, despite Angus being to blame.

She tried to impede the apology, "It's nothing, really."

"No, no, I'll get ya a couple bottles next time I go inta town."

"You don't have to."

"I know I don't," he faced her. "No one's tellin' me ta do it. *I* want to. *I* made the mess, *I'll* be the one ta clean it up. *What's so funny?"*

Hilly began to smirk, then laugh against her fingers as he went off.

Shaking her head, "Ruth gave me the sodas for nothing."

"... Well shit, why didn't you start with that?" a broken huff of a laugh left his throat.

"You wouldn't let me finish saying anything you horse's ass!" she shoved his shoulder, barely swaying him. The heat of his skin lingered on her palm.

"*Yeeeah*," he grinned, "Kinda do that a lot don't I?"

She shrugged. If he did, she didn't notice, or care. One of the two.

"Well, sorry all the same. Guess I owe *Ruth* the soda pops."

She doubted Ruth expected a favor in return for her charity.

"*Ugh*," he groaned, "Gonna have ta clean this up. Seats get sticky enough. No use startin' that way."

"It would keep the kids from falling out," she quipped.

Johnny laughed. His smile etched little lines in his cheeks.

The humor faded. "You should head back. Gonna be at this awhile."

"Okay," she agreed. Before leaving she pulled down one shoulder, stood on her toes, and pressed a kiss to a stubbly cheek. She hugged his neck tight. "Thank you."

For defending her. For not allowing another man to treat her like what she so often felt. A warm hollow to be filled. Traded like baseball cards, sold as cattle.

With that, she took the path so many had taken earlier. Down the midway to the backyard.

Until she disappeared between the tents, Johnny watched, touching where her lips had been.

HELPING HAND

∽ SHILZIE ∾

Men with badges are bad to carnies.

Threaten. Demand money. Run shows out of town. Arrest and hurt people for no good reason.

Whisper in black cars outside the Gate. Scribble de la Llum's name across the top of notebooks, underline, once then twice.

"Write this down. Tomorrow, I want a list of names, every adult traveling with the show."

"No children?"

"Do you have reason to believe a child is responsible for the murders, Mitchell?"

"... No."

"Men and women. How long he or she has worked the circuit, previous employment, hometowns-we'll check in on criminal records. Keep in mind men age twenty to thirty-five..."

"Why twenty to thirty-five?"

"In murder cases, the perpetrators are typically males of that age... I want to look into this show's history. There may have been prior incidents. We need the location of their winter quarters, associates in the business, supply vendors."

"Think it was one of them?"

"A strong possibility. Though, if the suspect is with the show, I don't believe the owner knows who did it."

"That hairy broad would lie to protect her kind, even a murderer."

"No need for name calling. She was sincere when I showed her the pennant."

"How do you know?"

"In her eyes. Eyes don't lie. She doesn't suspect a killer could be right under her nose."

More murders. Lots more Detective Wydell didn't tell Mama

about. Not only the two teens and their families. Others. More discovered every day. Found along a trail leading to Jackson. *This town.*

The detective planned to come back tomorrow with papers, photographs, and news clippings in a nice and neat file chronicling the recent deaths. He might take Mama to the police station and ask her questions. Show her telegraph slips of communication with other stations, other policemen, confirming the carnival paid for lots on privately owned land, filed for permits to work city land, or passed straight through. Stopping only to refuel or stock up on supplies.

He will interrogate Mrs. de Barcsy, working toward a confession, for her to freely give up the man, or men murdering across three states. *Three, he's connected to the carnival so far.*

A working man sits first chair on Joseph Wydell's list of suspects. Sick, he's found in his thirty-seven-year career do not often commit murders, though charged with the crime more often than Normies.

This Normal man, or men, were criminals most likely before shacking up with the carny. An easy escape from previous crimes. Slipping through the cracks into new states, traveling miles away, across the country in months. Never to be caught. Hidden in the marvel and fancy of whimsy and glee.

Under cover of darkness this killer—motive yet unknown—goes stabbing and mutilating. Mauling until dead. *Strung up on headboards, from rafters.* Left to suffer until succumbing to blood loss, exposed organs rotting, or being eaten by pests and rodents.

Shilzie didn't want to think about it anymore.

It's why she asked Vincent if she and her sisters could ride Carrie.

If Evro couldn't start her up, she could still sit on Falada and pretend he galloped around and around. Sitting on the pretty white horse made Shilzie forget the strange men with badges and funny hats.

Evro *did* start her up: *for one ride.*

If Mama hollered at him, he planned to tell her it was only a test run.

We're closed? Oh gee, Mrs. Boss Lady Ma'am I didn't know! Forgive me. After all, I'm just a greenie, boy howdy, I see the error of my ways. Never again Ma'am never, I will be careful next time, honest!

"How far along is Sabina now?" he asked.

"Coming up on four months," Rolan answered.

"Pick any names yet?" Evro hung onto the pole beside Falada.

Shilzie looked at his hands. A ring for every finger, sometimes two. One pushed down to the first knuckle, the other higher up, halfway to a fingernail.

Gold, silver, etched with designs, some with crystals or other colored stones. Black and red mostly. On the hand hanging at his side, he wore a thin silver ring with a cloudy blue-violet stone mid-pinky finger.

Pretty. The jewelry pushed thoughts of murder and police and the hot sun even further away in her mind.

"*No*," Rolan's nose wrinkled. "Sabi thinks it's bad luck. This one," he patted his sleeping daughter's tummy, "didn't have a name for a whole week after she was born."

Evro chatted with Rolan as she reached near Falada's nose and touched the jockey's jewelry.

At the prodding of little fingers he asked, "You like my rings?"

He allowed her to take his hand in for closer inspection.

Shilzie grinned, nodding.

"Nylee, darling, *please* slow down," Vincent watched her sister closely since she got off the carousel. Expecting a fall, scraped palms or knees, a fainting spell. Splinters when she took a turn around the fence. Swinging wide off of the pointed picket to keep up speed. Thirty minutes of running and swinging, hopping and dancing.

Nylee didn't listen. Breathing too hard, giggling too loud, too focused on staying ahead of her sister, of going as fast as her legs could muster.

"*OooooooWooWooWoo*," Elvi hooted softly, arms outstretched like an owl in flight, taking a left around the carousel, soaring after her sister.

"*MmmmmMmmMmmmm*," Nylee hummed between breaths, pumping thin arms.

"Here," Evro took the silver ring with the purple stone from his pinky, "let's see if this one fits you." A little big on the middle finger, he moved it to her thumb. Now it stayed in place. "There we go."

She smiled big, twirling the ring around by the stone. A glow of bright color within foggy edges. The moon beneath clouds. A full purple moon.

"My grandmother called it *fluorspar*," he told her, "She said it would protect those who wore it from danger."

She could use something like this *fluorspar*.

Protection from the person hurting customers.

The crooked man with the crooked smile during the crooked hour in his crooked shadow using his crooked knife.

The detective and his partner said someone died, and suspect one of the carnies did it. *Her family.* What if the men with badges are right? What if someone here killed that man last night? What if it was someone she knows?

Pulling from the vibrant stone she looked at those around her: Vincent, her sisters, Rolan and Helda, and Evro. She didn't want anything bad to happen. Not to anybody. They are all her family. That's what Mama says. That's what Shilzie believes.

Patricia watched the triplets while Vincent and Mama went into town. So did Sabina, Lavi, and her daughters. She'd known so many of these people the whole ten years in the show. What if one of them were killed?

Poor baby. She knows something's up.

Aloud he said, "How about you take care of it for me a while?"

Shilzie nodded, it would make her very happy, it would make her feel safe. And if she was safe, her loved ones would be safe. That's how it works. As long as she wore the ring, those around her would be protected by the purple stone. The stone is for protection, and that's what it will do.

Thump.

Shilzie and Evro turned at the sound.

"*Oooh…*" a gentle gust of wind. "*Owow*," Nylee's lips pursed, holding her left knee.

Ow! That hurt!

Nylee are you okay? Elvi ran up, patting her shoulder.

Owwie, owwie.

Vincent knelt beside his little sister in a matter of seconds.

"Oh, sweetheart," his furry hand brushed down the back of her head, "Are you alright? Let me see."

She held up a hand, showing him a bubble of blood on the tip of her index finger. A tiny bloom of the same bright crimson blotted her dress at the knee. The more she moved and rocked, the more dots appeared. With them, smears and streaks.

"She okay? Need me to get Sabina?" Rolan asked, concerned.

"No," Vincent held the underside of Nylee's knee in the cradle of his hand. He studied the scrape and wiped off dirt and grit with tender care. "I should clean it and get her changed. *Come here sweet girl,*" he lifted her into his arms.

Elvi crooned worriedly, reaching for Nylee's dirty hand.

"Elvi, we will return soon."

Is Nylee okay, Shilzie? Where's Vincent taking her?

She's okay.

But where are they going?

My knee hurts. I'm up really high!

"Take her with you, I can watch Shilzie until you get back," Evro offered.

Her brother's eyes went from the girl in his arms, who still tapped her wound, uttering little *'ah, ah, ah's,'* at the pain, to Elvi looking at him with questions, and over to the third girl sitting on her favorite horse.

"Shilzie, do you want to stay with Evro?" he asked, allowing her to decide. Brotherly instinct did not *want* to leave Shilzie behind. He couldn't bear to be away from her, almost as much as she couldn't from him.

As much as she liked Evro, she readied to jump off of Falada and join her brother. A voice stopped her. Feelings.

Wanting something. Being sad. And mad. Hurt. That one most of all. From someone nearby.

Who is that? Why so sad?

Who is sad, Shilzie?

Owwie!

Shilzie nodded, she would stay.

Come with us!

Yeah! Maybe Vincent will let us play doctor!... My knee hurts. You two can be nurses!

I have to find him. He needs to not be sad anymore.

"Listen to Evro and Rolan."

"We've got her, don't worry about a thing," said Rolan.

With a nod, he started for the backyard, Nylee in his arms, and Elvi clutching the bottom of his vest.

Once Vincent was out of sight, Shilzie worked at unfastening her belt.

"Here you go sweetie," Evro helped her down and held her hand until she stepped off of the platform. "Careful."

Shilzie continued holding it. Pulled him.

Hurt, anger, sadness, blood, tears, pain. Old wounds. No trust.

I can't believe he would do such a thing.

"Shilzie? Where are we going?" He tossed a look over his shoulder.

Rolan shrugged, unable to follow without waking his daughter.

"Okay, we'll be right back."

Betrayed. Doesn't want to see him, and *only* wants to see him. Jealous, jealous, jealousy came to her. Hurt, hurt in his chest. Comfort in his company. He makes him want to smile, but he can't, it hurts to smile. He wants to talk to him again, doesn't want to see his face. Wants to see his face, his smile, his eyes. Wants to scream at him for what he did. Shout. Ask why, why did he do it? He hurt him. Why did he have to hurt him too? Thought he was different. Makes him feel. Connected. Wanted.

They came around the banner line and Shilzie saw whose emotions flowed through her. Emotions she knew, didn't know, felt through him, though never experienced herself. Not in this way.

SHOUT AT THE DEVIL
∼ MORGAN ∽

"*Nah, nah.* Yah gotta spread yur feet 'part furtha, you."

Morgan did as Varlyn instructed and widened his stance.

"Dat's it," he nodded, dreadlocks shifting, catching in his collar. "Try again."

Morgan threw the bean bag in his right hand upward, in the same instant attempting to toss the other in his left beneath it.

"Nah, not like dat," the Crab Man corrected.

As before, for the last half an hour, Morgan *caught* the toss to his right hand, *thrown too hard, too fast*, and allowed the sack arcing before his eyes to plummet to his feet. He *also* threw incorrectly. *Again.* After being told he did it all wrong to begin with.

"*I can't do it*," Morgan tossed the blue bag at the dirt and covered his face. A poof of dust sailed into the hot breeze.

He failed to learn on his own. Fumbling with an old leather set scavenged from the baggage trailer like a bumbling clown. Unlike a clown, there were no comedic intentions *each* and *every* time a bag bounced off his shoulder, hit the caravan, and ultimately landed in the dirt.

It looks so *easy*, he thought. Believing he could instantaneously rotate the three leather balls between his hands first try.

Varlyn and Wells can do it.

I *swallow swords and eat fire, of course* I *can juggle.*

Fucking idiot.

After twenty minutes of self-humiliation, he gave up and begrudgingly went in search of the Midway's barker, or the resident Crab Man. *Whoever Morgan encountered first.*

Only for his act. To learn a new craft was he able to summon the will to ask for help, and even *with* that help from a professional, he *still* failed.

How did he learn to swallow a sword with no guidance? Could

have died on his first attempt of shoving a spoon handle down his esophagus.

No, easy as can be.

Throwing three balls into the air and catching them? No. Not even two. He dropped *one* when first asking Varlyn for pointers.

"*Nah*, you gonna get it. Need practice. Yah tink I wake up jugglin' one day?" He motioned a cleft hand from the Ten's bally, "Give me dem sacks."

He sighed, swooped one hand, then the other, retrieving the stitched, bean-brimming spheres and placed them in Varlyn's palm. The Crab Man dropped two sacks beside his stunted legs.

With a single bag in hand, he held his forearms parallel to the stage, and his elbows close to his sides.

"Now, I know yah dun wanna juggle right 'way. But ya gotta practice, you." Varlyn tossed the red leather sack in an arc, hand to hand. Right to left. "Jus like wit yur swords, had'ta practice ta do it. Same with tha jugglin'." Left to right. Right to left.

He knew all of this. Stunts take practice, every feat in his performance he learned slowly to perfect. Hours, days, years of time.

Juggling seems so simple compared to others. Piercing flesh. Cutting. Eating glass. Regurgitation.

And I can't fucking do it! I can't concentrate, I keep dropping the balls. I can't fucking concentrate!

Because of *him*.

This newfound knowledge of his supposed *friend*.

Why inform Morgan? He spoke of so much else. Jokes and stories. Stories and jokes. Couldn't find somewhere during one of his tales of riding the rails from California to Washington, Washington to Minnesota, Minnesota to Oklahoma to inform him of his side business?

Selling himself to Johns during show hours. Were his goods for sale *after* as well? Allowing strange men to touch and use. Paid in dollar bills for intimacy.

The image wouldn't leave his mind.

Hunger. Pleasure. Want for more. Lust. Arousal reawakening at the front of the pat's slacks as the green bills slid up Evro's chest.

Morgan's empty stomach turned. Evro's lips, his incessantly

smiling mouth, around that man's…

"Practice like dat, jus one atta time," Varlyn's dark claws passed the bean bag back and forth, arching and across, arching and across. His eyes stayed with Morgan. Focused, practiced hands seeking each catch. "Here, try again." He tossed the red sack.

Morgan caught it, sighed, rubbed a thumb between his brow, and lightly tossed it without much enthusiasm.

"Higha, up ta yur eyes. Yup, dere ya go." The Crab Man approved the technique. "Jus like dat," he shrugged, *simple as that.* "When ya can do it with yer eyes close. Startin' with *eitha* ya hands. *Den* ya bring in anutha." He peeked at his watch. *Lunchtime with the missus.* "I gotta go, me. But you keep practicin' yeah? Den I show ya how ta do more."

"Thank you."

"Notta problem," he scooted off the stage and lowered into his wheelchair. "Take care, yeah?"

Morgan nodded and held up a hand as Varlyn wheeled off.

Alone again. With the damn juggling balls. He squeezed the bag in his hand until the beans scraped against one another.

I hate you. Stupid fucking things. Why can't I just juggle?!

"Shilzie honey, sweetie, *where* are you taking me? Vinnie's gonna be back soon I promise." a voice crawled beyond the Ten's Annex, down by the games, from the carousel. The voice warmed his ears before stabbing him in the chest.

The hairs on the back of his neck stood up, his arms broke out in gooseflesh despite the heat.

"Ugkee," *Lucky*, Shilzie tried to pronounce.

A small hand tugged at Morgan's scarred wrist. Recent wounds stung. Reluctantly, he turned. Only for the little girl. He knew who else he would be face to face with when he did so.

"Ugkee wan see yu Ev," she told *him*, now pulling the jockey forward. "Wan tahk tue yu."

Morgan's brow furrowed and lips tensed at the man.

"Well," *that fucking smile,* "not sure why Shilz dragged me over but-" fingers choked by rings wiped through the air.

Wipe all you want, scrub and scrub, my memory will never be cleaned of what you did.

"-Hi there. Been awhile." He swallowed with some trouble.

Good. Perhaps he knows. Knows what I *know he did.* Does.

"So, how you been?"

Morgan scoffed and turned.

"I say something?"

He took his jacket from the stage. The collar snagged a bulb framing the front and snapped it off. Littering rounded, jagged pieces of glass across his boot.

"Morgan-"

"Don't!" he warded off the jockey's advances with the jacket as he gathered the red, blue, and green bean bags.

"What's with the brush off? You never came by Carrie after the show last week. You've been ducking me at dinner."

"I said…" he reeled, stomping close enough for the jockey to feel his breath, *"don't.* Don't talk to me. I am *done* with that."

Shilzie waited where the pair initially stopped. Hands clasped above her belly.

Watching. *Observing* the men, as if understanding more than she should. More than she could possibly know.

"Don't talk to you?" laughter—*not of the humorous sort—* saturated his words. "You gotta tell me why. What did I do to get you so sore at me?"

He won't let up, he won't stop.

Disbelief gave him a good chuckle. "You want to know *why* I never showed up?" Facing him, he continued, tone searing like fire. *"I did.* I went to Carrie after my first show. *You,"* he pointed, fingernails digging into the seams of a bean bag, "weren't there."

Evro stepped back, brows drawn and listening.

"Some roustie was at the controls, do you remember that? You asked him to cover for you?"

Slowly, the jockey solved the mystery ending of this tale.

"You left your jacket and popcorn with Ruth at the concessions." Morgan licked quivering lips. *"The box truck.* I saw what you were doing." *Mouth on him, turning away to spit when he finished. To spit out that man's…* Morgan's stomach hurdled again. "What you were *paid* to do. Is that what this has been about? Was I your next mark?"

He rolled his eyes. *"Yeah.* I spend time with *all* my tricks. Sure you've seen the Kootchie girls hangin' around the lot with their Johns plenty of times over the years. After all, *they're* paid *to do the same thing.* Don't see you giving them grief."

Morgan shook his head. "You lied to me."

"About *what?*" he laughed the word. "You never asked. And how could I fit *that* into conversation? *Oh, by the way*, I hook on the side for extra greenbacks*, what's for supper?... Dawn* knows about it," he whispered, leaning in, *"I give her a cut of what I earn.* Just like the girls... What do you think I was up to when the show picked me up, huh? On a street corner, half naked in the cold, crossing my fingers and toes hoping for *a carnival* to come by and offer me a gig?... What does it matter anyhow?"

"*You* didn't tell me, and I had to find out like-" he bit back the tremble of his bottom lip and narrowed steely grey eyes against the sting of liquid. *It's not tears! I'm just fucking angry!* "Like *that.*"

"I didn't think you would mind." *Didn't about his Gypsy heritage.* "I don't-I *truly* don't understand why you are *so* upset."

"I-" *don't care,* Morgan started, swaying with shifting feet. *I don't! I don't fucking care!* He lied to himself.

Evro listened, waited, didn't blink his big brown eyes.

"Because..."

Words *could* have described why he felt so betrayed.

Words, a funny concept. The deadly mix of frustration, anger, and hurt drained him dry of articulation.

Morgan could only react.

No thought to act, no inclination came to mind before throwing down the jacket and juggling balls. Before logical thinking and planned speech could stop his hands, they cupped Evro's jaw.

Fear, which has staunched Morgan's actions all of his years, watched as he pulled the jockey's face down—*missing its chance to halt, to forbid such brazenness*—and press his lips against his mouth.

Evro staggered, unprepared, stunned, wide-eyed the first few moments before letting his lids drift closed.

Their mouths parted.

Morgan breathed shakily. Heart racing as betrayal swelled alongside fondness, admiration, and torment. Fear covered its face, rocking in the corner of his mind.

What did I do? Don't look at him! Why did I do that?! Leave, fucking leave! Did I really do that? Why did I do that?! Fucking pathetic. Grabbing him like I know what the fuck I'm doing. Just fucking go back to your caravan before you do something else. Fucking idiot!

"Wish you would have let me know you felt that way sooner," Evro spoke softly, leaning close until their foreheads touched. "You're a great kisser," he smirked.

"Stop," he shoved. "Don't fucking mock me. *Don't."* Tears rippled on the surface of his eyes.

"I-I'm not…" he dropped the jests. "…Morgan. I didn't know… I thought you only wanted to be friends. Nothing more than that."

"Why?"

The aftermath of the box truck returned. The anger, the hate for everything, everyone. People hate and inflict pain on others, use them for their own gain. The cycle never ends.

"Why what?"

"Why did you do it?"

"Money…" Evro shrugged, "I've been doing it for years."

"Not that… why did you-" his lips trembled. Losing nerve, *"Never mind."*

Morgan scooped up his things.

"Why did I do what?"

Let me go! "Please move."

Humiliation. *Morgan does have a friend after all! Several. A whole group of pals to meet for drinks every afternoon after work.* Fear. Panic. Self-hate. *Misery isn't the only one who loves company!*

"Tell me. *It's alright."*

"You…" *are sad and lonely and more worthless than he could have ever imagined. He's going to wish he never wasted time on you. Why can't I just fucking speak?! Just say it! I can't fucking explain it! How can I explain what I don't fucking understand! I'm going fucking crazy!* "I can't!"

"Try." A warm hand went to his shoulder. Without menace, without cruel intent.

Instinct warned him to shrug it away. Unaccustomed to touch. *Fearful of it.*

"You… talked to me," tears fell. *You put in effort to make me laugh. Did anything you could to make me smile even a little. A scoff gave you satisfaction. You made the mute, the bystander, the outsider express* amusement *of all unfathomable phenomena.* "Then you… I saw you… why did you do that to me?"

"I… I'm sorry." Fingers of silver, gold, and colorful gems rose tentatively, touching strings of grey hair falling over Morgan's face, weaving through to sink around his temple. "I didn't mean to hurt you."

You did. You and everyone else. Everyone meant to care for me.

He had no right to blame him, but this man is the only person who Morgan felt may truly care.

For the first time in his life. Someone who may give a fuck if he were to die unexpectedly. Someone who would miss him: Morgan, *the person.* Not the employee, the performer, the means to a continued family line.

His face burned hot in Evro's hand.

The pulse branching from temple into scalp bulged, thrummed. Evro brushed at tears with his thumb.

This man is so much more fragile than Evro first suspected. So damaged beneath the surface. Real pain. Scars as old, as new, as those on his arms. A constant bleeding wound.

His fair skin and attractive face merely a Persian rug covering a splintered floor. Weathered with rot, scuffed, and creaking, with a jagged hole where past boots stomped through the weak point.

Tears dripped off of Morgan's eyelashes in perfect synced droplets onto his cheeks. Dewdrops from a flower during the morning thaw. And like a petal under pressure, he wilted against Evro's hand. Clutching his wrist and gasping a breath from the warmth of his palm.

He wanted someone to trust, to believe. Someone who might hold him. His heart ached to be held close. The warmth of another. Arms that were not his own to wrap around a shuddering body. Someone he could empty himself into. Let go. Let his pain be seen, and mended with words, with a touch. Not left alone to suffer in silence, to drown in memory. To awaken in fear.

Someone who would let him cry without need for explanation, simply allowed to feel, *as Evro did now.*

So tiresome to do it alone. *He was so tired.*

"*Shh,*" he soothed. "Come here," and brought Morgan's face to his shoulder, pulling him into his arms. Folding him in tight. "*It's okay.*"

The man with the Devil's lucky streak. The man who did not fear death or falter to physical pain trembled under the sweltering heat of the south. He clutched the man, the Gypsy, the prostitute, the ride jock, as tears soaked his jacket. Gasping against sobs during the first embrace of his life. The only hug, the only comfort from another human being's arms he ever received during a twenty-four-year existence.

"I don't know who hurt you so badly," Evro whispered, petting white and red strands, "but I'm going to help you forget about them. Okay?" His own words thickened with emotion the harder he squeezed. Until he could feel the speed of Morgan's heart thumping against his sternum, until the pressure of his arms slowed the quivering, soothed the tears.

Shilzie left the men alone in front of the bally.

Twirling the ring around her finger, smiling. Knowing she did something good today. On a day starting so badly, she made it better for someone who needed it.

STRIKE

ᘓ ? ᘒ

The carnival's heart ceased to beat by lunchtime. Finishing touches showed signs of life, stuttering the beat into a weak rhythm. Tightening of screws. Bulbs. Nails. Refueling rides that would not spin.

For patrons that would not arrive.

Metal shrieked, brushing against itself in the dark. Spooked, afraid of its own shadows. Cages, bars, boney windows.

The Wheel of Fortune spun, clacking its toggles against a wooden arrow.

Seats dangling from chains like hanged men jingled behind the one in the dark. He waited here, amongst the chains. The cool steel rippled in his grasp.

The imposing Shadow's Eye opposite him. Its strutted frame brought to mind a sort of ribcage. Seen through the eye of a kaleidoscope. Fortifying protection around a delicate center.

Easily broken, if he wished it so. To send its hearts, the little children, falling, flailing. Angels with broken wings. Cracking heads, snapping spines against the unforgiving density of the ground below.

How they would scream. Little rabbits in distress. Squealing. Unaware of the trap willingly, *happily* stepped into. Right into the camouflage of danger. So innocent. Safe they are told.

Yes, death can be sweet before it devours.

Tonight wasn't for the children.

Tonight is special. Tonight, the shadow's eyes locked on only one. This one should be in bed. This one shouldn't have come out after dark. This one would regret it.

"Fuckin' asshole… Thinks he can tell me what to do," the drunken man took a swig from his bottle, clumsily avoiding support posts. "Ain't scared of you. Ain't scared of *shiiit!*"

The shadow stepped forth. Chains shivering.

"And that damn gash… what my money? *Won't take my money.* My money's no good... Bet I'd give it to her better than he does," he set down the bottle. Unbuttoned his trousers and pulled out a knob of pink, wrinkled flesh. "Johnny's *Girly*," spittle clung to stubble as he laughed. "Split her wide and fill her up till she's drippin'… *ahh*," he groaned, pissing a spray of yellow onto the ride's seat.

The splatters began to pool, running to one corner and filling like a glass of hot, steaming tea.

The thin silhouette of Hercules passed over the shadow's face, flexed arms became bulging horns sprouting from his head across the dirt.

Tools leaned against a shuttered game joint in neat rows. Soldiers ready for inspection, ready for duty, ready to fight and die for their cause. One trooper stood out in particular. Chest puffing at attention.

Inspired, he reached for a spiraled handle.

"Tear that ass good and proper. That's right… *ahhhh*."

A step. Two, three, four, he neared. Swinging the pendulous implement at his side, clenching his fingers around smooth wood.

He shook his pecker, sending droplets across the front of his pants. Bent for his drink and turned.

"Barnum!" he jolted, focusing. "What the? -fuck are *you* doin' out here?"

The shadow lifted his weighty accomplice.

"Hey, w-what are you doin' with that?"

As the Herculean hammer came down, he could only inhale. Garble on his own hooch-flavored saliva as the flat head cracked the tender bone of his temple and squashed the pulpy grey matter within.

The body, no longer a man, but a sack of flesh keeping what floated inside from spilling out, fell. The ground shook. Sawdust shifted under dead weight.

Ding. The shadow grinned.

EARLY RISER

∾ RODNEY ∽

Oh, Barnum, oh, Bailey, oh, Barnum, oh, Bailey.

Rodney never thought those carny holy men's names would stick to his lingo upon joining the show. Growing up Normal as he did, he swore on his Health and wellness, not to codgers so old they predated the Cure by over a century.

Stuck the names did, like tacky glue as he ran for the donniker clutching his crotch with one hand. The other steered his course, reaching from a distance for the wooden latch. Ready to lift, swing, lock, and go.

Screw that!

Let the door rock on its hinges. Tinkling for all the lot to hear. Not like any *could* hear. Too far away from camp, too early. Still a few hours of sleep to be had before Johnny starts hollering.

Wish he wouldn't do that.

Can't he nudge the end of his foot or give the pallet a rattle? That's how his daddy woke him on the weekends for fishing. Bass mostly, large and smallmouth, crappie, carps, and catfish.

Weekend fish fry. He could almost smell it. The sharp tang of lemon, the itchiness in his nostrils from fresh ground black pepper. The meat fell apart, melted on the tongue. His mouth watered at the memory.

Otis never cooks fish. Something about Dawn hating the smell.

"*Alf, Al, Charles, Otto, John!*" he invoked of the Ringling Brothers for the strength to not piss himself. "*Barnum, Bailey, BarnumBaileyBarnumBailey!*"

He got to the outhouse as that familiar pressure began. A hot stream bashing the dam of his bladder. Here it comes, picking at the bricks, soon to spray out the other side. Rodney hitched his step into higher gear before those extra winks of sleep before sunup became time spent scrubbing wet britches.

"*Oh*," he moaned, flipping the latch and knocking the door aside with his left butt cheek. Not bothering for privacy, he whipped out his pecker and pissed down the seat's hole. "*Ohhh* thank you, Barnum, *ohh*."

Done, bladder relieved and pants dry, he righted his clothes, wiped his hands on his thighs, and backed out the door.

"Make it in time?"

Put on a happy face Rod. Maybe if I smile, he'll let me go back to bed.

He spread his lips, hoping his teeth weren't too cruddy with plaque.

Johnny crouched beside the showers, rifling through a toolbox. Fresh clothes, and a towel weighed down rope of one temporary sheet wall.

"Uh, *yeah*. Had to go real bad," he laughed weakly, edging toward camp. Not far. He could see the edge of his mattress inside the tent. The flap caught on the corner as he rushed out. *On his Health, he swore he could hear it calling his name.*

Roooood. Rooooodneeeeyyy.

"Well," his boss eyed the kit, "since yer up, wanna run over ta Shadow? Looks like I forgot my wrench when I packed up last night."

Rodney's shoulders stiffened. *Noooo.*

Johnny saw the look of despair on the greenie's face and could hardly contain a smirk.

That'll learn him. Never run into your superior before work officially begins.

"*Aww Johnny,*" he whined.

"Come on, I gotta git the showers goin' before folks're up my ass about it. *Told Dawn heated water'd make 'em more spoilt than a barrel'a rotten taters.*"

Run over yourself! He wanted to say.

"Do me this solid and I'll owe ya one kid."

Sighing, he scraped his heels and pulled up the straps of his suspenders, "*Yes sir.*"

"*Sir*," Johnny laughed.

You should do it. Your tools, not mine. Not my fault you forgot a darn wrench.

Snores taunted Rodney in the midst of camp. Each fart forced a snort of laughter into his fist, a lapse of forgetting this pre-dawn errand while others get to sleep.

Johnny will surely wrangle him into assisting once he's back with the tool. Tasked with: *hand me this, hand me that, hold this, hold that.*

It just isn't fair.

"*Doo do do do do doo do do.* Fine as a fettle," he sang under his breath.

Damn Blake! Wouldn't quit with that song last night.

Over and over, sharpening a pocket knife beside the fire. Nicking fingers as he sang, "*Fine as a—ow—fettle. Fit as a—ow—fiddle.*"

"From her head," he glanced the lonely midway, watched his feet, still singing with hands in his pockets, "down to her-"

A stain marred the dirt.

"-pretty little... feet."

Rodney followed the black oblong smudge. It turned brown, lightened, brightened up Shadow's black tower.

Feet. Why are there feet? And not pretty little feet as the song went.

Boots, work boots, the same brand Rodney wore to bed last night. Too tired to kick them off after a long, rough day of relaxation. Thanks for the vacation day coppers!

These floating boots were scuffed, the outsole coming undone in the front.

Got to fix that.

One snag on a board or stepping over a spike and he could pull it right off. He needs new shoes.

The overalls up there have the same stain as the ground. Dark. In lines, spurts down the front. Like he'd wet himself—Rodney thought he would do such a thing when he woke up from that dream.

Dreamed of screwing in bulbs during show time and the show couldn't start until he finished. Dawn glared down below with the crowd, yet somehow also above when he looked up. Chin hairs a springing corkscrew tickling his head. She wouldn't let him leave to take a piss: he's got to finish the job.

Had to do it now or the show wouldn't open!

The rides were still, crowds waited at the Ten, at the concessions. They all watched him up on the ladder with his box of bulbs under an arm.

He ached to take a leak, but he must finish screwing in the bulbs. Every time he put one in, another fizzled out.

Complete the task or else he'd be fired!

Screw in the bulbs, Rodney!!!

"*Oh,*" Rodney covered his mouth. "*Barnum...*" he yelped.

The round top of the tower pushed at the man's ass. A posthumous pelvic thrust.

Slumping off the lewd gesture was the overall's bib. The underside of the white belly dirty, hairy, and smeared a ruddy color. Flaking, congealed, leaking at the top of the man's thighs, where something *should* be.

Rodney should have been looking at another man's private parts. But there was nothing. Hair, and red. A red shiny hole surrounded by stains.

Stains covered the inside of the bib and streamed down heavy limp legs. Like piss. But it wasn't piss. This wasn't fucking piss. The man had not pissed himself 'cause he had nothing to piss with!

"Oh, Barnum! Oh fuck!" the greenie bit his knuckles. Eyes reluctant, yet eager to move higher.

Up the rumpled shirt, dirty with sweat and grit and those dark stains.

Black across dirt, but he knew closer they would be red—brownish when it dries on clothes. Dark, dirty, copper. The color that smells like pennies, *like copper*. Just like copper, the same color and that smell. Copper, the police, the police that came yesterday. *Dirty coppers.* That old joke about pennies.

What do old pennies and a crooked police force have in common? Dirty coppers!

His face! Jaw slack to the side like a ventriloquist's dummy whose mouth has popped out of joint. *Ladies and Gentlemen, I'd like to sing a song for ya but my mouth's a little screwy!*

The dead man's left eye bulged under a saggy brow, a brow sunken inward under its own weight.

People weren't supposed to look like this! Rodney had never even seen a *Freak* who looked like *this!*

Bits of white, and grey, and red so bright it became neon pink. Some of the grey slid down the side of his neck, sat perched on the tip of his ear. Over-chewed gum saved for later. On his ear so he wouldn't forget.

His daddy use to do that. Use to gross out his mother and his sister, but Rodney always laughed. Clutched his belly so his sides wouldn't rip at the seams when Mom gagged as Dad plucked the gum from the top of his ear and dropped it into his mouth.

His eye looked at him, big and round and staring. Staring from the center of the wheel, the Shadow's *eye.* He hung by his arms in the Shadow's pupil. Dislocated arms sprawled and strung by chains across the bulbs. Lashed to char-black spokes.

Every day he had to check the bulbs like his dream. He had to check that the circle in the center lit up, and the circle around the frame lit up. If not, the wheel didn't look like an eye at night.

It didn't look like an eye. Not a shadow's, not the dead man's. Not Angus's bloody eye resting on the top of his cheek, judging from above while Rodney stared.

Day after day, start the ride, check the bulbs, the bulbs have to light up.

Can't do it. Not now, not today. Angus won't let him.

Rodney can't check those damn bulbs because Angus is dead and hanging from the Shadow's Eye with his own eye popped out and watching him!

"Fuck, fuuuuck!" he tripped over a support pole and hit the dirt. He scrambled toward the backyard, wanting, needing to get as far away from the eye, *his* eye, as he could. Screams echoed throughout the carnival, "He's dead! Angus is dead! Oh, Barnum, he's dead!"

End - Part One
To Be Continued

★ ★ ★ ABOUT THE AUTHOR ★ ★ ★

Megan Crowe has been fascinated by carnivals, circuses, and sideshow performers for as long as she can remember. This love for the subject is what led her to create the FRK-32 series. A series that will focus on various traveling shows and individuals in a world affected by a failed disease curative known as FRK-32.

She has never been *With It*, but she sure is *For It!*

Email — MCCroweAuthor@outlook.com
Instagram — megan_crowe_3134
Facebook — Megan Crowe